Salty Stories From The Chair

Ralph Hill

authorHOUSE®

AuthorHouse™ UK Ltd.
500 Avebury Boulevard
Central Milton Keynes, MK9 2BE
www.authorhouse.co.uk
Phone: 08001974150

© *2009 Ralph Hill. All rights reserved.*

No part of this book may be reproduced, stored in a retrieval system, or transmitted by any means without the written permission of the author.

First published by AuthorHouse 6/30/2009

ISBN: 978-1-4389-7086-8 (sc)

This book is printed on acid-free paper.

Dedicated to

'THE NORTH WEST VENTURERS YACHT CLUB

And in particular to David Swinton who supported and helped my single handed Round Britain trip in 1990 for the Macmillan Fund and to the members who provided so much help with the 'Chinkie' stories and for the wonderful chair - JO!.

ACKNOWLEDGEMENTS

I must thank Rodney Sutton - sometime graphics artist for Boat Owner magazine - for his magnificent front cover, depicting Chinkie, sitting in his favourite old chair, UNCLE JO! This chair did exist for many years in a North Wales Yacht Club and the vista probably remains the same today, a pretty bay with dozens of boats. My grateful thanks to the club which paved the way for so many stories and I hope I have not done any member a disfavour. All characters were a pure figment of my imagination.

My thanks to June Bevan for the illustrations accompanying a couple of the Chinkie stories. Although not a yachtswoman she has captured both the appearance of a Silhouette Yacht and the atmosphere of the place perfectly. I am just sorry that I could not persuade her to do more.

My thanks to Serif for the Page Plus software which so helped me with this publication. I have used their products since they first came on the market with PP1 and they have kept me updated ever since through 12 new editions so I now have a 'state of the art' desk top editing program PPX3 (It would have been PP13 but for superstition!) for a very low price

    Finally my sincere thanks to all my friends in the Venturer's Yacht Club and particularly to Gerry for a new mast and David Swinton for continued support throughout my own venture round Britain.

Foreword

The following stories I wrote some years ago, some for a sailing magazine, intended to help those new to sailing know some of the things to look out for, but instead of a manual of seamanship I wrote a series of novelettes, in I hoped an amusing but entertaining manner. I have interposed these with short poems, beginning with a nonsense poem and then a true tale of a short cruise in 1999 where everything seemed to go wrong finishing with the a record of my sail round Britain for charity in 1990.

Since first writing the magazine stories, times have changed, particularly with respect to equipment and most sailors today use Satellite Navigation to know where they are when out of sight of land. However, if this fails a knowledge of basic skills in dead reckoning or use of a sextant is a tremendous help. If sailing even short distances always ensure you have a good anchor and enough chain, lights, a radio telephone, safety equipment (life belts, life jackets etc.) and warm clothes. Finally, like meeting a stranger for the first time, always let a friend know of your plans, someone you trust to remember that you just might have sailed into danger.

Sailing is fun and very invigorating but keep aware of weather patterns and don't set off with a steeply falling barometer. Nobody, but nobody wants to be out in a gale if it can be avoided, and never be afraid to ask for advice, but know your source, e.g. a harbour master, a fisherman or trained skipper.

When I sailed round Britain I took many photos but the heat in the boat ruined the negatives. In order to have some illustrations for the talks I gave to yacht clubs I painted several pictures on A3 and the best of these have been reproduced in the story presentation, albeit in monochrome.. You may wonder why there are none after Falmouth but the west coast from Lands End to Anglesey is well known to the clubs where I gave talks. I hope the the ones included add another dimension to what was, for me, one of the really high points of my life.

I finish with one serious note. If you are in charge of a boat, you are responsible for all who sail with you. Don't take children unless you have the right safety gear for them and are sure you can control them in an emergency. Two adults are the minimum for four children under fourteen and all should be able to swim.

I have sailed many thousands of miles and had my moments of fear and problems and plenty of very hard work during winter lay-ups for refitting etc, but in the end, sailing has given me my greatest moments of happiness and joy. May it be the same for you.

By the way, Chinkie is the club's old hand, my invention, as are the people who feature in his tales.

CONTENTS

PAGE NO   SUBJECT

4	Acknowledgements
5	Foreword
7	Contents
8	NAVIGATOR
10	Uncle Jo and the Anchor
15	SAILING
16	Uncle Jo and the Surveyor
22	THE ODD SAILOR
24	Uncle Jo and Racing
31	TEINGMOUTH ELECTRON
33	Uncle Jo and the Batteriess
40	THE CORMORANT
41	Uncle Jo and the Missile
46	THEY NEVER FADE AWAY
47	Uncle Jo and the Little Cruiser
52	A POEM
53	Uncle Jo and the Pragmatist
61	No Fair Winds
72	I almost made it. Didn't I?

Poems are shown in UPPER CASE

THE NAVIGATOR

When the square on the circle is twice the hypotenuse,
Where can the azimuth be?
I've doubled the sextant and added a tangent
But all I can see is the sea..

'Two and two make four' I'm told,
But it depends on the ink in your pen,
If forced to use pencil to write on your stencil
Then you haven't got all the gen.

How can I find my way in the dark
When stars are all I can see?
If I stand on my head it could often be said
I am not earning my fee.

I do try my best to follow the way
That Columbus and Magellan knew,
But mathematics evades me, it cannot persuade me
That as navigator I could crew.

N.B. My brother was a navigator in the RAF and managed to navigate his way from Belgium to Spain in 1943 after being shot down in his Lancaster. Later, as a trainer for Pathfinder Pilots he was killed at Chipping Ongar in broad daylight in Sept. 1944 when his plane flew into a hillside with cockpit covers on to simulate night flying. A totally stupid, and unnecessary excersize, described later as 'Pilot Error' during a fighter affiliation excersize, despite the rear gunner not being aboard (the one member of crew who could have seen out!) and only three engines. There is a plaque in their honour in the little church - the oldest wooden church in England - at Printsted, Chipping Ongar. The tail wheel had caught the top of a pear tree just as the hill flattened out and the plane pancaked some 50 yards on. I believe they were attempting a surprise pseudo attack on North Weald Aerodrome, just some 5 miles away, at 100 ft to avoid being seen on radar. The plane would have passed the Southern Sector Oporations Command at Blake Hall, a half mile right of it's flight path! Brave - very, Foolish, maybe but 'Pilot Error' - never.

UNCLE JO AND AN ANCHOR

By CHINKIE

Uncle Jo squeaked as I moved my hips to avoid the loose spring. Sometimes the old chair seemed to bite back at you if you sat down too carelessly. Poor old Jo: he needed re-springing and a general overhaul. I sighed and stretched my legs.

"Been far?" asked George, busy making a Turks Head. In the end of a piece of rope. "Only to the point and back. It's bumpy out there and I didn't fancy dropping the hook out on my own, not when there's an on-shore forecast." I reached for a cigar. "What the devil d'you do with those things?" I asked, pointing to his rope work.

Mike drew noisily on his pipe. "They forecast a deep low approaching Ireland. I thought we'd be OK for the weekend but there, another wasted in this ghastly summer!"

"Darling, I told you we shouldn't have come. You could have done the lawns this weekend. Besides, it's time we visited mother." said Mary.

Mike looked at me and raised his eyebrows. "Two things I detest. Lawn mowing and ...." he looked at his wife. "Cold yorkshire pudding?"

She laughed and poked him with her knitting needle. "Never mind, you can collect that anchor from the chandlery."

"What are you getting, Mike?" asked George.

"A 30lb Fisherman's. We're off to Scotland in a fortnight and my plough won't hold in kelp."

"Ah!" said I. "I found the same. I carry one on the cabin top"

"Yes, I had noticed. You've got the kitchen sink up there. I saw a large Danforth too. Haven't you got an anchor well or at least chocks?"

I laughed. "OK, OK. I have got a well but I carry a Thames Marine in there - super anchor that I got with the boat, and apart from kelp it's not let me down yet."

"Three anchors. My God!" said Mike.

"Four, actually. I carry a 10lb grapnel in the cockpit locker." I added. "How about you, George?."

"Me - I carry a 35lb CQR main and a 22lb as a kedge. Like you, I take a Fishermans to Scotland. It's a devil to stow, though."

"I used to have a Bruce but couldn't come to terms with it and sold it to Jack." I said. "It was perhaps too large for me...I couldn't get it to dig in. I dried out once when I had a bilge keeler and found it lying on it's back! Maybe if I'd had a lighter one it might have worked. Anyway, Jack likes it so that's alright."

Rob joined in. "Why do you have so many, Chinkie?" he asked.

"Belt, braces and saftey pin!" I quipped. "No, really I use the T.M. most of the time. It's just 22lb and easy to handle, but in a gale I drop the Danforth in tandem. In Ghigha last year, for instance, I spent three days gale bound, for a short time rising storm force. The only thing I lost was my dinghy and the postmaster brought that back later when the wind dropped, bless him. The only other boat there dragged twice to my certain knowledge!"

"Have you tried dropping a weight down the cable?" asked George. "It stops you yawing about, specially if you use warp."

I shook my head.

"Hey, there's an article about that in PBO." said Rob. "It suggests you could use a pile of chain - as a weight!"

"Stand up Mike." said Mary.

"What d'you want?" he said, rising reluctantly.

"I want to try this for size." She held up her knitting to his chest and we saw a white sweater with a pattern of anchors on the front.

"No boat name?" I asked.

"Good God, no. D'you think I'd let him wear a sweater with ELIZA written on it? Anyway, it's those anchors that started this boring conversation: reminded me of the one Mike's got to collect!" She said, pulling the knitting into shape.

"Sorry Ma'm" I apologised.

"Do you know why she thinks it's boring, Chinkie? Because I haven't got a winch!" said Mike.

"Why the devil don't you do the anchor work?" I asked.

"What, and let Mary loose at the engine controls? D'you know what happened when we went into the lock? She only put it into 'Full Ahead' instead of neutral. We hit 'Golden Sprite so hard they changed her name to 'Golden Sh....'"

"Mike!" screamed Mary. "Don't you dare!"

He grinned sheepishly. "Guess I'd better go and collect that anchor," and walked out.

I looked at George. "It's all go, isn't it?"

Mary was knitting again. "It was awful." She went on, by way of explanation. "We'd just entered the dock and Tom was shouting for the stern rope. It got in a tangle when I threw it short so I thought I'd better go into reverse. I forgot the small lever was the accelerator or whatever you call it. Oh dear. Mike was furious! The man from Golden Thingumybob was alright, though, when he saw there was no damage. He was more concerned for me and kept saying 'It's alright, Princess. Not to worry,' but I felt so embarrassed I just wanted to cry."

"Has Mike shown you how to throw a rope?" asked George.

"No, not really. I've never asked him , I suppose."

"Well, next time you must take the coil over the fingers of your left hand - you are right handed, are you?"

She nodded, her needles still.

"Good, take the coil in your left hand. Then take about a third of it in your right hand to throw. Then, as you throw it - underhand - keep the fingers of your left hand straight and the coils will just slip off one after the other."

"Don't forget to tie the inward end to something first, though." I added.

"Look, I'll show you" said George, getting up. "There's some rope outside, I'll fetch it".

Mary started knitting again. "D'you ever get it wrong?" she said to me.

I laughed. "Not as often as I did but I still sometimes foul it up. Everyone does. All I say is 'Take your time', don't do anything on a boat in a hurry. Go into the lock slowly and it won't matter if you miss with the first throw. Aye, and if the chap behind you starts honking - just ignore him."

George returned with a coil of rope and showed Mary how to throw it. He was very good and made me envious.

"Do you throw horseshoes as a pastime?" I asked.

"Of course." He said, and neatly lassooed my upraised boot.

Suddenly there was an almighty crash outside and much swearing. Mary ran out to investigate but returned with a delighted, smug grin on her face.

"Its only Mike." she said, sitting down and taking up her knitting again. "He's decided to drop the anchor!"

Sailing

Feet on the grating, feeling the tremble
Of water that's rushing, tumbling, shaking
The very timbers that hold you afloat.
Wind on your cheek, the sails in ensemble
As winches are busy at sheets a braking,
Holding your course on your wonderful boat.
There is great joy in sensible sailing
Tiller is easy and nothing is ailing.
Out on your own in a gentle breeze,
While you traverse these pleasant seas
Sun up behind you. It cannot blind you
Yet it is hiding the lowering skies.
A sudden darkness betokens the change
A front is approaching, well in your range
The wind starts to rise, your course you must change.
So you look behind you and see it's no lie:
The stronger new wind, now up to a five
And still increasing! If you don't move the tiller
You'll soon have a jibe.
Tiller goes over as rain squall now hits you,
You turn to face the still growing wind
As sheets are quick shortened,
The winch dogs all taughten
To take up the strain on the over pressed side.
But then it is over! You turn your Sea Rover
Back on the course that you hope to maintain.
This little skirmish is just what you needed
To stop being complacent, to face wind and rain.
The joy of sailing is the thrill of maintaining
The course that you planned at the start of the day.
Come wind, come weather, it's extraordinary what pleasure
Attends you when your harbour or Port is regained.

UNCLE JO & THE SURVEYOR
BY CHINKIE

Where's George?' asked Jim.

I was sitting on 'Uncle Jo', the only comfortable chair in the club house. Some well meaning idiot had just bought fifty 'serviceable, imitation leather chairs...neat, don't you know' but not made for reclining in after a long hard beat up the sound. I had made a straight path for Uncle Jo, as comforting a land mark as the fairway buoy on a foggy night.

'He's getting his dinghy up' and I nodded towards the beach.

'Ah - he wont want any help.' He sat down. We both knew George's pride in his physical fitness. 'Wanted to ask him about surveying.'

'Oh, are you buying or selling? '

'Both. I've found a lovely Miller-Fife: beautiful teak, lying up near Chester. Good price too, but the insurance people want a survey'.

'Yes, I expect so. If the boat you want is more than twelve years old, home built, or made of wood - they'll want a survey that's for sure.'

There was a cold draft from the North Easter as George came into the club house.

'Over here, George. Jim wants a word.'

He grinned, bluff and good humoured as ever but red faced from his exertions. 'Watching me suffer, were you?'

'I always have to do the washing up.' I said in a mock whine, and we all laughed.

'It's cold out there. Blowing up a six, I reckon. I see you are at the jetty' he said, turning to me. 'Reckon you'll be better off there than on your mooring.'

'Could be' I said, 'I came up for water and diesel. Jim here wants some advice on surveys.'

George looked across at him. 'Hello, 'ello, so you've sold Mary Lou then?'

Jim nodded. 'I've seen a lovely motor sailor, a Miller Fife.'

'Haven't you had enough of wood? You spend all winter scraping, caulking and painting Mary Lou and now you want to start again. You must be mad. Concrete, me boy, that's the answer. Carry a bit of ready mix and a trowel and you can go anywhere'

'Aye' I added, 'and pray for a gale to get you moving.' But Jim wasn't listening: his heart was elsewhere. 'She's lovely, George. Solid teak. 'Course the engine is shot but I can fix that, easy. The boat, though. Lovely lines.'

George thought a moment. 'Double ender, about 8 meters?'

'That's it. Wheel steering and a super doghouse - the lot.'

'I had a double ender once', I added, 'a clinker ships life boat conversion. Leaked like a sieve in a seaway but a lovely mover, very stable.'

Jim's eyes gleamed 'Ah, this one's carvel built - sound as a rock.'

'Back to George's concrete barge.' I quipped.

'What d'you want to know? ' asked George, turning to Jim.

'Well, apparently I have to have it surveyed before I can get it insured. Who should I go to? '

'First, me lad, it'll cost you! Compared to what you stand to lose if you bought a dud, though, it's worth having done. Second, you can use a good survey to help sell the boat later, 'specially a wooden boat. Now, where to go?' He thought for a moment. 'Go local if you can. The boatyard should help you...preferably not the one you're buying from; after all they are trying to sell so they might go for an easy survey. Where is it, by the way?'

'Oh, it's here now! I've had it brought down on a low loader.'

'So you've bought it already, before a survey?' said George.

'Yes' he paused, sensing our disapproval 'but it looks so good. It's not been in the water for five years.'

We looked at each other. 'You bought it without a survey?' said George, surprised and Jim nodded, shamefaced. 'Right' said George, ever practical. 'Go round to John Wilson and ask his advice.' (John, by the way, is our local boatyard boss.) 'You want a member of the Y.B.D.S.A or whatever they call themselves now, or a good probationer.'

'What's a probationer? ' asked Jim.

'Some one with proven experience in the boatbuilding business who has studied surveying and serves five years apprenticeship as an occasional surveyor. Full surveyors are very busy with insurance claims after all these gales so you may have to wait a while.'

'Is a probationer cheaper?'

George smiled. 'I shouldn't think so - he's a qualified man - like a doctor waiting to become a consultant!' (I winced, hoping there were no doctors about: we had a couple in the club and one of those was a consultant who had had trouble with a survey!)

'What will it cost, anyway.' asked Jim.

'There's a scale of charges which is drawn up, I think, by the YBDSA - what? Oh, Yacht Brokers, Designers and Surveyors Association - though I believe that it's split now into Designers and Surveyors. They charge to a formula. Let me think.' He paused.

'I know,' I spoke up. "I've just had a survey done on mine. It's length times breadth in feet divided by 1.4, the answer in pounds.'

'Yes, that sounds like it.' said George. 'Of course, some charge more if they think their reputation deserves being recognised. You're paying for experience, after all.

'Cor' said Jim, doing some quick mental arithmetic. 'That's about a hundred and fifty quid, isn't it? '

'Plus VAT' says George. 'Of course, if he finds anything seriously wrong at the start he'll likely save you money by cutting short the survey. Oh, but you've bought it anyway. Well, if he knows that, he'll give you the works. If you had paid a deposit 'subject to survey' he would probably try and save you money if he could see it was a dud. They know that time cost money and they are busy men anyway...at least the good ones are..'

Jim muttered 'You think well of everyone.'

'Go on, stop worrying. I expect you've got a real bargain anyway, knowing you. It'll be just a few less beers for the next few weeks, and speaking of beer....' George put up his hands and made a great impression of a panting, thirsty dog.

Jim grinned and rose to buy drinks. I nodded at his suggestion.

George watched Jim's retreating back thoughtfully. 'He'll have picked up a bargain - he always does. Lord knows where he finds 'em.'

'What happens if something goes wrong after the survey? A friend bought a boat after survey but when he got it out to sea the rigging parted and his mast came down. He couldn't get anything out of the surveyor.'

'Then his surveyor was not YDBSA cos' they are all covered by an indemnity insurance and he can claim from them.' George said which left me thinking and wondering if mine had indemnity insurance. I reached for a cigar and George lent forward with a light.

'Are there 'horses for courses' with surveyors? ' I asked. 'Mine is GRP, but what about you with your concrete hull? '

'What? Oh, I see what you mean. A good surveyor can work with all hulls. Obviously he knows more about some types than others, but those chaps all talk to each other and I expect they compare notes. Of course, if you are looking at GRP, especially home made, then you would need a moisture meter and not all surveyors have them yet'

'What's that for? '

'It measures the amount of water in a small patch of the hull material. Sometimes water gets into the GRP past the Gel coat. Frost gets at it and it blisters and possibly delaminates. In some hulls, where filler has been used and it's had a lot of chalk in, then unless it has been well sealed with 2 pot epoxy paint or good gel coat .....squish! It's different with concrete of course. With a new boat, you have to keep it wet for ages while it cures.'

'Is that how Noel found out about his rudder?' A voice spoke over my shoulder - Mike had joined us and had been listening to George.

'What's this about a rudder?' I asked.

'Noel found his rudder feeling odd, sort of stiff and heavy, so when he hauled out last week he had a look.' said Mike. 'Apparently he drilled two holes in the bottom and about 5 gallons of water came out!'

'My god, what's he going to do? ' I asked.

'Reckons he'll fill the holes before launching and then do the same every year. I wondered why he didn't inject polystyrene foam? '

'Yes, I heard about this. Apparently John Wilson used his meter and it read saturation values.' said George. 'As to foam filling, it sounds like a good idea but I suppose it might react with the steel shaft, sort of stop it drying out. What they call 'poultice corrosion', I think.'

'Oh, clever clogs. You know it all. How d'you do it?' asked Mike.

'If I didn't know you were a superannuated electrician I'd guess you had an interest in surveying'. I said.

'Less of the superannuated, if you don't mind. Some of us have to work for a living.' He replied.

' Anyway, you'll never sell your boat. I reckon you'll have it as a monument on your grave.' I smiled.

'He'll need a cemetery all to himself with that great object.' laughed Mike.

Jim returned with the drinks, bearing a glazed look. 'I've been talking to the new bar maid.' He handed me a beer absentmindedly. 'She says she might crew for me next year.'

We all burst out laughing - Jim had done it again, new boat, new girl! Now I knew the meaning of the saying 'Lucky Jim'.

The Odd Sailor

Walking on the high tide line
With wind upon my back.
I dwelt upon that other time
My feet on bladder rack
When I had seen that oddly boat
Struggle on a tack.

I stopped to watch as the sailor moved
To tighten up the sail.
A kind of hopeless thing to do
When surely he must fail
For wind was with the tide that day
And not so very strong.

He tried to start his engine:
In this he also failed
So he dropped his sail and grabbed the oars
And slowly made his way
Towards the bank near where I stood.
I went down to his aid.

The boat was small, and up the sand
We pulled her safe away
And then I looked, could not believe
In what he'd sailed that day.
A tiny boat, a wooden boat,
Made of bits and pieces.
The sail a sheet, the mast a threat
Of bamboo canes, all bereft
Of any strength, better spent
Supporting tomato seedlings.
The outboard engine, old and tired
Lashed to a beam, nailed to a seam
That would reject its loading.

The whole damn thing should be afired!
For there was no sense in sailing
Such a piece of junk

The owner was a fruit farmer
With time upon his hands.
The crop were sprayed and watered
So to sailing he turned his hand.
No licence do you need to sail
No office to inform.
You can make a fool of yourself
If to that is what you're born.

The sad thing, the cruel thing
Is for those who have to spend
Their time in trying to rescue
The sailor in despond
And risk their lives for idiots
Who really shouldn't be there.
Oh save us from the half wit
For whom we have to care.

And now I walk the tide line
Free of any stress.
Looking for any brick-a-brack
That I can then assess
To use at home, a piece of foam,
Some drift wood, a garden gnome?
'Cos if you walk the high tide line
You'll never know what's next.

UNCLE JO & THE RACING SCENE

By CHINKIE

I had settled into 'Uncle Jo', my favourite armchair, just in time. Gerald bustled in: he never walked anywhere. He always 'bustled'.
    "Taken root, have you?" He said to me. "Ought to have been out sailing, boy. Every time I see you, there you are - stretched out like a stranded Grampus!"
    "Stranded, Gerald - me?" I asked placidly, but he ignored me.
    "Lizzy, Lizzy." He bellowed. "Bring me a Brandy, will you?"

He subsided noisily into one of the so called easy chairs. "I can't find Jilly James anywhere." He said. "Have you seen him?"

Jilly is our Vice Commodore, responsible for the sailing and racing programme. I believe his nickname came from the fact that he could always be found 'jilling' round the start line of every race, eager for a quick start. I'm not a racing man, though a great friend of mine, Blondie Hasler used to say it helped you to know your boat better, but I like Jilly - he enjoyed his racing, win or lose, and I never heard him raise an objection: I suspect it was because he was not averse to trying the quick dodge himself if he thought no one was looking. I once came upon him going the wrong side of a buoy in a race but I pretended to be looking the other way, busy with a riding turn on the winch.

"I saw Jilly about ten minutes ago." I said. "He and George were on the slip."

"Never there when you want him. Damned Portsmouth Yardsick ratings. He's got mine too low - anyone would think I'd got a racer instead of an old scow!" He grumbled.

Let anyone call his boat an old scow and they'd get an earful. He had a beautifully maintained Vega which would be fast in hands other than his. As it was, he insisted on staying dry where the Vega, when pushed, is a trifle wet to say the least. Lord alone knows how he stayed dry and shining on army manoeuvres and I have a mental picture of him followed by a faithful batman holding a brightly coloured golfing umbrella.

"Here you are Colonel." said Elizabeth, avoiding his hand. "Your own glass too, see! I remembered this time." She winked at me, doing a little dance to avoid his hands as she waited for her money.

The Colonel only played around while Jim was safely out of the way and I noticed that he had half an eye on the door. I suppose every club has one, an ageing Lothario.

"Is Jim coming in for a drink?" I asked her, holding out my empty glass. "Or is he going to be varnishing all day?" Jim had just bought a Miller Fife and was busy lovingly restoring it to its former glory.

"He said he'd be in this evening." The door opened and we looked up to see Mike and Mary come in. "We've got to decide on a name." she continued..

I noticed the royal 'we' but let it slide. "He's going to change the name then?" I asked. "I thought it was registered."

"It is, but who wants a boat called 'Tipsy Turvy'?" she asked.

"Tipsy? You're sure you don't mean Topsy?" I smiled. "I have known better names, but if he wants to re - register he's going to have to pay a lot of money out to change it! Besides, is it lucky?"

"I don't know about luck, but he's thinking about something called the Small Ship Register."

"Oh, I see." I said.

"What's he going to call it?" asked Gerald. He wasn't going to say 'you'!

"Oh, we've not decided yet." said Elizabeth, blithely unaware of the effect of her words on her audience. She smiled at Mary as she sped off on another errand: she was a happy acquisition as a bar maid. There was a budding romance here between Elizabeth and Jim, but some of us were wondering how serious that young man was, whose first loves in the past had always been his boats.

"Thinks she owns him already." said Gerald, sotto voce. "'Spect she'll be choosing the curtain material next!"

"Don't be mean, Gerald." said Mary, sitting next to him, much to Mike's annoyance : he detested our Colonel. "She's a nice girl and it's time Jim settled down. Now, are you happy about the race?" she asked.

"I was telling Chinkie here, I reckon I've got the wrong handicap. That damned Twister put it over me on the beat out: he was carrying a much bigger Genoa than is allowed for on his boat."

"Oh, come on Gerald, he only put it up before you." said Mike. "Besides, a drop in the wind had been forecast so he was taking a reasonable gamble that paid off."

"I'm going to ask James about those ratings, and the buoys on the race card." He ranted.

"Poor old Jilly, trouble again." said Mary, and turning to me: "I see you weren't racing, Chinkie."

"I've got neither the competitive spirit or the rig for racing. Besides, they forecast a drop in the wind this afternoon and, like George, I need half a gale upwind." I replied.

"You Junk sailors - you're all the same. Always some excuse. Too many bits of string to play with." she said.

There was a sudden influx of members returning from their boats and Gerald leapt up to accost Jilly James. I could hear them arguing in the background as Mike, now joined by George and Veronica, homed in on me.

"Why don't you race, Chinkie?" he asked.

"Get a round of drinks - here, take this." I handed him a fiver "and I'll tell all, as the driver said to the traffic cop."

"I'll get them" said Veronica. "I want to talk to Elizabeth. No, no, put your money away." but I insisted: it was a small price to pay for retaining the embrace of my beloved chair.

Mary guessed. "He won't leave that old chair so you may as well take his conscience money!" she said.

I looked at Mike: "I don't race because a) I'm not competitive, b) I haven't a racing crew and c) I hate inquests,...that's the worst part of playing bridge. Your opponent trumps his partner's ace and the whole room knows for the next hour!"

Mike grinned. "You're sure your opponent does the trumping"?

I ignored him and paused to rearrange Uncle Jo to my bulky frame.

"My son gave me up long ago when I changed to a Junk rig. There's nothing to do, Dad' he said, and of course he was right, but that's why I like it. It's lazy sailing, no deck work for these old bones - easy reefing. I did race once, in the Falmouth Classics in 1990 and I came second but I didn't know 'till a couple of days later - I had not stayed for the race report or prize giving. I was tired." I shuffled about and found a cigar which I lit. Mary here said there were lots of pieces of string. She's right, of course, but when a piece of string breaks you just tie in a new piece, no fancy gadgets to break far from help. In any case, only two ropes are used for most of the time: the main halyard which is, if you like, your accelerator and the sheet which is your brake. Both from the cockpit, simple, and no stowing unruly mainsail or flapping foresail!"

"I've heard a mainsheet called many things, but never a brake," laughed George.

I eyed him thoughtfully: "What happens if you let go of both tiller and mainsheet?" I asked.

"O.K. You win - you luff up." he replied.

"Exactly." I beamed. "If you want to go faster, pull up a bit more sail. Slower, either drop some sail or let go the sheet and possibly the tiller. Of course, it's not perfect! When the wind drops you're pushed to make to windward in a junk. The flat sail doesn't have much drive below a three."

George spoke up. "I've just read in the CA Bulletin about a chap who reckons you can overcome that. He seems to have developed a sort of fully battened gaff with roller reefing genny."

I nodded. "I saw that. Sounds interesting."

Mike then said "Ben Souter has just taken delivery of a new Westerly and that has a fully battened main. He's very pleased with it 'cept the top batten tends to catch on his back stay. It's easy to reef - runs in lazy jacks like yours."

I was immediately interested. "Where is it?" I asked "and who's Ben Souter?"   "He's new to the club." said Mary, taking a drink from Veronica's proffered tray. 'Lives near you I think, Chinkie. Doesn't he keep his boat in the new Marina, Mike?"

"Are you talking about 'Sentinel'?" asked Veronica, handing me a beer and my change. "I went aboard yesterday. It's lovely inside, all bright and airy. I'm not sure I'd like it when it's rough," she added. "A long way to fall without hand holds. They'll be good club members, though - offered me some home made wine. It was very good too." She chuckled.

"What's the wife called?" asked Mary.

"Louise - they're coming in tonight so I'll introduce you." she said.

I returned to the rig: I have an almost one track mind."I reckon that a fully battened Bermudan main is a good compromise for a cruising rig. Easy reefing, high aspect ratio to stop wave blanketing of the wind, and good windward ability if the sail battens are thin enough to take up an aerofoil shape." I said.

"Hello, 'ello," said George. "Are we in for a change - is Chinkie going to come in out of the cold? Watch this space!"

"I'm not the only one with a Junk." I laughed. "There are three of us now, don't forget. Anyway, you've been racing all day yet none of you has said how you got on. Who won?"

There was a pause. "Well, we did." said Mike, looking at Mary, "But Gerald thought we'd gone the wrong side of number three on the way back and wanted us disqualified. We showed him the race card which said you could pass either side on the return leg but..." He held up his hands.

"That's mainly why I sat beside him." said Mary, grinning.

"So that was it. I thought..." began Mike.

"I know what you thought." Mary interrupted, and then with a wink in my direction added: "I said that was mainly' why I sat beside him." and she ruffled his hair.

"We went the landward side of B3 to avoid the worst of the tide: scraped the sand a couple of times too.....on the ebb!" said Mike with an endearing schoolboy grin. "Most races are won round here by knowing your tides, working depths and, when you touch bottom, having a heavy crew to heel the boat!" He dodged Mary's hand.

I may have mentioned that we are mainly a cruising club: we don't take our racing very seriously, at least most of us don't, so my thoughts went back to the new members. Home made wine! Now that is another matter entirely. I did say that I had an almost one track mind, but cigars and wine.......!

THOUGHTS ON TEIGNMOUTH ELECTRON

I sit, warm in storm proofs, embalmed in fog.
Listening, not looking: the ears seeing through the gloom.
Searching, searching, while the eyes see only compass,
The tiny lumined needle hovering, the wind
From forward of the beam, enough to fill the sails
And turn to weather but for tiller's hand,
Forever cheating wind and waves to gain a westing.

Listening, I hear the chunter of the waves,
Not menacing despite the fog, but reassuring:
Movement is all through this long night of pain
Where every bend of leg sends messages to the brain
Of ague, ache and heat. The nerves,
Confined in pulsing heat transmit the flame.

Ah! Such pain, born of Ramsey Sound
Where jiving, tumbling waters threw me down
Into the cabin, hammered my leg
On fractured engine casing -
Useless anyhow with clutch awry.

The clock says four, the morning wakes.
The fog seems thicker, yet no sound outside the ship
'cept wind and waves.....I hear a voice repeat a phrase:
'Come here, come here'.

I raise my head and seek the source: nothing
But rope on sail, creaking in the wind.
A tired mind hallucinates, making double
The meaning of a simple trouble, talk
Of ropes and blocks, sails that knock,
Creaks and sighs, wind that cries in rigging.

Was this what witched the Teignmouth skipper 'oer board?
Was he bereft of sense by troublesome cord?
The chattering, chuntering blocks on tortured mind!
To hear them say 'This man I find.....'
At full court from wind, from rope, from creaking dory,
That might suggest a judge and jury?

We'll never know, but sitting here I feel
An understanding of what might have been
Were I so tired, were my dreams so o'er trod.
But no, the fog is lifting. I head for Padstow,
A mere 5 miles. There is Trevose light!
JUNKETTE sails on, out of velvet night.

I wrote this while in hospital in Truro in 1988, waiting for an xray on my leg. I had been thinking of a friend of a friend who had entered the Around the World yacht race in an ill prepared boat called Teignmouth Electron. He had fallen so far behind that he carried on broadcasting spurious positions while staying in waters off the east coast of South America. Eventually his boat was discovered abandoned and his log showed his fictitious voyage. I imagined what he might have felt had he heard the noises that had accompanied me during my night in the Bristol Channel while in some pain.

UNCLE JO & THE BATTERY

By CHINKIE

I struggled to light a large cigar I had been given: I had no cutter with me and had to use my boat knife to prepare the end. The cigar was old stock, passed on to me by a friend who had given up smoking. It had kept well, a good wrapper leaf that had sealed both ends. It had come in one of those awful metal tubes, but at least the tube had stopped it drying out too much. The trouble with modern marketing techniques - practical but not aesthetic. I got the cigar drawing, looked up and felt strangely at ease and comfortable. The reason wasn't clear to me at first, but more of that later.

"What's the topic today then?" I asked of the half dozen members who were staring out of the window at the beach activity. We had just had lunch.

"Come off it, Chinkie, that's a conversation stopper if ever I heard one." said Veronica, sipping her coffee. The companionable silence continued for a minute or so.

"I was talking about batteries to John." said Mike. "He's just taken a new batch into stock. Someone advised me to go to an agricultural dealer for a tractor battery - apparently you can get a better deal in heavy duty batteries, but John said 'No, they were no good for deep cycling,' whatever that means. D'you know, George. You're an electrician."

"Yes. For a car or tractor you have a heavy drain on the battery every time you start the engine but the generator soon recharges it and most of the time it is fully charged. On a boat or caravan though, you have a slow discharge over a long period before recharging - deep cycling, see - so the construction needs to be different. Best thing is to have two batteries if you have an inboard engine, an engine starting battery with high cranking power... a car battery to you.... and a larger service battery for your electrics designed for deep cycling. 'Course, you'll need a change over switch for charging or you won't get enough power back into your service battery from the alternator."

George, as usual, was a mine of information. He went on to add "I should avoid the 'Sealed for Life' type whatever you get. They may not spill when you heel over but they can't take a continuous charge without bursting and leaking".

"Make sure they both have proper carrying handles" I interjected. "Batteries in boats are almost always in inaccessible places, unlike cars, and without a lifting device you can do yourself an injury - more backs done in by lifting batteries out of bilges than you get by pulling up fouled anchors."

"That's a matter of proportions, Chinkie," said Rob. "More boats with batteries low down than fouled anchors. They shouldn't be in the bilges either! Sea water and batteries don't mix."

"O.K., O.K. You win" I laughed, "but you know what I mean - batteries are usually very low in the boat."

"Why's that?" asked Mike. "Why can't they put them in more accessible places?"

"Weight, my dear chap. Keep the weight low down for stability." said George.

"Ah yes, silly of me." said Mike ruefully.

"Don't feel too bad about it." said Rob. "I saw a boat last week - the chap was fitting the hull out himself and he'd put the batteries on a specially made shelf, all boxed in, just under his control panel and actually above the waterline. I tried to tell him but he wouldn't listen. He'd given himself two problems, too high and too near the ignition switch. If the switch sparked he could blow the boat up." He paused, then added "That's the problem with boats you fit out yourself - sometimes you don't know what trouble you're laying up for yourself."

I looked at Rob. He was a University Lecturer when he wasn't sailing his Silhouette which he cared for meticulously. I liked Rob for his quiet integrity and thoughtfulness, not in the least 'pushy' or overbearing - his students would like him. We rarely saw his wife who, like his daughter was very shy.

"Rob's right." said George, who'd built his own concrete boat. "Sometimes you make a basic mistake without realizing it until it's almost too late. I went over my plans again and again, thought I'd got it right, but it was only after we'd begun installing the engine that I realized all too well of what I'd done!" He looked round the group. "I couldn't reach the stern gland so I had to cut a hole in the bottom of the cockpit which I should have done at the start. Going back to batteries, though, I saw a note in a recent owner's magazine warning about the dangers of sparking during charging.   When you charge a battery, there's a lot of hydrogen given off, that's what's in the bubbles in the acid. Now if you have a spark, say the ignition switch or even disconnecting the charging leads while charging, the whole lot can blow up in your face. It happens every year, especially when batteries are very low and put on a heavy charge prior to launching after lay-up. Switch off before disconnecting, and don't let Chinkie anywhere near with that cigar in his mouth."

"Do they really explode?" asked Mary. "I hope you are taking this in, Mike!" Benny spoke for the first time, unusual for him to be so quiet for so long. "I saw a demonstration of a new petrol driven charger last week. Portable, electric start, charges at 8 amps and gives over half a kilowatt of AC. It's both light and quiet too, made by the motor bike people, Kawasaki or something - the suicide squad. Anyway, I've ordered one for 'Spindrift' - it will fit in the cockpit locker. It's super!"

"And I shall be able to watch Wimbledon on TV without being shouted at for running the battery down." laughed his wife in her inimitable American brogue.

For those of you who don't know Benny, let me tell you about him. He's a rare visitor to the club because he runs a very successful shoe factory in the midlands and is always dashing round Europe. 'Benny the Boot' we call him! Now I know why I feel so pleased with life, .Benny and his lovely American wife Lynne always give you this feeling of camaraderie, of life being a game and great fun. On the few occasions they are with us they spread an aura of warm friendliness. They were also a shining example of a 'happily married couple' with two children in university. He adored his pretty wife and she was so proud of him. No wonder his shoes were becoming a household name. Despite all his material success he could still wax lyrical about a battery charger: he could say 'super' and get away with it.

"A quiet charger is a boon - you won't beat mine." said Mike, grinning.

"He's boasting again" said Mary, smiling at him. "He went and bought a solar panel at the boat show for £300! Now I shan't be able to sunbathe on the cabin roof. Anyway, I claimed a new bikini: if he's going to find the sun to charge his batteries he can afford to give me a bikini to charge mine!"

I grinned at her. "You'll charge everyone's battery in a bikini."

"Chinkie, I wouldn't think it of you." She replied.

"Oh, I don't know." said Lynne in her delightful American drawl. "I reckon there's life under that cigar haze."

The two girls began to talk about clothes as Benny asked Rob what his plans were. This was part of the charm of the man: despite having the largest boat in the club he showed a lively interest in a member with the smallest boat. Benny's boat was 47 feet while Rob's was 19.

"I think we shall try for Lundy this year in August. The club's going up to Scotland but I can't keep up with them so we'll probably go south." said Rob.

"You know what 'Parkinson' says: if ten boats go North the wind'll blow from the North. Should give you a fine run down south." said Benny.

"I reckon 'Parkinson' is a bit like 'Kilroy' - he's been everywhere and said everything. But thank you for your encouragement." Rob replied.

"Will you be fishing?" asked Benny.

"If he's not careful, he'll catch a sprat that will tow him to Lundy!" said Mike with a grin.

Rob smiled and turned to Benny. "Only Mackerel. At our sailing speed we are usually just about right for trolling for Mackerel with feathers, 2 or 3 knots."

"Don't denigrate yourself, little 'Shellduck' sails very well. I've seen her!" said Benny.

Lynne had looked up at the word 'Mackerel'. She was a very good cook. "Ooh, have you tried them soused?" she asked. "Fillet them and put them in a jug covered with a mixture of vinegar and lemon juice for twelve hours or so. They're better than Herring, meatier, aren't they, darling" she turned to Benny.

He nodded. "Super! We always try for Mackerel first. Two for Lynne and two more for bait. Trouble is that if you land in the middle of a school you can catch too many. I've seen a boat take 24 and when he got back he couldn't give them away - everyone had caught Mackerel."

"They are such beautiful fish." said Mary. "I'm always sad when we pull them aboard."

"What do you catch with your Mackerel bait?" asked Rob.

"Depends on where we are." replied Benny, elegantly trapping a fly on his knee cap with a well aimed paper swat. "Anchored over a wreck its Pollack, Ling, Conger or perhaps Cod. Over rocks it could be Coalies and Pollack and over sand there'd be Rays, Doggies, Tope....a fair range."

"I've heard of most of those, but what on earth are 'Doggies' and Pollack or Coalies?"

"To you, Rock Salmon" said Benny with his infectious grin. "A euphemism used by fishmongers - who'd want to buy Dog Fish, 'cos that's what 'doggies' are. Filleted on the fishmonger's slab they're sometimes difficult to tell from Cod. Coal fish are a gray pink on the slab but become sparkling white when cooked."

"You often get Coalie with your chips and peas at the 'chippy'." said George. "Especially the cheaper ones. During the last war it was mostly doggies and coalies that we got in the shops since deep sea fishing came to a halt and these are available from inshore waters. They can be a bit like eating paper, though... difficult to swallow, sometimes."

"Ugh" shuddered Lynne. "I'll keep to cod, thank you, or Clams!"

"Ah, a New England Clam bake! Now that's something special." said Benny, his eyes gleaming with the thought and his hand closing on Lynn's in some private memory.

"Come on" said Mary, rising and pulling at Mike's hand. "The tide is coming up, time we got the dinghy inflated.

We all rose to make use of the day when there was an explosion.

"God, what was that" asked Mike, rushing to the door. We all dashed outside, fearing the worst but found that it was just one of the crowd having trouble with his car backfiring.

Mary whispered in my ear "Oh Chinkie, I thought someone's battery had exploded." She was shaking.

I smiled and patted her shoulder. "No, my dear, it only happens like that in books! In real life its the cinder in your shoe that causes the most discomfort.!"

The Cormorant

There it stands upon the pier,

It's wings outspanned –

Fills me with fear:

About to fly at me?

No, not so. See there,
It's drying it's wings in the salty air!

UNCLE JO & THE MISSILE
by Chinkie.

Rain was streaming down the club house window, the wind howling through the masts of laid up boats. I settled deeper into Uncle Jo, the disreputable armchair that had become my sheet anchor and listened to the endless tales being spun around me.

"Did I tell you of my brush with a missile?" asked Robin above the din and clatter around him. Robin was a man who had been a salesman and kissed the Blarney Stone could be guaranteed to tell a good yarn. There was a growing quiet.

"I was sailing down Cardigan Bay, not a lot of wind but we were going nicely. Sunny day, Barometer high and all well with the world. First time I'd sailed in those waters and well out of sight of land, but we were only keeping half an eye open when suddenly I saw something strange! A sort of platform, thirty feet or so square that looked as though it was loaded with old cars all painted white. No sign of anything on the chart but I did see the ominous words "Target Area and Buoys". I thought 'My god, that's a target, lets get out of here!' I am neither curious nor courageous... and started the engine."

He stopped, took a long pull at his beer. "About an hour later I reckoned that we must be safe and switched off. I hate the noise of the engine and our speed dropped again to around 4 knots. As you all know, I bought a Decca set at the boat show so I'd taken a fix of the target and knew I was now seven and a half miles downwind since we had the tide with us. I relaxed but the RT went at that moment: Aberporth Range calling a boat 12 miles north of Fishguard to identify itself. 'not us', I thought and checked both DR and the Decca co-ordinates. We were 16 miles off Fishguard on a sou'sou'west course. 'Still, I was wondering if I ought to check in when another boat spoke up and was asked to change his bearing to sail closer to the coast." He paused.

"Oh thanks, Mike" he said, accepting a glass of beer. Mike knew when to lubricate!

"Well," continued Robin, wiping the beer off his moustache, "that cleared us, or so I thought." He was interrupted by several voices." I know, I know," he continued, holding up a hand, "there's one born every day. Anyway, we saw no other boats ('are you surprised?' came a voice from the back) and yes, we had the sea to ourselves."

"It was just after five when the first shock came" he continued, frowning at his would be interrupters. "An old four engined bomber flew over towards the land. That was unusual in itself, but a minute later there was a loud screeching whine that lasted about half a minute. I looked around but couldn't see anything. 'What was that' shouted Betty who was preparing an early dinner - we wanted to be clear of plates and things ready to enter Fishguard harbour in a couple of hours if the wind held.

"'No idea - can't see anything.' I said, and again checked the chart... Fishguard about ten miles off. The penny still hadn't dropped. Ten minutes later, Betty served up dinner to me in the cockpit and a couple of seconds after that a modern jet flew overhead, very fast. Just as it was disappearing the screeching whine came again and this time I saw it!" He paused and looked around, ever a showman.

"It came in at around 100ft, straight overhead and very fast. It looked like a cigar with gyro blades on the back and travelling in the same direction as the plane. Betty was in the cabin, eating her dinner. ' Where are you going' she asked as I tried to reach the RT. 'Didn't you hear that?' I asked. 'I'm going to call the coast guard.'

"'Why?' came the calm reply, 'What was it'. I explained. 'Oh, well it didn't hit us' she said. 'Don't fuss. Your dinner will get cold. Call them when you've finished.' She was adamant that I eat and you know how she is when she's made her mind up!" (Didn't we just!)

"Well, I've never eaten a meal so fast. I called the coast guard."

"'Go 67 and wait!' came a brusque female voice. In the face of Betty's calm I hadn't thought I could reasonably say 'Pan,Pan' - five minutes had passed since the damn thing had gone over. Eventually the coast guard came through and I told them 'A missile has just flown over us, missed the mast by a few feet.' and I gave them my Decca co-ordinates.

"Wait a moment, Bero" came the calming reply, then "What direction did it come from?"

"From the sea, heading landwards." There was a pause, then

"O.K. Bero, there'll be no more firing tonight. You'll be alright now" and he signed off.

"When we sailed into Fishguard two hours later we passed under the stern of a small naval vessel and I'll swear there were several pairs of glasses trained on us." He thought for a moment. "I suspect they were looking for our non - existing radar reflector."

He took another swig of beer.

"The end of the Saga came the next day." He said, grinning. "As we raised sail, the Gaff broke, cracked in the middle, so we had to sail back home with a jury rig - two gennys, back to back. Not very efficient and a long slow drag north but I kept the shore in sight although we'd been assured that there would be no firings since it was a Sunday - they don't serve beer on a Sunday in Wales either!" He added, resentfully.

"In the late morning we came across the actual target - I think - a platform with lots of radar reflectors on it and a Ministry of Defence warning to keep clear. I wondered if what I had seen on the way down had been the actual missiles, perhaps remote controlled or some monitoring device."

"Why didn't you have a Radar reflector on your boat, Robin?" asked George.

"I didn't because if you remember, last year when we were sailing together I asked a coaster if he could see me on his radar screen and he said I gave a stronger echo than you did with your 'catch rain' device. Since then, though, I've changed my rig so perhaps I don't give as good an echo." He finished his beer.

"I think you'd better get one, don't you?" said George.

"Where would I put it? I've no cross trees and the mast head is already cluttered with aerials."

"Why" asked George gently, "don't you get one of these cylindrical reflectors. I've changed to one on my boat, it doesn't chafe the sails and you could hoist it on a spare halyard?"

"I think I might." answered Robin. He paused. "D'you think that broken gaff was trying to tell me something?"

"Like what?" asked George.

"Well, a warning from 'the little folk'?"

We all laughed. "More likely you saw the 'little folk' flying over on the back end of a broom stick, Robin." said George, chuckling.

Betty entered at this moment, in time to catch George's remark. "Have you been telling them about your apparition, Robin?"She asked, and turned to us: "He can't think of anything else at the moment. Wanted to spoil a good dinner by crowing to the coast guard. It's his own fault for buying a yellow boat. I don't blame anyone taking a pot shot, if that's what they did, even little green men!"

George: "I take it, then, that you don't like yellow, Betty?"

"Like it? I hate it. I can't find anything to wear that doesn't look ghastly against it and Robin wanted me to wear those horrid yellow boots which clash even more. Come on Robin, you've done enough gossiping." and she herded him out.

"How did his boat come to be called 'BERO'?" asked Mike.

"It comes from Betty and Robin, the first two letters of each name." George said . "A lot of people do that." He thought for a moment. "I thought he'd have trouble with that gaff though, I saw him rigging it.... he had fastened his main halyard to a saddle near the centre instead of sharing the load by fitting a strop from the end of the gaff to the saddle.."

"You'd better tell him then." I said, but my mind was on Betty and the intriguing thought that Edward De Bono must have learnt a lot about his theory of lateral thinking from women: who else would put Robin's errors down to a colour scheme, except perhaps a wife hiding his failings, not least of which was a tendency to garrulity and an eagerness to be the centre of attention.!

They never fade Away

When old friends die and leave the scene, They do not fade away.
Mine stay with me in memory and often join my way.
I sailed alone round Britain with Blondie Hasler by my hand,
Though he had died some years back he kept me safe from land.
My father will oft abide in dreams that will not fade
I see him clearly, fondly, as if 'twere bright midday.
Brian, dear friend, joins me when on route to market town
Though he's been dead a full four years I still can see him frown.
Then there's Bob, a farmer's hand who ploughed a straight furrow.
Captain of his cricket team he is still a wondrous fellow.
These are but a very few who join me any time,
Like neighbours calling in to see if I'm still keeping fine.
Yes, there are many, many more. And though they may have died,
I tell you this – it is no line, they are always by my side.

UNCLE JO & THE LITTLE CRUISER

By Chinkie

Rob sailed the smallest boat in the club, an old Silhouette. Despite the small size of his boat, Rob and his family still manage to sail great distances.

"Of course, I don't sail far from land. We haven't room to store water for more than a couple of days," said Rob when we were talking about this business of cruising areas one day. "But day sailing about 15 miles or so, you soon get around. We'd like to get to Lundy and perhaps to Instow this year.

"From the North West, that's a fair step in a small boat," I said. "D'you have to wait for a time of high pressure?"

"It helps, but she will sail - well reefed - in a six. It's not comfortable and we don't set out in anything forecast over four, but that still gives you a lot of time on the water."

"Shayne Acton sailed 'Shrimpy' round the world, didn't he? His boat was about your size, wasn't it?" asked Mike.

"Yes, but didn't 'Shrimpy' have a single keel. I'm not sure what would happen if 'Shell Duck' capsized. We make up the ballast!" He grinned.

'We' included his wife and teenage daughter. Since their Silhouette had only room for two berths, they had removed theirs to sleep a diagonal 'port to starboard' - all very 'matey' but no good in a sea-way. Shayne sailed half way round the world alone and then picked up an attractive girl crew so 'mateyness' was natural, but they still had bunks.

"How on earth do you carry everything?" I asked.

"How did Blyth and Ridgeway find room for three months supplies in a row boat across the Atlantic?" He replied. "Or the Pyes, for that matter. No, you improvise. We have one of those 'Panic Boxes' with the watertight screw lids which we tow behind us filled with milk, butter, bacon etc. A sort of cool box, you could say. Charts are rolled up and stored in a plastic drain pipe and the one in use I put in a plastic envelope to keep dry. We only use the local tide table, no heavy almanacs, and our clothes - in plastic bags - make up our mattresses and pillows."

"What about cooking?" asked George.

"Your missus helped, by introducing us to the 'Dry Pan'. It doubles up as an oven, a saucepan and a frying pan. We use a primus or solid fuel tablets...I don't trust gas with having petrol on board for the outboard. Of course we do as much pre-cooking on land as possible, don't we, Shell?"

His daughter Shelley, a very quiet - rather shy - girl nodded. "Yes, Mum's got one of those big vacuum jugs as well as a large thermos so she makes a stew during theevening on shore and after breakfast she warms it up and puts it into the flask." She blushed, surprising herself with her eloquence and Rob smiled at her affectionately.

"We were talking about anchors the other day. You won't have room for much, will you?" I asked.

"I've a small spade anchor with three fathoms of chain and the rest warp. If I need a stern anchor I either find a large stone off the beach and tie it to a mooring warp or use an old mill weight I keep in the bilges for extra ballast."

I looked at him in growing admiration. "I suppose you use a lead line?" I said.

"Of course" He said innocently, "and a torch."

"A Torch?"

"Yes, to find the bottom in the dark...and to signal with: no navigation lights!" His eyes looked at me roguishly and I decided to quit the unequal contest. I, who had everything - twice over – now shown how to live fully and completely with a penknife, a stone and a sense of the absurd. He was a lucky man. A lovely man.

He sensed my discomfort. "It's alright. Your 30 mile sail is equal to about 10 for us - perhaps less, but we're closer to the water and see more." He laughed. "Sometimes we're so close I don't think I need fishing lines - just dip my hand overboard and flip up a Mackerel, a bit like tickling for trout. Anyway, it means we can slip into little anchorages that are too shallow for you to even see."

"My dear Rob." I said, settling back into Uncle Jo, my beloved old chair, for reassurance, "I'm not belittling you - I admire you. If I were younger and more agile I'd willingly swop places with you for a week,....well perhaps for a couple of days." I said, on reflection.

"I'm not sure I'd want to swop with you" he replied. "No offence, but I'd be always reminding myself that I needed at least six foot of water, and if I was wrong, the damn boat would fall over."

"Don't think I don't often feel the same." I said. "These fin keels are alright for racing men or if you're in a hurry, but there's a lot of comfort in bilge keels."

"What first put you on to boating, Chinkie? You were a RAF man weren't you?" asked Mike.

"There is an RAF yacht club, you know! It was long before that, though - I'd be about 14 - I read ALAIN GERBAULT'S book 'Fight of the Firecrest'. It was the true story of a young Frenchman sailing his thirty something foot cutter across the Atlantic. I remember I was so thrilled about his 'hanging from the bob stay by one hand' that I just had to go to the library to find out just what a 'Bobstay' was! Of course Arthur Ransoms' books helped - but it was the Firecrest that started it all for me. If a Frenchman could do it I was sure I could."

"How long have you actually been sailing?" he asked.

I laughed. "A long time. starting with 'Broads' cruisers - about 50 years, I suppose. I know when you started ...all I say to you is what we used to say in the RAF ...'get some time in'." I grinned at him and confess to making a rude sign. I turned to Rob." What about you?"

"Oh, only when we bought 'Shell Duck' off a friend who was going abroad. It was Jen's idea we should get it - help Shell out of her shell ....oops! Sorry, that was accidental. Is it six or seven years, Shell?" he asked, ,turning to his daughter.

"It was eight years ago, Dad, just after my seventh birthday after I'd learnt to swim."

"Do you like sailing, Shelley?" asked George. He had a wonderful way with youngsters who seemed to expand under the warmth of his personality: he was the ideal commodore for a family club.

"Oh yes. Some of the places we go to are so lovely." She paused, this normally quiet and retiring girl and we all waited, expecting more.

"A fortnight ago, we were in a little cove. We weren't supposed to be there 'cos there was a notice warning people off the beach because of bird's nesting. Dad said they'd have finished by now but we stayed aboard anyway and anchored in a little shallow pool for the night. I woke up early and it was all misty. I got up to look out and heard a bark - and there, only a few feet away, sitting on a rock, was a lovely seal." She paused, her eyes shining with the memory, "His fur was all wet and shiny and we looked at each other for ages and ages till he slipped into the water and vanished. He was so - so beautiful."

What could we say - this child had just summed up what was, for all of us, the greatest joy of cruising in small boats: meeting up with the unexpected, the joy of finding out what is just around the corner.

A Poem, clear as a running stream.

A poem is like a jig saw, each piece must carefully fit
In colour size and meaning, there's really no remit.
No matter whether it rhymes or sings,
It must have truly bottomings
And tops all true - from side to side
The meaning must abide.

Each stanza must a picture be
So that the poem runs straight and free
Saying just what you're aiming to,
Telling all that you feel true.
The meaning must abide.

If possible it should easily read
So others, unknown can all agree
The idea is clear and understood -
Nothing left for one to brood.
The meaning must abide.

The use of rhyme gives a sense of lilt,
As in a song, it is inbuilt,
But break the meter now and then
To give suspense,
Give happenstance
A chance for latent thrill.

UNCLE JO and THE PRAGMATIST

by Chinkie

I was standing with two new members at the club house window, enjoying the scene. It was a warm, sunny afternoon, a few sails flapping in the almost non existent wind and the occasional swoop of a gull.

"What are those men doing?" asked Martin. "Surely they don't work on the buoy down there!"

I looked and saw that number three had been brought ashore for its biennial overhaul. The locals were collecting their supper.

I explained: "No. It's the lads taking the mussels off."

"Mussels?"

"Yes. The buoys are brought ashore about every other year for repainting and general overhaul. While they're afloat they become covered with Mussels so that when the buoys are brought in, word gets around and all the chaps come down for their share of the plunder."

"Do they eat them or use them for bait?" He asked.

"Good heavens, they eat them. Number three's had a good two years since it last came in so they should be a good size."

Martin looked bewildered. I think he only thought of Mussels as a poor bait that wouldn't stay on the hook. "They grow about an inch a year so a two year old Mussel is good eating, at least it is at this time, well after spawning. Besides, Number three is in deep water so the shells will be clean, none of the grit you get in beach or trawled mussels. Quite often you have to keep those in a clearing tank to clean them out!"

I glanced casually across the bay. Surprisingly, there was a speedboat being motored fast between the moored boats. We don't get many lunatics here but....."Hey, lend me your glasses a mo" I cried to Louise who had been lazily swinging a pair of binoculars by their strap.

I snatched them and noted her surprise but hurriedly put them to my eyes. I had trouble adjusting them but then I began to search the far side of the bay. I spotted it, a small dinghy with two young boys fishing, at least they had been fishing but now they were hanging on as the wake of the speed boat tossed them about. They had tied their dinghy to a mooring buoy on a short painter which seemed to be snatching at the bow of the dinghy on the surges. The lads in the speedboat were turning for another sweep. Surely, I thought, they wouldn't be so foolish.

They came around again, closer this time and as they went past the little dinghy nose-dived - it went down. The speedboat sped on.

"Quick," I cried, thrusting the glasses back at Louise. "Help me...two lads in the water!" I dashed out to the dinghy ramp. Tim was dragging his dinghy up.

"Tim - Tim," I cried. "There are kids in the water, there look." I pointed. "They're way out."

He looked at me, then looked where I was pointing. "Can't see..." He began, but then turned his boat back to the sea and Martin and I helped him pull it down. Martin found the boys with his glasses. "They're hanging on to the buoy." He said.

"I'll row." I said and Martin made as if to join us. "No room - go call the coast guard."I cried, and then, to Tim "You start the outboard....never was any good with those things."

"How do I get the coast guard?" shouted Martin.

He was a new member, of course. "Phone. club house" I called and saw him turn back.

"Damn!" said Tim. "Iv'e flooded it - it's still hot"

"Do what you can" I puffed, rowing in short strokes, feeling the strain on my stomach. The tide was helping.

"Let me row" said Tim.

"You get that bloody outboard going. I can't cope with Seagulls - don't know 'em." I snarled.

I kept rowing, glancing over my shoulder and wondering if the buoy was getting any closer. There was a splutter and the engine coughed into life, ran for five seconds and stopped. I glared at Tim and grabbed the oars again.

Suddenly the engine caught and we were motoring hard. The bow went up so I leant back as far as I could, staring into the spray.

"I think I can see them." said Tim , but my glasses were useless in all that spray. I faced forward and hurriedly cleaned them and then turned round again. Almost at once I saw the boys and one of them saw us: he gave us a wave but the other lad looked all in. A few yards off I saw him lose his hold and sink below the surface.

Tim is older than me and the boy in the water was struggling to hold on himself.

"Cut the engine, I'm going in." I shouted, pulling off my boots and jacket.

"No. Wait till we reach the buoy."

A second or two later he had hold of one lad and I dived overboard, the dinghy leaping about like a mad thing. God, the water was cold! I duck dived, trying to judge the strength and direction of the tide. It was very murky as I kicked out and down. I saw something pale and caught what felt like an arm. I hung on and pushed for the surface. Luckily the tide was very weak and I soon surfaced. I saw the dinghy about ten feet from me and shouted. Somehow, Tim had got the other lad aboard, shivering and helpless - and now put his weight on the oars.

As Tim got to me I grabbed the stern and pulled at the limp arm. Tim helped and almost turned the dinghy over: there was no way we were going to be able to get that lad aboard.

There was a shout and the work boat came alongside.

"Early dip, Chinkie? Here, let me have him." said a voice as I hung on.

"He's out" I said, stupidly.

"Give him a bunk up as we pull" said Peter from the work boat and soon both the boy and I were on board. One of the men was giving the kiss of life and then thumping the sodden chest. I watched shivering as the engine powered up to take us ashore, Tim tied on behind. I was watching the lad.

Had I been in time, and anyway, how long did it take for someone to drown ? Suddenly he started to splutter and vomit in the bilges. Thank god he was going to be alright. Reaction had set in and I was shivering violently. Coats had been put round the two boys and Tim had passed mine from the dinghy as we set off back for the club house.

"We saw you rowing like a mad thing," said Peter, "We thought at first you'd seen someone on your boat but when you headed out here we knew something was wrong."

"How on earth did you get this launched so quickly?" I stuttered.

"We'd pulled her up the beach when we'd landed number three. We were getting the mussels when you went down the beach." He explained. "Don't remember seeing you move so fast before, Chinkie! Anyway, with five of us it was no trouble."

"Don't know what we'd of done without you. Thanks." I said.

"What happened?"

"Two idiots in a speedboat: their wake overturned the lads' dinghy"

"Ah," said Peter, "Lucky you saw them then. Whose speedboat was it?"

I shivered. "No idea, I've not seen it before, it's not from round here."

By the time we'd reached the beach there was a coastguard landrover by the slip the Coastguard using his walkie talkie.

"There'll be an ambulance in five minutes." he said -"Take you all for a check up." He looked at Peter. "What happened?"

Explanations - endless questions - names, name of boat (no one knew, of course), when, where, why.....!

"I'm going to the clubhouse." I said. Some members had come down to see the excitement.

"I'll come with you!" said George. "You want a hot shower."

"I've no clothes, they are all on the boat." I protested.

"We'll find a blanket. Shower first!"

"The boys....."

"They are going to the hospital for a check up, they'll be getting baths, I expect." said George.

"I didn't see their fishing gear." I said."I suppose it will have gone with the tide."

"I imagine that's the least of their worries." said George.

Later, wrapped in a blanket - George had gone off to my boat for some dry clothes - I sat in dear old Uncle Jo, my beloved armchair. ""Here you are." said Veronica, holding out a mug of tea. "Quite the hero, then!"

"Oh God, no!" I said as this sunk in. "No. Veronica, I don't want to talk about it."

I closed my eyes, thinking of that dive into the cold sea, of the yellow jacket which had saved the boys' life - I'd never have seen him without it. What had I been thinking of. I'm no hero, far from it, but somehow there wasn't time to think: I suppose when the crunch comes, there never is. If you stopped to think or consider - you'd never do anything.

I could hear murmuring but kept my eyes closed. I felt drained, my head ached and my guts were on fire. Most of all, though, was a burning anger, a hot blazing anger at the blind stupidity of youth. A game gets out of hand; barracking starts as a laugh and becomes a lynching; an argument becomes a fight, the fight a battle! At the time it was just anger: the rationalising comes in writing it down, in attempting to relate simple boyish pranks. I had once been party to the forcible bathing of a fellow recruit in the RAF, but that had at least the justification of the fellow being indescribably dirty! On another occasion as a youth I had vandalised a swimming bath: for that there was no excuse. Fortunately for me, I had owned up and was forgiven but all I can now remember was the stupidity of it.! Was this how it felt after the Huysel Stadium disaster?

I heard Veronica saying "Leave him, he'll be alright. I'll stay, George."

I knew tears were streaming down my face and felt a handkerchief thrust into my hand. I covered my eyes, feeling weak.

"Not now, leave him be" another voice which faded off.

I was shuddering. "Here, drink this!" I looked up. A strange face: "It's alright. I'm a doctor. Just drink this." I drank the strong fluid, feeling it warming me - hot rum and peppermint, it tasted like.

"How are..." I stuttered.

"They're alright. Now you take it easy. Don't do anything at all until at least half an hour after the shivering stops. You'll be alright then. You look as strong as a horse."

I looked up and tried to smile but felt myself break down again. "Damn them, damn them." I cried and closed my eyes again. For some reason I thought of the man I had met at my secretary's wedding: he had been at Auschwitz and had not forgotten the games they played with the prisoners!

"It's the reaction, we saw it in B.C. when someone had an accident with a saw and the guys who brought him in used to..." the Doctor's voice faded into the background. Was it British Columbia that had taught him to use Rum, I wondered. I guessed it was more likely that they drank whisky in those climes.

Sometime later I found Mike sitting beside me.

"Why, Mike?" My shivering had stopped. "Why do people behave like they do? Those lads in the speedboat - they must have known!"

He looked at me and waited. Then "They were playing, Chinkie. When they read about it tomorrow they'll feel a twinge of conscience perhaps - but I expect next week they'll be at it again. Look at drunken drivers - they never blame themselves for long. Just thoughtlessness."

"Isn't there a God?"

He chuckled. "Must be - think of Peter and the boys on the beach, so handy to the launch. But a God of retribution....I hope not. It's inside us, Chinkie. We make our own heaven and hell. It's your hell today but come tomorrow and you'll be back to watching us all again. In that armchair you're like a spider, sitting in the entrance of its web, feeling all the vibrations. Don't think we don't know!" He laughed.

"Oh Mike, sometimes I hate the world." I paused, looked at him and sighed. "I like some of the people, though."

"That's enough! You're getting maudlin. Ah, here's George with your togs. Bet he's forgotten something!"

George came in with a sail bag full of clothes.

"You're coming back with us tonight." He said. "Vere's gone off to make a hot pot for supper."

"But my sleeping bag's on...."

"D'you think Vere'd let you bring your sweaty old bag into the house? C'mon, get dressed."

The next morning, sitting down to a civilised breakfast I asked "Will they find the lads from the speedboat?"

"I think the police know who they are" said George "But proving it...!"

He drank some tea and then added quietly "By the way, they told me that a speedboat's been found holed below the water line over at the point. Must have broken from it's mooring!" Veronica was silent.

A God of retribution ? I thought of what Mike had said. He was right, of course, so there had to be a pragmatist somewhere.....the lads on the beach, friends of the boys? I would never know, nor did I want to. I have to admit that I don't ordinarily like pragmatists: they're too full of prowess in their practicality, their methods usually lack originality or imagination....usually!. I helped myself to more toast and smiled at my hostess.

"The sun's come out." I said as a warm ray of light shone across the table and we talked of other things.

NO FAIR WINDS

A new member, Mike Aldridge, having bought a K22 Junk rigged boat in Penzance but having very limited experience of sailing in dinghies, accepted my offer to help him bring the boat by sea back to his home base near Sittingbourne in Kent in late summer of 1999..

We drove by hire car to Penzance on Sunday August 1st, arriving in the early afternoon to book into a motel that Mike had kindly arranged so that we had at least one night of peace. After booking in Mike decided that he needed to find the farmhouse where 'Tilley Hats' were imported before being distributed throughout the U.K. He was determined to buy one that fitted, having and poor experience with salespeople in Chichester. We didn't find the place but located the area and saw the signs leading to it. That evening, before returning to our motel we found a restaurant for a meal. In Penzance everything closes down at 9pm so you have to go out into the country if you want a meal. I had the strangest meal I have ever had, Chicken Breasts with Asparagus tips. It sounded delightful but when it came I had no idea what meat was on my plate. It tasted more like well boiled Salmon and looked like that. The asparagus was in tiny chips in a cream sauce. It was all rather horrid and not a good harbinger for the trip.
The next morning, before going to the harbour to work on the boat, off we went to hunt the hat! Up tiny lanes with high hedges, past hidden houses and outbuildings we finally located this secret venue. A charming Cornish lady then proceeded to make sure that Mike tried on the full range before he finally bought one. I was so impressed with the whole procedure including finding the place that I succumbed and bought one myself. Never have I paid as much for a hat - £45 – but it carries it's own insurance, is guaranteed a lifetime's use etc. etc. It makes me look like an Aussie backwoodsman and I feel I should be singing 'Waltzing Matilda' although it is an American design.

After this we returned to Penzance, but now this rather dismal place was thronged with people who, because the weather was damp and dark, had forsaken the beaches for the lure of the shops. We could not find anywhere to park! An hour later, after lunch was over we finally found a spot not too far from the boat and started to unload. The tide was out so we made four journeys over the mud, with all our gear around our shoulders. The last trip was with the dinghy pulled behind us so that we could get ashore when the tide came in. This was the moment for me to fall flat on my back in the mud!

Once aboard and sorted out, and with the afternoon rapidly waning we had a good look around at what Mike had bought. The hull was sound and clean. Inside, though full of unsorted gear we had brought, all seemed well. On deck the story was very different. The anchor cable and the anchor were so rusty that the first task was to use a hack saw on the chain and let it slip back through the hawse pipe for later disposal. The anchor shackle was so rusted that there was no way of unscrewing it and as it was a bit too much for our baby saw we left it and shackled the new chain and warp to it. We were to regret this later!

The mast, being a junk, was through deck mounted but the jamming wedges were loose and could be slid up and down the mast from the fo'csle. The first big blow and they would have fallen into the boat, the mast left to float in it's collar with possible disastrous effects. We had the awful job of getting all the old gunk off the mast, cleaning it and hammering the wedges home until all were even, using – for want of a mallet – the end of a socket spanner. The retaining band had obviously slipped so we removed it and packed the mast beneath it with some webbing strapping before remaking the joint. At some stage in the future, this would have to be removed and replaced by a pair of jubilee clips but it should get us home.

The running rigging was looking pretty tacky but by this time it was starting to get dark and we needed to clean up and clear up inside the boat. There were more problems. The Echo Sounder didn't. No oil in the tube so that was easily rectified, but for how long had the previous owner sailed the boat in this condition? The log also did not work but I did not dare try and pull out the transducer as I was not sure if the cover cap was either the right one or if it would fit. Fortunately Mike had bought an electronic trailing log so this failure was not important. More basic was the fact that the masthead anchor and tricolour lights did not work either. I pulled Mike up the mast in a bosun's chair but he could not easily reach to find out how to get the cover off and we had to give up. We did have a bicolour and fitted this later so that we were legal if night sailing. The stern light at least was operational.

The engine, an old Evinrude 6hp twin, looked O.K. but we would not know until we had tried it out for real. It started alright which was a good sign and the owner had told us it had been marinised over the winter – something that proved to be either untrue or very badly done. I understand that the owner had bought a new boat but I cannot for the life of me understand how he could have let his existing boat, which he assured us he had been using, get into it's present state. Quite plainly, it was not safe to take to sea in the condition we had found it.

On Tuesday morning, the 3rd of August we left Penzance at 0630 in light winds which meant we had to motor until 1030 when, approaching Lizard Head we had enough wind to sail at 4 knots. Now we had a new problem. When we started to round the headland we had a west going tide and an easterly wind. The sea became choppy and the motion was uncomfortable. Mike soon succumbed and went below with sea-sickness. We had feared this might happen and I wondered if I would be strong and fit enough to take the boat all the way to Kent alone. After an hour or so he came up and once past the Lizard light the motion eased and he improved. We reached St. Mawes at 1700 but after a very short while, decided to sail to Falmouth Yacht Haven so that we could buy some new rope for rigging. The standing and running rigging was very much the worse for wear and the yard Hauling Parrel down to only one strand of a 3 strand 4mm rope! It was a great delight for me to meet again, and be remembered by Molly Minter, the Berthing Supervisor whom I had not seen for 9 years. Her only accession to the passing years was to wear a pair of glasses. Because there was so much to be done to the boat we spent two days in Falmouth, making good rigging, electrics etc. If you have to have a stop over then I can think of few better places to do so than in Falmouth. However, the weather on our second day was foul!

Mike had some pills which he decided to try out to see if they would get rid of his problem of being sea sick. I really felt for him. I have only once suffered myself, in someone else's boat when I doubted whether they had full control. For me, although not very sick, I had a very uncomfortable couple of hours.

We left Falmouth for Plymouth, again facing head winds and motor sailing into force three Easterlies again. This time a new problem occurred. The electronic trailing log that Mike had bought at great expense (£140) stopped working. It transpired that the connectors did not mate up properly and Mike was able to get it going again by fitting a very tight cable tie around the whole instrument so that the contacts were pressed together. This worked after a fashion but looked untidy and later, on one of the longer legs we discovered that the log went from 99 to 323!! Instead of dead reckoning which I had hoped to teach Mike, we made almost constant use of the GPS. We anchored for the night in Cawsand Bay, not having the time to go into Plymouth proper, and the next morning set off for Dartmouth. Before leaving we decided to check on the engine spark plugs: it was sometimes misfiring. When we had them out we could see they were badly oiled up and very worn. They must have done some hundreds of hours and the engine certainly had not been marinised. The sacrificail anode was in an awful state. Fortunately the owner had left us a pair of new plugs.

Dartmouth is a long haul for a small boat from Plymouth, and again we were motor sailing into the usual Easterly winds for a total of eleven hours in very murky conditions and occasional showers. Here we anchored in the river opposite the Town Quay which was full, of course. The H.M., when arriving to collect his money, told us of a boat which had dragged and dropped down onto another boat, causing damage. He had collected it and tied it up to a large tanker buoy using his own ropes as he could find nothing suitable on board. Pulling in the anchor chain he found it woefully short, almost too short to reach the bottom of the harbour, a depth of around 20 ft! I thought of the "Three men in a Boat" story —yet another sailor woefully unprepared for sailing.

The next morning found us lounging about, together with another four boats, waiting for the man on the fuel barge to arrive. Instead of an 8.30 start we were delayed until nearly 10am. Obtaining fuel (Petrol) was to become one of our major problems. At this stage we had a running tank carrying 5.5 gallons and a further 3 gallons in two carry tanks. With the endless Easterly winds we were almost continuously motor sailing. Late as it was we set off for Weymouth. I debated whether we should stop off at Lyme Regis but it was unlikely that we would be able to get into that tiny harbour which we would not reach until gone 7pm so decided to soldier on. This was an awful mistake because, due to our late start we got to the Bill as the tide turned against us. We were well out but when we started heading north to take the inside of the Shambles, we caught the edge of the west going race and for nearly two hours we were almost standing still, though motoring at around 4 knots. There was another boat in front of us and we held station for two hours before the tide slackened enough to let us through. By now we were desperately short of fuel so decided to anchor off the beach rather than possibly have the engine fail at the entrance to the harbour. This at 4 in the morning!

It was a dreadful time with the bumpiest four hours I can remember and we were delighted to be able to start the engine and crawl into the harbour after an early cup of tea. We made for the fuel barge – NO PETROL! We were advised that there was a garage near the supermarket some half mile up the town. We motored up to the holding pontoon, reserved for boats wailing to go up river when the bridge did it's bi-hourly rise. Mike went off with our two cans and made two trips to get petrol, first to fill the ready tank and then to have spare fuel. Mike was proving to be a real mate and a first class companion, not averse to hard work. I had to cope with the H.M. who came to tell me that I was breaking the by-law which restricted the use of the pontoon for onward river traffic. I told him what I though of a harbour without fuel and he went away without taking any action. There was little he could have done because Weymouth was jam packed with boats, mostly up for the Eclipse.

We were glad to leave and headed East, again into Easterly winds. Praying had turned out to be spectacularly useless, but then I am not a religious man. You cannot expect a cobbler to make bread, or a Deity to listen to a heathen.

At the sensible hour of 4.15 we stopped at Lulworth Cove where we dropped anchor for the night. My but how we needed a quiet night to make up for the previous 24 hours. In the morning we dinghied ashore and walked to the village about a mile away for fresh bread and milk. It was pointless moving off before midday as we would have been needlessly heading the tide so we dallied ashore. At 12 we returned to the boat and just as we got aboard I realised we were moving, the anchor was dragging. I started the engine while Mike began to retrieve the anchor. No anchor! The shackle had finally given up the ghost. All we had left on board was a small fisherman's anchor which just might have held the dinghy. We set off for Poole!

Motor sailing into an Easterly, of course. Now another tragedy. In our haste to leave Lulworth Cove we must have made a bodge of tying up the dinghy. This was understandable because the boat was dragging her anchor as we boarded and everything was done in a hurry. Once round St Alban's head we realised that the dinghy had gone walkabout. It was pointless to turn back as we would have no idea where to look. This was a brand new dinghy, less than a fortnight old. I called the Solent C.G. to explain in case some one later found it and thought there might be a yacht in trouble. Five minutes later they came back to say that Portland C.G. had been advised that the dinghy had been seen and collected by another yacht who would leave it at Dartmouth Marina for collection. Another long drive for Mike when we finally got back home but at least he had not lost his dinghy.

In Poole we were able to tie up at the town Quay and the next morning Mike went to the Chandlery just opposite our mooring and bought an anchor and some more rope. In the town he also found a small hurricane lamp which we would need for an anchor light. So far we had used my battery lantern shining onto the deck when lashed to the rigging. Mike was unable to buy any paraffin, no-one seemed to stock it, so he came back with a small bottle of scented lamp oil. The lamp took about two thirds on one filling!

It was while at Poole that we met our first other Kingfisher owner. NEP, a K20 was moored two boats out from us. We chatted with Roy Clare but he did not stay for the night as he had a mooring in the area.

From Poole our next step was to the Solent where we spent a quiet night at anchor off the North shore a little way up from Lymington, ready to call at Portsmouith the next morning for fuel. We called Gosport Marina and explained that we wanted a short stay to buy another fuel tank – we were sure we should have two ready tanks, one each side of the engine ready for quick changeovers – and to get petrol. The marina was full to overflowing but we did get a temporary berth on the North wall. It was as we were entering Portsmouth Roads that the eclipse occurred. It lasted about ten minutes and the skies, already heavily clouded, darkened to the West but stayed light and clear in the east. As if to celebrate the event, all the lights went on in Ryde and Mike suggested that we should switch on our Nav. Lights as a warning to other boats. I thought this would be gilding a very tarnished lily and declined the idea. Very few boats did light up. Having bought our supplies from the chandlery and stopping for lunch, we left our mooring and approached the Fuel Barge. NO PETROL!

We went back to our temporary mooring and the indefatigable Mike got hold of a trolley, loaded it with all our fuel tanks and walked to the nearest garage to fill up. Fortunately there was one just outside the gates of the Marina. I offered to help but Mike was quite adamant. I suspect he thought I might have a heart attack if I did too much. His job is to ferry disabled people around for outings and holidays and he must be a whizz with them. He treated me as though I were an invalid: never was I allowed to go forward to anchor or adjust the rigging, even though he is himself a non swimmer.. I discovered later that my not wearing either a life jacket or belt worried him. He was not sure he would be able to recover me if I went overboard. Truth is that I never wear a life jacket and only rarely a life line. This is a foolishness that goes with old age: do as I say, not as I do!! He is about the best person one could have to share a cruise with

We finally left Poole and time was now running short. I suggested to Mike an all night stint, to which he agreed, but I insisted that during darkness we should not use the engine but sail, albeit in long tacks. The Easterly winds still hounded us. They were long tacks, in time at least. I watched the lights or Worthing for most of the night and a check of the chart shows that we covered one mile in two hours. But the sky was a myriad of stars, a sight rarely seen nowadays because of the glare of town lights. Twice other boats passed us, sailing in the opposite direction with wind and tide both aiding. It was all very frustrating. Eventually the next night we rounded Dungeness and anchored of Dymchurch in the shallows, both very tired.

The following morning, after another bumpy night we woke to our first Westerly wind and had an exhilarating sail up to Ramsgate which we entered at 4pm. We were both lucky and unlucky. It was the first day of Ramsgate Regatta and we arrived before the major influx of boats. The wind had freshened to a Westerly 6, blowing straight into the Marina. With this in mind and being told over the radio to take a vacant finger berth I naturally chose one upwind and we tied up nicely. Then, a courtly figure with white hat and gold braid at his chest asked me to move to the opposite side, down wind, as the space I was in was reserved for one of the regatta boats. I assumed he was the berthing master or H.M. and very reluctantly agreed to move. He offered to go round and take our lines. I knew it would be a dicey procedure since an outboard in reverse is just about unsteerable. I tried backing in but the wind was too strong and I had to turn. The wind then took hold and despite revving up in reverse we hit the jetty as this benighted man just watched and waited for a line, making no attempt to hold us off! I discovered later that he was the Vice Commodore of one of the visiting clubs and wanted the space for his mates. Meanwhile I found I had holed the bow!!! This surprised me as I had understood that all Kingfishers had a steel or lead plate down the bow behind the Gelcoat. This was obviously not true as we could see daylight! Fortunately the Chandlery stocked Epoxy putty and it was a simple job to fill the hole. Mike was amazing. I had holed his boat, albeit accidentally, but he kept his cool. I just wish I had been more spirited in defending my rights to keep the first berth we had entered but I admit to being dead tired after some eleven hard days and nights. The Marina at Ramsgate is a wonderful place and the best and cheapest we met in the whole trip. There is a short stay Marina where you don't need to lock in and a long stay Marina for those staying a few days. The harbour exit leads straight to one of the best and cheapest restaurants and we had a wonderful meal with a bottle of wine for less than £20 FOR THE PAIR OF US!

The next morning we asked where the fuel barge was – NO PETROL! This at the start of the Regatta week! The berthing attendant offered to take us in his car after nine ocklock to the nearest garage but we could not afford the delay and set off just after 8.30am. We did have three gallons and if the usual Easterlies were there again we would have plenty. We had missed the forecast but being so nearly at the end of our journey we took the chance. A grand sail up to the East Margate buoy, but in a Westerly, yesterday's wind! Would you believe it. after ten days of Easterlies we now had a Westerly heading us yet again down the Thames. It had eased from the levels of the previous day and was around a three to four. I tried sailing and for a time we had the tide with us. This, of course meant a lumpy sea and Mike disappeared below feeling ill. He had done very well so far, only very occasionally feeling sick but never actually being sick. He could not have chosen a worse moment. My eyesight is not good and I had great difficulty in trying to find the buoys. I was tacking in short timed tacks which made DR impossible. It had to be either GPS or eyeball. We had no autohelm and I could not handle the steering, GPS and a chart so did the best I could. Suddenly I noted broken water ahead. I changed tacks and Mike appeared at this moment. From then on he was by my side as we made our tortuous way up the Princes channel. With hindsight I can see that we would have been much better off on the inshore channel but chose what I thought would be the safest route in terms of depths. Since we only drew 2.3 ft. the inshore channel would have been perfectly safe. When you are very tired it is difficult to make rational decisions, at least that is how I defend myself.

The tide changed by mid afternoon and from then on it was a battle royal to get to the Medway. We had the Power Station cooling tower in sight when the engine stopped, out of petrol. I tried to tack but the tide took us slowly but surely eastwards. I got as close to the Isle of Sheppey as I could and we dropped anchor, advising both Thames C.G. and the Medway Port operations of our position. We had so little paraffin left that Mike was waiting until the last minute to light it. The decision was made for us when a catamaran pulled up alongside and told us he had found us on Radar and were we in trouble. We thanked him and said we would wait for the tide tomorrow, lit the lamp and settled down for yet another bumpy night. I got up to attend to the needs of nature at 3am and as I got into the cockpit the lamp went out. Back with my electric lantern.

The next morning Mike had a look at the running tank and reckoned that there was still a lot of petrol left in it. We drained the little 2hp outboard into a jug and got about a litre of fuel. Then Mike lifted out the Evinrude and while I held it, removed one of the ready tanks, put a funnel into the other and upended the used tank. Almost a gallon of fuel came out so everything was put back and with the gauge of one tank now ready a quarter full we set off, with the tide but still with adverse winds for our final destination. We were able to sail until well into the Medway, a joy after all that motoring. The Junk rig really is a 'B' upwind in anything under a four and cannot cope with a three knot tide, but then, very few rigs can, I suppose.

I had set out to teach Mike seamanship during the cruise. We started with basic knots and moved on to anchors, chain scopes, charts, reading distances and making allowance for tides. I was unable to teach him dead reckoning because of the faulty log, but I believe that he not only learnt the purpose of the various rigging ropes on the junk but could now sensibly read a chart and understood the significance of tides. Also he learnt the extreme power of sail compared with an engine: only three panels taking us on a beam reach at over 5 knots in a force six. I don't think the engine could ever have reached five knots on its own! I would have liked to have done so much more for this delightful man, for instance briefing on R/T procedures, river bars, the effect of atmospheric pressure on depth etc. but we were always pressed for time. I have no doubt that working to deliver the boat as we did rather than have it taken by road has taught Mike so much more than he could have learnt in the sterile atmosphere of a night school class room. He will not attempt to motor with the engine cover on, for instance, and will not let any battens move further forward than 90 degrees to the boat centre line. He knows to aim for a 5 deg. slant between wind and sail and he understands how to try and avoid a jibe though I had no opportunity to teach him to sail by the lee: we never had following winds! Yes, I reckon Mike is now an "Able Seaman"

Mike's friends were waiting for him on the pontoon. We had said we would try and get to the club jetty by 3pm on Sunday 15th August. After some 400 miles in mostly opposing winds we arrived, 10 minutes late!

I NEARLY MADE IT, DIDN'T I?

Dedication

I dedicate this story first and foremost to the wonderful Coastguards who protect people like me who sail our coasts, backed up by the RNLI. Secondly to the Cancer Relief Macmillan Fund for whom I have the greatest respect and for whom this journey made some funds and finally for all those folk who spend their time in small boats sailing round the coast of Britain. I hope this tale may encourage those who use their boats as sea borne caravans in Marinas to venture to sea and enjoy new friendships.

FOREWORD

In 1990, I chose to sail round Britain single handed because in 1980 I had been given a poor prognosis after an operation for cancer and from which my best friend Peter had died ten years later in January 1990 from the same disease. In his case he had left it too late to save himself by asking for a second diagnosis. The trip was by way of a memoriam to Peter and I decided to collect for Cancer Relief Macmillan Fund who do so much for the families of patients and can now record collecting about £5000 for their funds. As a result of my operation I am a colostomist and this added it's own complications to the trip.

This record starts at Hesketh Bank. Something that very nearly didn't happen at all because on the preceding Friday night, while loading the boat, I had fallen from the ladder onto the safety rails and from there into the mud of the river bank. Fortunately the tide was out and I just missed hitting a stanchion with my back. I managed to see my GP on the Saturday morning but luckily I had done nothing, no more serious damage than a few bruises and scrapes to my back and arms and despite his advice that I should put off the start for a week I decided to go. After all, the TV cameramen had been booked and all my friends would be there to send me off.

JUNKETTE AT HER MOORING JETTY

The following report takes me from Hesketh Boatyard round Britain to Anglesey, a distance of around 2500 miles, mainly single handed.

From Hesketh Bank to Ramsey

On Monday, 23rd April – St. George's Day – I set out on the great adventure. TV Cameras watched my every move as I raised the new sails 'in anger' for the first time and turned out to motor into the flooding tide from the Douglas boatyard at Hesketh Bank, down towards Lytham at 9 am. Cameramen were running along the bank to catch my attempts to improve sail shape etc. and my friends to keep me in sight for as long as possible. The weather was fine and sunny and all augured well for the start of my 'cruise'.

Hesketh boatyard, much used by yachtsmen (I mean the sort of yachtsman who builds or maintains his own boat, usually on a shoe string with what's left from the groceries) because of the excellent chandlers - the Campbells had built their Junk rigged schooner here - lies on a tributary of the Ribble near Preston.

JUNKETTE LEAVING THE RIVER RIBBLE

There is not much water (but plenty of mud) so you leave as soon as you are afloat, and with a little luck you reach Lytham as the tide turns to allow you to rush out eleven miles through the shoals to the sea. If you misjudge the channel then you are going to be on the sand for a good many hours. The buoyed channel silted up a year ago so the training wall was breached and now the new 'southern' channel is only marked by a few fishermen's buoys. Of course I lost sight of them and was soon on echo sounder and prayers. I must admit at this stage that my eyesight leaves a lot to be desired and I was to have continuing difficulty in locating buoys throughout the trip.

There was a slight north westerly - right on the nose so it was a case of motor sailing but by 11 am I was at last in deep water and could relax and give a radio call (T.R.) to the coast guard. From now on I was to keep the coast guard continuously aware of my movements, with TR's (transit reports) morning and night so that if anyone wanted me they had only to speak to coast guard to find me. This was important because of keeping contact with Cancer Relief committees and also Radio Manchester who were monitoring my trip with fortnightly radio broadcasts.

In mid afternoon I was 'buzzed' by a large fishing trawler. This was to happen once more in Scotland. I guess it was because at some time they had been troubled by a thoughtless pleasure boat. Whichever way I turned it would try to steam across my bows so that I would foul its nets. It was a Belgian boat and too big to argue with. A similar thing happened to a yachtsman in the channel when a French fishing boat sailed tight across his bows and then claimed new nets. They towed him to France and he had to pay up over £1000 pounds for 'careless navigation'. Eventually the Belgian boat left me.

This is the time to admit that the Irish sea is no ordinary sea: it is a Celtic sea and not all the 'little men' are in Ireland, nor do they all come out of a barrel of 'Poteen'! Somehow they have become aquatic and their mischievous antics abound in these western waters. Their origin is obscure but they could be the spirits of Irish Saints or of more recent unhappy souls from that tortured but beautiful land. Whatever, I doubt not that one was at hand on the bridge of that Belgian trawler! Consider the fishing trawlers lost here at sea: how often has one of these gremlins been known to cloud the periscope mirror of a submarine at the crucial moment. I sacrificed a glass of gin to them: not too dissimilar to poteen!

At 7.40 pm. I saw Mangold light on the Isle of Man but I now had the tide against me and progress was slow. Eventually I entered my first port of call, Ramsey, at 11 pm. and I had a familiar re-introduction into the problems of single handing: how to tie up in the dark at half tide. I found a ladder in the deserted harbour, and heart in mouth I ascended with a torch, taking both bow and stern warps with me to find something to tie on to. It was pitch black and everywhere seemed to be covered with builder's bits and pieces but eventually I found a bollard for the stern. All I could find for the bow was a wheel-barrow some distance away (a huge one!) amongst the builders rubble as this side of the harbour was being rebuilt. I only had just enough warp to reach it.

I had been up since 6 am and at the helm since 9 am and was knackered! I retired to my bunk and went out like a light. The following morning, when I could see my way, I moved JUN-KETTE across the harbour to tie up alongside another yacht and began to make enquiries about publicity. The main purpose of the trip being to raise money for Cancer Relief, it was essential that the local media knew of my presence. My first set - back was to discover that no one in Ramsey knew anything about my visit, but that was soon put right and the press came, radio arrived and I found I was the lead story on the midday Manx news.

I found myself suffering a dichotomy about press coverage as time went on. I am not one for much personal publicity and I had hoped that the Cancer Relief organisation would look after that side of things. However, partly due to the fact that I could give no clear time table and that I often visited ports where no local committee existed, I found I had to make arrangements myself. Holding out the begging bowl was also not quite me and there were times I wished I had the panache of a Botham.

Since my last visit to this lovely harbour, arrangements for visiting yachts had changed and now they are welcomed to the inner basin, the bridge being raised for boats when required as there is much more room beyond the bridge. However, I stayed in the outer harbour, ready for a quick get away at half tide. Far from having a rest in Ramsey, I was so feted that I was glad to depart and start the serious business of sailing again. People were invariably kind and helpful when they knew what I was doing and exceedingly generous. A Scottish Skipper, Bryce Walker - a retired farmer, insisted on standing me a dinner on my second night in harbour and the Commodore of the Yacht club spent a considerable time with me, promising me a great reception on my return and complaining that they had not been warned of my arrival. I am only too sad that force of circumstance dictated against me actually getting back to Ramsey. I know I missed out on a superb reception.

There was one very warming occurrence when a young lady asked me to tell her about the voyage as she was doing a project on the harbour for school, and when I finished, asked if she could take a photograph of me. When she came to go, she felt in her pocket and gave me 20p for the Cancer Relief box: *"It's all I've got left of my pocket money"* she said!

In the corners of my mind are memories of Manxland: for many years I had a pen and ink drawing prepared for the TV programme 'Jackanory' by one of our designers, Paul Montague, who had given it to me as a momentoe after the programme. It showed a Viking ship approaching the island, full of helmeted warriors bearing shields while on the cliffs could be seen hordes of Manxmen waiting to do battle - all very fierce and illustrating the independence of the Island. Today the Tindwall (Island parliament), the oldest in the world still makes its own laws and the low income tax is an inducement to mainlanders to settle there, though shortage of building land is making it difficult for the Island to accept many more émigrés and the doors are closing.

Other memories include the notion that they must eat a lot of salt fish in Peel. There are more urinals in that town than in any

I have been in, either before or since! Douglas has a harbour wall made of spaghetti! At least that is what it looks like from seaward. My first visit to the Island was just after the Second World War when, with my mother, we went for a day to Douglas on the S.S. St. Tudno from Llandudno. We spent all our time gormandising: after five years of pasty grey bread it was a treat to eat a lovely fresh, crispy crusted white loaf spread thickly with butter, and to have it with fat Manx kippers. There were trams in Douglas then; reminders of the transport we had used back home in Leeds in the thirties: hard seats, rattles and clangs, whines and bells, but no smells of petrol, of rubber...just dust.

The Island has its own flag, three legs forming the spokes of a wheel on a red background. The sensible and courteous yachtsman wears the flag at his yardarm when in a Manx harbour. I wasn't sensible: I had left mine at home, a poor return for all the friendliness and courtesy shown to me. The idea of wearing the flag of the country you are visiting is not only a nice gesture but advises other boats that you are a visitor (which they would see from your ensign if abroad) and may need help or advice. Of course, it can count against you in some places. Even in British waters some sailors have found the sight of a red or blue ensign in Northern Ireland an invitation to have their moorings cast off during the night!

From the Isle of Man to Port Partick

I left Ramsey just before midday, heading for the Isle of Whithorn on the Solway Firth. I had a good south westerly to help me on my way, but just north of Ramsey the Autopilot began to play up: this was to go on until I reached Stonehaven right round Britain on the East coast! The pin broke this time so 'George" went sick. At 3 pm the wind increased rapidly to a six and I had to reef down, but got caught out and jibed so that the only wooden batten I used (the rest were nylon) broke under the strain. I was faced with lowering the main or losing the sail if I jibed again. I first began to haul in on the jib reefing line, but with an eye on the main I didn't realise that the foresheets had become tangled with the sail and I got a snarl up with a great flapping envelope of sail.

    I quickly lowered the main and then, after fitting safety harness and line, went forward to try and clear the tangle and tame the foresail. It took thirty minutes of cursing, praying, and panicking until I realised how to untangle it. I got it furled and then let out enough to sail on, but now I had missed the tide advantage (it takes longer than you think to clear a tangle like that) and spent an hour covering the last mile into the Isle of Whithorn, sailing on reefed jib alone.

The tide runs very fast across the entrance and there is a long reef to port as you approach. There used to be a perch - there was on my last visit - but now there was just a small red buoy. I discovered later that this buoy had been put down by the local chandler (Bob's buoy) after the perch disintegrated (over a hundred years old) early in the year. The jib alone was insufficient to drive me against the tide so I started the engine and motor sailed into the bay. The tide was now too low to enter the harbour so I anchored off and went ashore in the dinghy, having to haul it a considerable distance over the foreshore of rocks, sand and pools to the foot of the harbour wall. This was my first introduction to what I called 'the sweat'! ie. getting the dinghy off the cabin roof and into the water. It was really too heavy for one person to handle easily and I began to regret that I had not bought a rubber dinghy, but knew that in extremis, the double skinned 'Dingo' would prove a safer vehicle since I had no room for a life raft. At least it was easier to launch than to retrieve when I then would have to drop the life lines to get the boat over the gunwale.

While trying to telephone home one of those spontaneous acts of kindness which I kept meeting occurred and Bob Rowley, the local Chandler, recognised me and invited me to his home for a meal and a bath. As I emerged from the bath I saw through the window that JUNKETTE was in trouble. The mainsail was in the water and it was obvious that the lazy jacks that hold the sail to the boom must have broken. Bob had also seen this and we hurried down to the harbour.....to find a Coast Guard landrover on the pier and the Kircudbright life boat standing by JUN-KETTE! Apparently a town local, whom I later met, (full of abject apologies and rather the worse for drink) had reported a yacht in distress with its sail in the water and the 'Round the World' skipper also in the water unable to get back on board. By chance, the harbourmaster, who knew where I was, was himself on a Coast Guard training excersize some miles away. When apologies had been made the lifeboat crew took Bob and me back aboard JUNKETTE (with the sail all neatly stowed and lashed down by them) and we brought the boat into the harbour and onto the visitors berth from whence we repaired to the Inn to restore both ourselves and my good name!.

Next day, my luck was really in because Bob turned out to have been a professional rigger and in no time had fitted new lazy jacks, splicing eyes in the ropes some seven feet above the deck as though it were an every day event. Because he had no stock of cleats, he carved me two from a teak block so that I could tail the rope ends on the boom. A remarkable man, who found a pin from a seagull engine that I managed to fit to my Auto Helm which then became operational again. I had to butcher the case to fit it and that in turn lead to future troubles, of which more later.

  Good fortune was to smile on me yet again as the boss of the quayside Inn, the Steam Packet, offered me the 'family' room for the night free of charge. In it I found the largest bath I have ever seen: I could almost have had a swim in it and I did have a glorious soak. Later, I was to meet again with Bryce Walker who had sailed his boat from Ramsey to Girvan The following morning I made the first of my radio broadcasts with Greater Manchester Radio on the 'Susie Mathis' show, broadcasts I was to make about every fortnight all round Britain. I should have made one as I left Hesketh bank, but I had forgotten to switch my R/T set on and did not hear them calling me.

I spent the rest of day helping repair the lazy jacks and removing the wooden batten pieces. When a wooden batten breaks inside the sleeve, it is extraordinarily difficult to extract the sharp, needle like pieces of wood. I replaced the broken batten with a spare made of Nylon (all the others were nylon) and I was to have no further troubles with any of the six battens for the next 2000 miles. Many Junk sailors carry spare battens on deck since the compression loads when running can be very destructive, but the flexibility of nylon with the inherent strength of the material prevented any breakages.

Of course, unlike a Junk, JUNKETTE has her battens end at the mast where the luff of the sail, like a gaffer, is laced down the mast. As a result the stiffness of a Junk batten is no longer required: indeed this is why westernised Junks are so poor to windward in light airs when the sail cannot take up a proper aerofoil shape. The Chinese used bamboo battens which are reasonably flexible but not easily obtainable in the right lengths here in Britain.

Whithorn, safe in all winds is a lovely harbour at the mouth of the Solway Firth, an area of shoal waters and fast running tides, no place for deep keel boats but very beautiful with small refuges at Kippford and Kircudbright and in Luce Bay. It is the last stop before the Mull of Galloway when heading North. On the other side of the estuary lie Whitehaven and Barrow, and further south the town of Ravenglass on the river Esk, a small inlet used by boats taking part in the three peaks race because of its proximity to Scafell Pike. Sadly Ravenglas, although a beautiful little refuge is no longer as popular as it was because Windscale is close by and researchers can be found most weekends measuring the radiation levels in the seaweed. If, by chance, you dry out on a piece of weed you could be subjecting yourself to as much radiation in 24 hours as the average person would get in a year. I was told this by a Green Peace researcher who showed me his Geiger counter, rattling away like a machine gun some foot away from some kelp. Fortunately the tides seem to keep Whithorn clear from infestation of this hidden enemy: the large volume of water flushed out of the Solway Firth by each tide ensures that the sands are properly scoured. The layman can be excused for being scared: perhaps the Geiger counter would have shown as much radiation from the face of my watch with a luminous dial, but then....you cannot be sure, can you?

I do know that when Calder Hall, the world's first atomic power station, was first opened (the original name of Windscale) the event was televised and a mobile camera control room and gear went up from Manchester to provide pictures. While setting up, one of the engineers found the largest hairy caterpillar he had ever seen. There was talk of taking it to a Zoo or specialist biologist as he thought he might have found a new species. However, it vanished overnight and despite a thorough search it was never recovered. Of course at that time we knew little about possible mutations caused by radioactivity, but looking back it could well have been that news of our discovery reached those channels that felt that any speculation should be nipped in the bud lest there was a great public outcry. People were then reading 'The Day of The Triffids' and it would not have taken much to set up a nation wide scare. We will never know whether memory amplified the view or whether we did indeed find a mutation.

The following morning, after tidying the boat, Bob and his friend Norma Whitton arrived and Norma presented me with a mascot, a small purple and white teddy bear which she had christened 'Big Bob'. At this stage I should explain the layout of JUNKETTE to those readers unfamiliar with sailing boats. At the back end of the boat is an open cockpit for the helmsman to sit in, with room for six and a tiller connected to the silent crewman, an autohelm or automatic pilot: essential for the single hander if he is going to be able to make meals, look at charts and carry out simple housekeeping. All the sheets and halyards (ropes controlling the sails) are fed back to this cockpit for ease of adjustment. There is a spray hood to keep me dry when it is raining, and a companionway forward, over the engine casing, down into the saloon. Here there are two bunks, one on each side, with a cooker to the left (port side) and chart table opposite. Beyond the bunks is a bulkhead (wall) with a sliding door to the heads (toilets) on the port side and a wardrobe opposite. Beyond these there is the foc'sle or fore cabin with two berths.

When sailing alone, I use the starboard saloon berth which is handy for the hatch and for the chart table, and store all my clothes in the foc'sle. Now I hung 'Big Bob' above the forward end of the chart table while 'Perky' (a small pink pig presented to me by my daughter and inscribed 'to someone special') was hung above the aft end of the table. These mascots were to develop a life of their own, a twee anthropomorphism brought about by loneliness.

I left at noon and carried the tide and a light following wind up to Port Patrick. This was my first chance to try out the new sail plan and it worked magnificently. There was no weather helm and steering was a delight, allowing me to make nearly 5 knots in a light wind, arriving at 6.30 with enough water to enter harbour, or you might have thought so, but I went aground on the sand and was stuck for the next three and a half hours! I have been into Port Patrick many times and it was foolish to get caught out, but I had just read the Clyde cruising club notes to remind me of the entrance and the words 'avoiding a rocky patch at the inner end of this point which is awash at half tide' were in the forefront of my mind, so that even though it was well below half tide and I could see the rocks, I headed to starboard....onto the sand!

My embarrassment was partly allayed when another boat, a 45ft ferro-cement (concrete) boat also went aground 20 feet away. He came off at 9.30 pm. and I followed half an hour later. As I entered the harbour he called out and invited me to tie up alongside but I decided to turn first (I don't know why!) and in doing so in the now dark harbour, I hit a trawler with my new bowsprit and with a crash....it broke!

I was devastated: for a moment I thought all my plans had come to nothing before I'd even properly started. This was the first accident I had ever had and I was trembling like a leaf. I continued to turn the boat until I was lying alongside the ferro schooner and they quickly took my lines. There seemed to be no one aboard the trawler, or at least no one emerged to acknowledge the bump. As far as I could see it had suffered no damage: not even a paint scratch as the bowsprit had given way immediately on impact and bounced JUNKETTE away from the other hull. As for me, though, JUNKETTE had a piece of wood sticking out from the bow like a bayonet and a tumble of wires and ropes festooned over the pulpit while I had a very dented and bruised ego.

Of course I wasn't used to the extra length of my boat, it had been 26ft long but was now 30ft with the bowsprit. Of course it was dark. Of course there was a wind funnelling across the entrance....but it shouldn't have happened. If there had been some one else with me, if I hadn't gone aground, if.....! I have been single handing for years and knew that everything must be thought out in advance, nothing taken on trust. It has taken me very many sea miles to learn this basic premis and I still make many mistakes. I tied up much shaken and was invited aboard the ferro for a cup of tea by the skipper, a fireman from Liverpool who was used to dealing with shock cases. At the chart table, 'Big Bob' had turned round and was facing the porthole, his back to me. I thought nothing of it at the time, assuming the cord had twisted.....I was to learn. That was a long, black night for me.

The next day I re-rigged the jib back to the bow roller after noting a rather ominous bend in the foresail roller reefing extrusion, and I sawed off the broken end of the bowsprit, some six foot of prime mahogany which seemed to weigh a ton, but not as heavy as my spirits. I would now have excess weather helm until I could get the bowsprit replaced, but at least I was still mobile. The crash had caused the Decca aerial mounting at the masthead to crack and the antenna leaned at a crazy angle. Yet another problem: I would have to go up aloft and try and put it right, despite the pain in my back. With the help of an Irish skipper on the winch, I went up twice and on the second occasion I managed to splint the mounting with the use of the bottle screw from the bobstay bound to the bracket with a couple of jubilee clips and some epoxy putty. It looked awful from the deck but I guessed it was fairly sound, provided there was no great vibration. Strange, but I found it easier working up the mast than staggering round the deck with my aching guts and bad back. I had not yet got over my fall from the jetty a week ago.

There was one thing gained from these antics: the Irish skipper promised a handsome donation to the funds if I went to Carrickfergus before finishing at Ramsey. I had decided against trying to fit Northern Ireland into my schedule, but now I would have to go and show my face. I had given my club a silver bowl, the JUNKETTE bowl for the best cruise to Ireland by a club member: if I wasn't careful I would find myself winning my own prize! Surreptitiously I fed a gin to my little friends (?) below the keel.

Port Patrick is one of the cleanest towns I have come across and waterfront amusements of the more vulgar kind have been denied planning permission to operate so that it is for me very superior to a lot of other sea-side resorts. It has a 'fun' golf course and some splendid pubs and eating houses, but since there are no charges and no harbour master (it is owned by an association based in Cambridge) the facilities for getting on and off boats are rather primitive and dangerous with some rusting iron ladders on two walls, the third being occupied by naval vessels.(1990).

I recall an occasion when I had been crewing for a friend and had been in great pain with stomach cramps (again) which had been with me for several days. We had had a round of crazy golf, and whether it was because I was having difficulty in standing upright or because I was past caring, I had the best round of my life and completed 18 holes in 60 - on a crazy golf course too! However, I seemed to have spoiled it all when I fell into the harbour while trying to get into the dinghy from a ladder. My friend dived in after me, afraid that I would be unable to swim, and we had both taken all our money with us so that later his boat was festooned with paper money drying on lines all over the cabin. For me, despite the ignominy of my unintended dip (my son was there to witness it) it had been a wonderful release: within three hours all my pains vanished. I can only assume that the sudden rush of adrenaline must have cured me, either that or imbibing some of the filthy harbour water!. However, I had absolutely no desire to try a repeat treatment although my stomach was giving me great discomfort.

From the Isle of Whithorn to Oban.

I was now behind schedule and Rolls Royce, who were lending me a couple of apprentices to help me through the Crinan Canal would be expecting me at Ardrishaig in three days. The Rolls Royce involvement was interesting. I had mentioned to a friend in Manchester that I would have liked to have gone through the Crinan canal to pay my respects to Blondie Hasler's memory (his home was close by the canal) but that I would have to go round the Mull of Kintyre because I had no crew. He rang me a little later to say that I must go through the canal as he had found a crew for me, a couple of Rolls Royce graduate apprentices from Glasgow. I was amazed as I had no idea that he even worked for that prestigious company, (he was director of training) but was delighted to accept his offer. I discovered later that the Rolls Royce apprentices had built their own boat in the Clyde, called - as you might expect - 'Merlin of Clyde'.

When I left Port Patrick, a popular venue for Irish Skippers sailing from Belfast, I had an uneventful sail to Corsewell Point and then anchored in Lady Bay at Loch Ryan for the night. I was using my new 'Delta' anchor from Simpson Lawrence for the first time and it was to prove an excellent buy and never let me down:

a CQR without a swivel, only 7kg for my length of boat and it was to hold me safely in gales on several occasions. I had bought it because of the light weight recommended for my size of boat, knowing that in Scotland I would often need great lengths of chain when anchoring and any reduction of weight would be a great gain as lifting is not my strong point. Of course, on this first occasion I had a somewhat restless night, left wondering how well it was holding and whether I had given out enough scope of chain - the pilot says that the holding ground is poor - but my back and stomach were not helping matters and doses of distalgesic became a regular four hourly routine. A year later I was to lose a boat from very near this spot when the anchor dragged during the night but this time lady luck was with me.

Loch Ryan is a lovely, enclosed stretch of water with a regular ferry service to Ireland. The harbour is no longer of much use to either fishermen or pleasure boats because the constant passage of the ferries seems possibly to have led to a silting up of the harbour entrance. It can only be entered for about an hour either side of high water and even then, not by deep keel boats. If it were to be dredged and given a Marina it would make a wonderful sailing centre for this part of Scotland, within easy reach of both Scottish and North of England sailors and could rival some of the southern ports such as Falmouth. The Clyde, further north, is much busier with commercial shipping and with the growing leisure market this Loch could become the pearl of the North. However, this is in the hands of the planners and in the meantime it is a little used anchorage, to be viewed with care by visiting yachtsmen because of the treacherous nature of the holding power of the ground.

From Lady Bay I motored up to Troon in thick mist, relying on Decca for position as my log was proving faulty. (I was going to have to wait for a replacement until I got to Perth) so I used my Walker trail log from then on. The only boat I saw was a small fishing launch with a dozen men aboard which appeared suddenly out of the gloom from Girvan and just as suddenly disappeared. The fog was strange: it kept lifting and strong sun filtered through for a few minutes, and then it closed down again for maybe an hour at a time. Luckily, the fog cleared just as I reached Lady Isle which suddenly shone in a shaft of sunlight, looking positively beautiful, and I was able to enter Troon without difficulty.

After settling in (and being given free berthing) I contacted the local press and a photo session was arranged for the following day   (out with the broken end of bowsprit: how the press love a trauma) another delay in reaching the Crinan! While in the showers the next morning, I met the skipper of the boat DALRIADA, sunk by a submarine in 1987. Peter Moseley, the skipper (an army chaplain), was held up by his daughter during his time in the water waiting for the lifeboat. Now he was sailing again, this time with a crew of raw army cadets, a very brave man. I believe the boat he was now skippering was called 'BRAVE WARRIOR'! He told me that although the Ministry of Defence would accept no liability, they did pay all the costs of a replacement boat and the lost gear without any quibble. I don't know, but probably a replacement boat would cost no more than a single torpedo. possibly less.

Troon is a first class Marina with excellent access to the Scottish coast and is used as both a wintering harbour and a staging post for boats travelling to the highlands. For me it had a major drawback: the restaurant food was poor and the coffee undrinkable, but that apart, it is just the sort of place to encourage 'harbouritis' and I was told that many boats spend more than 90% of their life in the marina. I'm afraid I relate to those vagabonds who live on their boats in some lost backwater in the winter, take short pecking runs out into the icy breezes of February and March and then take wing to far off places in April. The life is good. No, its great, and I have a great sympathy with all wandering and free spirits. They don't add to the great forward progress of man but they provide a quiet background of stability and peace, a sort of reference point for the busy executive or harried labourer.

From Troon I sailed through the lovely Kilmarnoch waters round the head of Arran where I had once almost run down a basking shark (but was now more likely to be run down myself by a submarine), to spend the night at East Loch Tarbert. The Kintyre peninsular is punctuated near the top by two indentations from the sea with a mile of land between. In 1093, King Magnus - 'Bare legs'- of Norway claimed that all the Western Isles round which he could sail with his rudder in position belonged to Norway, the mainland to Malcolm - 'Big head'- of Scotland. To annex the Kintyre peninsular, *Bare Legs'* proceeded to sail round the peninsular and had his dragon boat dragged, with himself at the tiller, across the mile of dry land between East and West sides of the peninsular at Tarbert (which means 'draw boat') gaining what he called 'a large land and better than the best land in the Hebrides'. It stayed in Norwegian possession until the thirteenth century when Edward I gave it to John Balliol, 0Malcom having lost his power) who was shortly succeeded by Robert the Bruce. Libby Purves in her book 'One Summers Grace' recalls that Robert the Bruce used to have his boat hauled over the land. I wonder if she mixed up the two!. There are several 'Tarberts' in Scotland though none with a more colourful history.

This wonderfully picturesque harbour lay tranquil in the warm May evening and I looked for a mooring in the soft light, at first without success, but then found one inscribed 'In use every day' and covered with at least a year's accumulation of weed. (Had *Bare Legs* used it?) As I picked it up a voice called 'Welcome to Scotland, Mr. Hill'. It was my apprentices from Rolls Royce who had come looking for me. I promised to be at Ardrishaig at 10 am the next day and they in turn promised to ring Bridget Hasler and let her know of my arrival, and to be ready to take my lines at the sea lock in the morning. I slept easily that night. I had been feeling ill for a week now and in considerable pain with my back (a delayed reaction to the fall, not helped by events in Port Patrick) so the night's rest was a blessing. Big Bob and Perky were smiling at each other!

Early the next morning I left my scruffy buoy and motored in the slight mist up Loch Fine towards the Crinan. On the way I passed two uncharted yellow buoys (my chart was new, and, I thought, fully updated) and was glad that the visibility was good enough for me to spot them in time as they were in the middle of the Kyle. At Ardrishaig (pronounced by the Scots as AH <u>DRY</u> <u>SHIG</u>), the early mist began to clear and the lads were ready for me, two very pleasant young men who had been waiting two days for my arrival. I rather think their supervisor was not amused at my lateness, but I never met him so maybe I am doing him a disservice.

The Crinan Canal (which Middleton says he used for his round England trip when I think he was talking about the Bowling canal) crosses the Argyll peninsular with some thirteen unmanned locks and two sea locks, and inland operations stop at 4.15 pm. (The sea locks stay operational until 9.30 pm). The locks are self operated except for those at each end and there are six manned bridges to be opened, so if you wish to transit in one day an early start is required, earlier than I had allowed. It is hard work and really requires a minimum of three people. We joined up with another boat whose skipper had two young lassies helping him. We soon worked out a routine where my boys operated the current lock while the girls went ahead and opened the next lock.

The day was brilliantly sunny and the banks aglow with the bright yellow of the gorse. The sound of the birds was everywhere, but not once did I see a Linnet, those natives of gorse further south. On my last trip through the Canal, it had been the West Highland Week and the Canal was full of boats, pushing and thrusting to get into the locks, sometimes six boats at once. Now there were just the two of us and nary another boat in the other direction.

We reached the very last bridge at 4.45 and a little money changed hands with the bridge keeper who had waited for us. The boat that had been transiting with us had engine failure just before the bridge. We had given him a tow but he decided to overnight in a small cove and we left him there: his two girls having already left to return to Ardrishaig.

THE LAST BRIDGE ON THE CRINAN

I spent the night just above the sea loch after the Rolls Royce staff photographer had visited us and taken some photos for their magazine. At this point the two young apprentices left me, first giving me a tie with the 'MERLIN OF CLYDE' logo and then the well known 'Rolls Royce' plaque in silver and black. "It has a part number" said Dave Greenhill very proudly while his compatriot, Derek Paterson, a more contemplative type, suggested thoughtfully "It would look well at the foot of the mast." And that is where I stuck it! (How many times have I been asked since 'Have you really got a Merlin engine?') With nearly 500sq ft. of sail I sometimes feel jet powered.

The weather was so wonderful that I decided to take a day off and enjoy the countryside. I did some sketching of the otter pool and the upper reaches of the canal as well as the Crinan basin. I was offered lunch on a boat in the lock, a wonderfully presented Golden Hind with a man and wife crew plus a man who had been fitting out a 'She' at Hesketh Bank and had seen JUNKETTE there during the winter. What a small world. It reminded me of a friend who, many years ago, took his family to Spain and deciding that he wanted a little peace, went off on his own, driving up into the mountains to a deserted spot where he left the car and started to walk. After a short time he heard voices and around the next corner came face to face......with his next door neighbour!

A similar thing happened to me when I was climbing down the cliffs at Lands End, having left the family for a little 'space'! I sat on a rock and enjoyed the view, soon to be improved by an attractive girl clambering down the rocks towards me. The impossible happened and she sat beside me. While I was working out what to say she said 'You are Cec Korer, aren't you?' I had to deny it and admit that I knew the gentleman as a colleague of mine, then a production assistant in television known to be talent scouting: she was a secretary in the same building as ourselves. She didn't stay long! Cec, incidentally, was responsible some years later for commissioning the first program to be transmitted on Channel Four: COUNTDOWN!

Talking to one of the loch keepers, I discovered he was a taxidermist in his free time and had just finished a Giraffe (yes, the mind boggles!) for a Dutch Zoo. I saw a Lobster which had been returned from Florida because it was the wrong colour....it had been cooked and was red: the buyer wanted the natural colour, blue-brown! I bought a lovely Tawny Owl after being assured that no animals were shot and those he used reached his hands as a result of authenticated accidents. He told me that his main market was America: it was interesting to find someone with such a distinctive occupation and we found ourselves comparing notes on the treatment of the profession in the TV comedy 'Two up, Two down!.

In the evening I met Bridget Hasler and daughter Diana and learned that Bridget's son Tom intended to take their Kingfisher 22ft boat PILMER to Norway with a cousin. His father, Blondie, a tough Colonel of Marines who had led the little ship raid on Bordeaux during the war (Cockleshell heroes) and had inaugurated the single handed transatlantic race as well as the 'Round Britain' race, would have been proud of him. I also heard how Blondie's remains had been given the last rites and his ashes spread over the turbulent waters of the Corryvreckan: a fitting end to a very great man. The boat for this operation had been provided by the owners of the Crinan Hotel, Mr. and Mrs. Ryan, friends of Bridget who were to prove equally friendly to me, providing me with wonderful fresh bread and bacon which was to last me until I got to St. Kilda.

It was now early in May and the weather continued sunny and calm with a high pressure area centred on Northern England. At this latitude it was still nicely warm without being too hot and I found that food was no problem to keep: an Iceberg lettuce would last a fortnight if kept in the bilges (the coolest part of the boat), and bread would last a week at least. Most important of all....there were no flies, that scourge of Scottish waterfronts throughout July to September.

After a final visit from Dinah, armed with eggs and cakes, I left the Crinan Basin bound for Oban. The journey up past Fladda light and along the side of Kerrera is a delight once the troubled waters of the Dhorus Mor are past. Here the tides meet and the sea literally boils under you in a quite disconcerting way. I sailed past some of the loveliest lochs in Scotland and it was a shame to have to hurry by them. Loch Craignish, Loch Shuna, Loch Melfort (where I once spent an evening drinking a fine malt whisky and talking to the kilted landlord until we had killed the bottle between us. *"What is it?"* I asked *"Ssh. It comes from across the water!"* He said. *"Islay?" "No, man, from Ireland!"*) , Cuan Sound and Easdale, Irene McLachlan of Arnamir - all places of fond memories. One of the saddest things about this trip was to be missing out on so many harbours that I would have liked to visited, but such a journey would take 5 years rather than 5 months.

Once, I had intended to visit Arnamir but it had looked crowded so I anchored in a little bay a short distance away. The next morning I went into Arnamir to pay my respects to the redoubtable Irene and she told us *"You should have come in last night. You missed a real sailor....Claire Francis!"*

I had met up with the Ocean Youth Club boat TYCHO at the Crinan and they invited me to tie alongside when I got to Oban since suitable moorings are now at a premium at that town. When I reached Oban by early afternoon I headed for the town quay and their friendly hull. A hale and hands were ready to take my lines. The skipper was a young man called Hugh Chisholm and I was very impressed with the way he handled his not inconsiderable responsibilities. The O.Y.C. boats take a dozen or so youngsters away for a week at a time and sail in all types of weather. There is a trained mate in addition to the skipper and sometimes a very small trained crew, but most of the actual sailing is done by the youngsters themselves. The work done by the O.Y.C. is really great for youngsters, as is that of the 'Sail Training Association' who run the tall ships 'Sir Winston Churchill' and the 'Malcolm Miller'.

I had to go in to Oban to pick up my mail, but I had not allowed for Public Holidays and the Post Office had not yet received my new log which would have meant waiting over the weekend to the following Tuesday, so in-stead I gave instructions for it to be sent on to Inchyra near Perth rather than waste time. My Walker log would have to serve a little longer and if sailors wonder why I consider that a chore I can only say that unwinding a knotted trail line is not an enjoyable occupation, and mine seem to reach that stage with great frequency. At sea on the oceans, the problem is almost non existent and the only difficulties are those of theft by large fish, but in coastal and weedy waters the trailing log is a menace if it snarls up.

In Oban I came across a culinary delight that I had not met elsewhere: when I called at the butcher he gave me my meat vacuum packed, so I bought three separate and different joints which would keep for three or four days unopened. I was then able to have pork, followed by a lamb cutlet and finish with a fillet steak. This is available from supermarkets in England but so far I had not met it in the high street butcher whereas in Scotland all the main towns seemed to have this facility. I did not purchase a Haggis: I had my first at MacTavish's Kitchen in Oban some years ago when there was a great celebration and it came at the end of a seven course meal. Even then, blown out as I was, it was wonderful and a great experience, once my ears had got over the shock of 'piping it in'! Of course, 'Burns' night is the time to have haggis: strange when you remember that Burns was a Lowlander and hated the things so he wrote the famous lines now read out as the Haggis is brought in, a parody praising the humble dish as royalty.

That experience had occurred during the West Highlands week when yachts come from all over Britain and Ireland for a week of racing ending at Tobermory. It is a time of great jollity and good humour and a wonderful sight as dozens of yachts fight for line honours, their multi-coloured spinnakers filling the sky as with bunting at a party, a crazy kaleidoscope of reds, blues, greens and yellows interspersed with billowing clouds of white canvas. The nights are long, noisy and happy with boats often rafted up twelve deep. The boats are stripped out for racing, carrying only the bare essentials and one young lady crew complained to me that her Irish skipper had had the loo removed and each crew member given a bottle and the use of a bucket.

There are quite a few girls who crew racing boats and it is no easy life. They are most often to be seen on foredecks, changing headsails, often in boisterous conditions, while the stronger men handle the winches further aft. Women are generally lighter and quicker on their feet than men and make very good crew, as Tracy Edwardes' team proved in the Whitbread race. I was to find out later that it was usually women who did any mast climbing that might be required too 'because they are lighter, don't you know'! Speaking for myself, the best crew I have ever had has been my own young daughter who, at the age of thirteen, helmed the boat in a force seven while I was forward trying to pick up a mooring buoy in the Menai Straits, and she made it first time, in the dark, with tiller in one hand, torch in the other and a foot taking care of the throttle. She does not like to climb the mast, but you can't have everything. I believe that women drivers are either very good or very bad whereas most men just think they are good.

On a boat, if a woman likes sailing she will invariably be good at it, but if she doesn't, she'll tell you and god help you if you ignore her! That is the time to sail alone....or take up golf!

I had got to Oban, some 260 miles, a tenth of the complete journey without crew apart from the Crinan Canal, and the tiller and I were just getting to know one another. The weather helm without the bowsprit was as bad as I had expected and in anything above force four the autohelm had difficulty in coping because it was permanently at the end of its travel, ie. the helm was hard over. I could overcome this by drastically reefing the mainsail, but my speed would then drop to around 3 or 4 knots which, in a good breeze, was unacceptable to me. I was going to have to wait until I got to the south coast and have the bowsprit replaced before I was able to sail at a carefree six knot reach, and in the meantime any good breeze meant many hours at the tiller.

I have been often asked what I think about when I'm alone on the tiller and I find it so difficult to answer because I really cannot remember. I only know that the time passes quickly and that I am constantly delighted with the changes in the colour and mood of the sea. In moonlight or low sun the calm sea looks like a silk lamé robe, shimmering in an intensity of glorious silver or gold and undulating as though moved by langourous limbs. Then there are the antics of sea birds, and of the fishing fraternity whom I suspect believe that any slow moving craft (I rarely use my engine) might be trying to raid their lobster pots. I met one fisherman in Wales who regularly had his pots raided. He knew they had been raised and emptied because the bait had gone even when it was wired. He once caught a young lad at it and recovered a Lobster...but only once! So far he had not lost any pots but that will happen. Its a hard life, that of a fisherman, inshore or offshore.

Speaking of sea birds, I am always amazed at the time Guillimots can spend submerged, chasing fry underwater. By comparison of lung size we would have to stay underwater for over an hour to compare! I believe they have some mechanism whereby they store extra oxygenated blood as do some aquatic mammals like seals. Since it appears that we all originated from the primeval seas an affinity with sea creatures is not all that surprising.

From Oban to St Kilda

I left Oban on Saturday morning, 5th May heading for Loch Sunart, but a head wind left me tacking up the Sound of Mull, most unusual for me as in the past I have always had a fast reach to Tobermory. I passed the Macleans family home of Duart Castle and remembered the last time I had called there when the Laird's daughter had been acting as guide. Our small party of four from two boats had come in just in advance of a coach load of trippers and had just been introduced to Lord Maclean when the large party arrived. The Laird's daughter told us all how she and her brother had their heights marked on the castle wall as children to see how much they grew each year and my daughter was delighted because we had done the same with her. Miss Maclean went on to talk about visits of the Royal Yacht and how they waved a table cloth out of the long window and saw Her Majesty reply in similar manner from the deck of the Royal Yacht as it had sailed up the Sound of Mull. When Ruth and I returned a few days later I had waved a tea-towel from the cockpit as we approached the castle, much to my daughter's disgust....she hid herself, but she need not have bothered, no one saw us.

Filled with these reveries I slowly tacked past the castle until the radio warned of pending North Westerly gales and I took refuge in the bay at Craigmuir, anchoring close to the jetty and disdaining the bright blue tourist buoys on the far side of the bay because I enjoyed watching the crowds boarding the ferries. The visitors buoys, more usually marked with a yellow can buoy, have been put in by the Highlands and Islands Tourist board for visiting yachts and are to be found in many of the main tourist areas. In some places they are very welcome, such as Tobermory where the water is very deep, but in Gigha where, at Ardminish Bay there was room for dozens of anchored boats in almost tideless conditions and a constant depth of 10ft with a sandy bottom, the board put in a dozen or so buoys with the result that a) they are difficult to use by boats with high freeboard and b) they restrict the ability of other boats to anchor. Where there had been room for more than 30 boats there is now safe room for about fifteen!

Incidentally, while mentioning the island of Gigha off the Kintyre coast which I had missed this trip, anyone coming to Scotland for the first time and not using the Crinan canal should consider a visit to this island, a natural stopping place after Port Patrick or the Irish coast. A large scale chart is essential to avoid the many reefs but a slow and careful approach will repay with a marvellous safe harbour (except, perhaps in an easterly) and a Post Office cum general store where cycles can be hired to tour the island and to visit the lovely gardens.

The wind brought a cold spell and for the first time I really felt it: I even wore my balaclava and socks in bed. I do not normally feel the cold but my general state of debility and damp feet from wearing sandals certainly affected me. Later I was to find my elder daughter's rubber hot water bottle and I admit to using it almost every night until I was well down the North East coast! It had written on it 'Vickie's private bottle. Keep Off!'

The following morning, with a good strong North Westerly heading me I began the long slow beat towards Tobermory with two panels of sail reefed down. After about an hour, as I came about to tack again there was a crash and the sail hung loosely to leeward: the end of the boom was trailing in the water, having broken about two feet from the end. I dropped the sail and lashed the boom down and then motored towards Tobermory.

I called the coastguard to ask if there were any boatbuilders who just might be able to help me and they suggested one not far from Tobermory in Loch Aline, but it was the holiday weekend and I wasn't going to have much luck. I was able to pick up a visitors buoy in Tobermory while I considered the problem. If I had been in mid ocean I would have had to repair it myself and I was trying to prove the efficacy of the rig, so I did just that. I made a sandwich of epoxy putty and the two halves of the boom and bound them with a rope which became the anchor point for the mainsheet. Therefore, when I pulled in on the mainsheet I would be tightening the joint. It was to work well and lasted until I got to Torquay many weeks later.

The crash of the boom had weakened my mast head repair to the Decca Aerial so that I had to ask a fellow yachtsman to man the winch while I went aloft yet again, this time to bend the aerial mounting bracket upside down and lash it to the shroud so that it would not fall on deck. My guest yachtsman (a seventy year old) asked if I was intending to navigate to Australia! He was very worried that I might fall in the water (I had dropped some tools overboard) and that he would be unable to help. I should point out that to climb the mast I use the main halyard which has a four fold advantage with twin sheave blocks at top and bottom so that I am able to haul myself up, only needing some one to gather up the spare rope. On the way down I caught my colostomy bag in the shrouds and pulled it off. When I reached deck level I was naturally eager for my helper to depart so I could go below and make repairs. He was upwind of me and left rapidly. This was one of the times I was glad to be single handing though a nurse would have been handy to repair the skin tears.

In the bay I saw what I thought was another OYC boat called 'Spirit of Merseyside', a lovely black schooner complete with young crew. I was to meet them again, later, in St. Kilda, and to discover that the boat was owned by the Fairbridge Drake society. At this time of year there were not too many boats about so you tended to note those that were sailing. They twice dropped anchor, no easy task in the very deep waters of the harbour where they were: I know because I had tried to anchor there on a previous occasion and had had to give up after finding a depth well over 15 metres.

I went ashore and for the last time in Scotland met someone I knew from home, a family from Cheshire who had heard of my exploits in one of the Sunday papers. On my last visit I had got a little high on Malt whisky (I am very rarely 'a little high', I don't often drink) and a friend had invited me back to his boat for coffee - probably to sober me up as he thought I might not get back safely. When I left at midnight in pitch darkness, I rowed back to my boat, no short distance, and as I clambered aboard I heard 'Goodnight Ralph'....he had followed me to make sure I was alright. Such is friendship.

I left Tobermory on Tuesday, May 8th and at 11am was approaching Ardnamurchan Head, sailing at four and a half knots close hauled. Wherever I went the wind now seemed determined to head me, but at least the boom repair was holding up well and the Decca working, although the aerial was upside down. I was a bit fed up that I had mounted the aerial in such an inaccessible place, but there is no doubt that I get much better signals at mast height than from a pushpit mounted antenna which is more usual and which I had on my other boat. JUNKETTE is looking very 'tatty' with bits tied up here and there, but all the repairs are sound and holding up.

My destination this time was the Island of Canna. I had never been to Canna before, but deciding to go to St Kilda via the Sound of Harris made Canna seem a sensible mid port of call. It also has a good anchorage. Shortly after clearing Ardnamurchan Point I was 'buzzed' for the second time by a fishing trawler. It again seemed he was trying to get me to cross behind him and get mixed up with his trawl: no matter what I did he turned to cross in front of me. After four changes of course and much time wasting I called him on R/T. *"Red fishing trawler on collision course with yacht JUNKETTE for the third time. What are your intentions please?"* At least now he couldn't claim I had carelessly broken his nets. It worked! I got no reply but he steamed off on a reciprocal course. Why do they bother?

I had hoped to meet up with a boat called 'Chloe' in the outer Hebrides and I was thrilled to hear another boat, 'Genista', call them. 'Genista' was going to Eigg and then to Plockton (another superb anchorage on the mainland above Kyle Akin) and so I asked them to tell 'Chloe' of my whereabouts if they met them first. I had met the owners of 'Chloe', Roger and Jeannie Burston, at Hesketh Bank and was very impressed with their achievements. Roger is in his seventies but still spends every summer in the North West of Scotland, Island hopping, even out to St. Kilda. He and Jeannie had given me many tips for the north western part of my travels.

By 4pm I had passed Rum and, as the wind had died back, or been blocked by the Island of Rum I used the engine to motor up Canna Sound and anchor in the harbour. There was only one other boat when I arrived but later a charter boat named 'Monacho' arrived with 14 Americans and a Scottish skipper. I didn't know it at the time, but 'Monacho' and I were soon to get to know one another rather well.

That evening I opened the last of my meat packs from Oban, a fillet steak with which I drank a half bottle of wine. I was celebrating being in the Small Isles and well on my way to St. Kilda. I suppose I was also drowning my irritation with the fishing trawler that had buzzed me earlier.

In the matter of eating and drinking, I made it a habit of starting each day by eating a good breakfast of bacon and egg when sailing since I never knew when or if I would get any lunch. I would try and eat some cheese and biscuits or a cup of soup at midday but there were many days when I just could not leave the tiller so I would wait till I anchored for the night and then have a good evening meal, fresh food if possible. I carried potatoes, onions, greens and tomatoes almost always and bought fresh meat whenever I could. As to drink, I made it a rule while sailing never to have more than one drink, a gin and tonic, before anchoring, and that never before noon. In the evening I occasionally opened a bottle of wine but was more likely to have a glass of sherry. I am not a beer drinker (though I was to suffer from this later when, after my return, I was found to had bladder stones due to taking insufficient liquids) and when the weather was very hot, would drink lemonade.

Another fad I had was to drink real ground coffee whenever I could. I would make it by the 'jug' method, and good it was too, but impossible while sailing, of course. My cooker is gimballed which means that I can boil a kettle while under way, but trying to do much with it on my own was often difficult because I was trying to keep my speed up as I had a long way to go. Cup-a-soup or tea was about the limit of my ability. Although there were times I cursed in not having a thermos of coffee to hand, somehow I rarely prepared one: I preferred the aggro of having to make a drink to break up the day. It's just too easy to take up a thermos instead of taking time off by heaving too and boiling up, but having said this I begrudged wasting more time than was absolutely necessary and waiting for a jug of coffee to brew was just too much.

CANNA

After my meal I scanned the shore of Canna and saw three churches, one to the left on Sanday, one to the right on Canna, both now in ruins, and a small chapel close to the farm. These churches were the reminder of the days of religious schism in

Scotland when Catholic and Protestant, High Church and Presbyterian bellowed across the hills at each other. Had anything changed? Later in the evening, the fishing fleet of about three trawlers tied up at the tiny jetty (they did not include the one which had given me trouble) with great speed and panache, considering the rocky nature of the ground close to the jetty and the darkness. They had obviously been doing it for so long that it was now second nature to them.

I was still in the middle of a high pressure system and my best winds were those of the afternoons when the warmed lands induced on-shore winds, sometimes reaching force five. In the mornings it was calm and I ended up by using the engine more than I would have wished. The previous day had been typical with a calm in the early morning and a breeze getting up around twelve which lasted until early evening. The morning after my arrival in Canna was just the same, flat calm, and I motored out of the quiet harbour to head west.

Shortly after leaving Canna shores I saw my first seal and also my first large fish which leapt, a shining brown and grey with a fleck of orange out of the flat, still water. I had no idea what it was but guessed it must have weighed several pounds. I was heading for Loch Skipport on South Uist and progress was slow in the light airs. However I had plenty of time and bided the afternoon adiabatic wind which arrived, a little later than expected, at 3.30pm and sped me on my way.

On R/T I heard another boat call 'Monacho' and because I had seen the boat in harbour, I did the forbidden thing and listened in on the conversation. The skipper of 'Monacho' apparently came from Oban and he was talking about the new houses they were building there. *"Och, they're very nice, but they are all being taken up by the white natives".* After further talk I believed he was talking about the English who were retiring to Scotland and buying up these desirable houses so that they were not available to Scots. I think he didn't like the 'White Natives' very much! Of course this is what happened in Wales where cottages were bought up as holiday homes by city industrialists and used for the short summer season, to lie idle for the rest of the year while the country labourers could not find anywhere to live. You might not agree with the fire raising tendencies of some of the discontents but at least you can understand their motives. The Scottish skipper went on to explain that he was taking a party of fourteen Americans on a walking tour of the Islands and that he would go out as far as St. Kilda, which interested me greatly: I might yet get to meet this interesting man whom I think they called 'Cubby'.

Just before the wind arrived, lolling about in a fitful calm I decided to check the gear box for oil. It was almost dry and I quickly refilled it. From then on I checked it every week and found it needed oil almost once a fortnight until I began to get constant winds in August. I decided to top up the engine too and this was to prove to be a major error further north! The single hander, especially when sailing in such unfrequented waters, must carry his own spares and be able to carry out as much as possible of his running repairs on the move. Garages, like banks, are few and far between so spare oil, gaskets, nuts/bolts/screws and washers must be available in the bosuns locker just as adequate funds for food are kept in a safe place.

I was carrying a reasonable supple of spares with more than enough tools, or so I thought but on the East Coast I was to find that I had no spanner big enough to undo a seacock, and that could have been a fatal omission! I also had no bolt cutter but fortunately I never needed one though it is an omission that I intend to make good before I go cruising again. I also carry more than enough mooring warps and pieces of cord. This was just as well because by the time I had finished my trip I had lost some three full length mooring warps and had one carelessly cut in half by friction. I also managed to lose three fenders but did get two second hand ones in Falmouth. Adequate fenders are a must and too often boats are equipped with tiny things, a pair of which would be better used under a transvestite's shirt.

By 6.30 I was creaming along at six knots, my arms growing longer by the minute because of the pressure on the helm, so reluctantly I reefed two panels and settled for 2 knots loss of speed. Half an hour later, Loch Skipport was in sight and I dropped anchor in an isolated spot behind Small Island, Shillay Mor and had a superb quiet night, disturbed only by the call of the sheep on the surrounding hills. At 8 o'clock I was cooking my dinner and feeling on top of the world, having completed 35 nautical miles. It had taken me eleven hours but it had, in the end been a very pleasant sail. I called the coast guard at Stornoway, my first contact with this unit who were to keep a friendly and fatherly eye on me until I passed on to the Pentland office.

Friends had told me to try Loch Skipport on South Uist as an anchorage if I intended to use the Sound of Harris, but I was enormously indebted to the Clyde Cruising Club sailing directions which give all the essential pilot information for these little anchorages and harbours. Thanks to that pilot, and because the wind had turned to a North easterly direction I made for the complete security of Caolas Mor where the sound of the sea was almost completely lost: a little pool surrounded on all sides by hills and the small islands of Shillay Mor and Shillay Beag. The quiet was astonishing, and when I heard an invisible sheep bleat it was as though a fog horn had sounded. The animals blended so well with the scree and boulders that they were difficult to see. Here there were no bird cries, only that occasional plaintive bleat. It was the perfect retreat, and one I would not have found without the aid of the C.C.C. directions..

The next day I left at 9 am for North Uist and Loch Maddy, convenient for entering the Sound of Harris. An early start was more typical for most of my journey. I would rise at 5.30 am., make a cup of tea and get the fishing forecast from which I would try and compose a synoptic chart (rather like the ones you see on the BBC weather forecasts or on the back page of the Telegraph) so that I could try and imagine possible wind shifts or changes in strength. I would then cook myself a breakfast, wash myself and the dishes and be ready to depart by a little after 7 am. However, today I was only to sail about 20 or so miles and had plenty of time so decided to use the tide to assist: it would be north going at 9.50 am.

The coast line of the Uists and Benbecula is lovely and there are countless little bays and harbours of refuge: friends of mine have spent as much as three weeks on this short stretch of coast but as usual...'full of care I had no time to stand and stare'....(Davies doesn't even get a mention in Daiches 'Victorian Poets'!) and tacked slowly up the coast in light head winds, arriving in Loch Maddy at 6.30 in time for a pleasant supper cooked in the superb quiet background of yet another Hebridean haven, having taken 9 hours to cover 26 miles in very leisurely fashion.

There was nothing I wanted from civilisation. I had bread, bacon, eggs and fresh vegetables so I did not go right up to the town but chose, instead, the little bay of Aird nam Madadh where there was sufficient shelter from the very light North North Easterly wind. I was feeling fit, all the pains of April had now departed and I was enjoying myself very much so that I felt the days were slipping by just too quickly. I had only one regret, that the 'sweat' meant that unless I towed the dinghy I rarely went ashore. However, I was usually tired at the end of a day's sailing so it wasn't too much of a hardship. I had a good supply of tapes to listen to and there was always the radio, John Dunne on Radio 2 if I anchored early enough or later talks on Radio 4. My favourite tapes were Crystal Gayle (what a wonderous looking girl with 'sit upon' hair), the honey voiced Karen Carpenter (what a sad loss her early death has been) and the smooth, South African tones of Roger Whittaker whose past tutor at Bangor University is a good sailing friend of mine. I also had some concert tapes such as 'The New World' and some French impressionist music by Debussy but these seemed at odds with the grandeur of the Scottish scenery which needed a Brahms or Beethoven symphony to do it justice. (Debussy's 'L'apres midi' came into its own on the Tay on my way up to Perth!) Besides, being on my own I valued the sound of voices. My daughter had also prepared a tape for me: her Radio 1 favourites, 'to keep me feeling young' and in fact I found most of them very enjoyable.

Of course, having worked in the media for thirty years I have a natural affinity with radio, especially radio drama where the scenery is always superlative and where you are aware of the change in style of writing over the years: like a painting where excess detail is often a sign of amateurism, a lot of modern plays have very loose dialogue where you have to use your imagination to fill in the gaps. Most refreshing - though sometimes modern young directors get carried away with Sterio effects which can be just too intrusive!

Like a painting where the eye can fill in the missing bits to produce a likeness, (a phenomenon brilliantly portrayed by Rolf Harris with a few strokes of a large brush) the properly introduced 'unspoken phrase' can be more telling than a page of dialogue, a trenchant sound effect more gripping than a scream. If only more advertisers would realise this: I am not a cigarette smoker but to me 'purple' spells B & H, 'Katy' is OXO! A black look from the guy I tie up to with inadequate fenders is much better than a dozen swear words. A colleague once made a program switching blunder of major proportions, but when his boss found out, instead of shouting at him he said a sad, downbeat, 'Oh, Geoff!' I have never seen anyone so deflated and so very sorry. Masterly man management.

I did consider sailing to the town in the morning for fuel and water but it meant I would have missed my tide for passing through the Sound of Harris so at 7 am I was on my way. In summer the tide through the sound runs South East for 10 out of 12 hours and in winter these are reversed. I had two hours of friendly tide!

I arrived at Cope Passage an hour after high water with just the remnants of the North going stream and had no difficulty in finding and entering the buoyed passage.

THE SOUND OF HARRIS

The Sound is full of reefs and shallows, and the buoys must be carefully followed, which is not too difficult in good visibility. As I approached, North Uist was bathed in patchy mist but this began to clear and I found myself counting the buoys out to ensure that I had not inadvertently missed one. Friends had warned of the difficulty and on their boat: while one had kept a sharp look out the other had steered. For me, I had the chart on my knee, binoculars ready round my neck and hand nervously on the tiller, ready to knock the autohelm off if the need should arise. I counted every buoy and marked them off on the chart!

I found them all except the very last: had I reached the end of the passage? I chose to exit via the Sound of Pabbay and Sound of Spuir as the most direct route to St Kilda, but this proved a mistake! I was soon among breaking seas with the echo sounder showing 1.5 metres! Time to turn back and find another way. I tried again round the south of Spuir. Unfortunately chart 2642 ends at Pabbay and I was now on the smaller scale 2841 and 2721 which showed clear water, but the echo sounder was fluctuating between 3.5 and 11 metres and I had no way of knowing whether these were rocks or shoals of fish or just weed. All this time I had been motor sailing in almost calm conditions and was mightily relieved when I finally got into deep water at 11 am.

Fifteen minutes later the wind came up and I could sail and stop the engine. By midday I was passing Haskeir Island and at 4 pm I had my first sight of St. Kilda, or to be precise, of Boreray. The wind was now freshening from the North East and I took in two reefs. At 5 oclock the wind freshened still further to the top of force five and I decided on two more reefs as the weather helm was becoming impossible. I lay a'lee and lowered the sail, but the spray hood was raised so I couldn't see what I was doing and the gaff came down the wrong side of the lazy jacks. I had the main stuck, half up and impossible to get down further. I decided to motor across the wind so that the breeze would help me get it the right side of the spar, but the jib sheet was in the water and when I started the engine the rope wound itself round the prop so that I had no mainsail, no engine and no jib (the jib sheet was taught under the boat). I put on a life line and went forward to cut off the trapped jib sheet and reeve a new one through the blocks. I now had a jib working and could sail downwind, fortunately towards St Kilda as the wind was North easterly, but with little ability to steer because of the effect of the mainsail which I dared not jibe,and knew that in no way would I be able to enter Village Bay. The wind was rising, now about a six so I lessened the effect of the half mainsail by trycing up the lazy jacks but had a bag of sail that kept flogging in the wind. Village Bay was no place to be in an Easterly but I had no choice: at least there was still a lot of North in the wind.

There was nothing for it but to ask for help. I knew 'Monacho' would be at St Kilda so I called them and they asked my position. Because of the state of the mainsail, every time I left the tiller the boat went crazy and bounced about like a mad thing, throwing me every which way. If you can imagine being rolled down hill in an oversized barrel, then that's how I felt! I managed to give my decca bearings and said I thought I was about 5 miles from St Kilda which I saw on my Starboard bow. If I had been able to look at the chart I would have seen that the Island I saw was Boreray and not St Kilda, but in that sea with a half full and uncontrollable main sail it just was not possible.

Back on St Kilda, 'Monacho' and a fishing boat 'J.B.T.' were trying to make out where I was from my conflicting reports. The fishing boat agreed to come and find me and he buoyed his anchor to save time and set off at around 8 pm. An hour later they found me and took me in tow, a wild ride at about 8 knots to avoid the wind in my mainsail having any effect. I had doused the jib and was stuck at the tiller, trying to steer off their port quarter to relieve the load on my forestay. This was a major task at this speed and by the time 'J.B.T.' had re-anchored at 10.15 pm I was almost at the end of my tether.

Unfortunately I was not yet out of the wood because when I dropped the tow and anchored myself, I was only a few feet off the rocks. Valiantly, 'J.B.T.' again dropped anchor and towed me further out where an inflatable from the boat 'Spirit of Merseyside' pulled out and took me in tow, heading towards shallower but safer water where I finally dropped my anchor. While hanging on to 'J.B.T.' I had the greatest difficulty in not having my bow stoved in on their sides as the seas were quite horrendous and we kept banging into each other. They found a huge fender cum buoy with which one of their crew ran around the deck, thrusting it between us everytime I looked like crashing into them. This went on until the dinghy could pick me up and at some time in that dark period I felt a tremendous bang on my leg.

While tied to 'J.B.T.' in the harbour I had been able to loose the mainsail from the lazyjacks and stow it properly. This was a major task as I had to find something long enough to reach the gaff. I considered climbing the sail, using the battens as steps, but if I had freed it I would have fallen to the deck with the sail, rather like standing on the branch you are sawing off! Instead, I used a very long oar a friend had lent me and managed to lift the gaff over the offending lazy jack. On a tossing deck in a high wind this was quite a feat and when I finally anchored I was done.

I had given my only bottle of whisky to the men on 'J.B.T.' so there was no stimulant to take: a gin and tonic seemed hardly adequate. In future I shall have to have some brandy for these occasions. Instead I made a pot of tea, a cheese sandwich....my first food since a lunchtime biscuit, and then slept like a log after I had noted, with great surprise, that 'Big Bob' did not have his back to me. Apparently he had approved of my puny efforts!

The next morning broke fine and clear with little wind but I felt the effects of the night before, and I had some difficulty moving about the deck. If there was an area of me to ache, then except for my arms it ached: my leg, my chest, my back, stomach and neck. After breakfast I watched the large inflateable from 'Monacho' take the party of Americans ashore to start their bird watching sortie on the Island.

ARMY HUTS AT ST. KILDA

St Kilda is now owned by the Scottish National Trust, the most westerly of the outlying island of the U.K. and a resident warden looks after the Island for the trust. Theoretically permission should be obtained before landing but provided that visitors behave with due decorum there is no problem although it is as well to report your presence and duration of stay to the warden.

I had called the warden to explain my predicament but had been unable to obtain an answer. I had been hoping to find a diver among the army personnel who also occupy the Island, a Radar early warning station, such as I had worked on in the late forties in Hampshire.

After the Americans had disembarked, the skipper of Monacho came back to talk to me: no, to 'grill' me would be a better word. He could not understand how a yachtsman could possibly get a rope around the prop. "How long have you been sailing?" I replied about fifty years. "Ah, but how much time is that? Once a year?" I explained that I sailed about 2000 miles each year. "Ah, but are you qualified?" He was slowly mellowing and when I mentioned an RYA qualification he finally accepted that perhaps I was the victim of ill fortune rather than an idiot. He didn't say as much but instead offered to try and get me help in the form of a diver from the shore.

I wanted him to think well of me...don't we all? But I was very aware of his earlier comments on 'White Natives' and far from feeling abused I felt that I had somehow to show that I was neither a poacher or a fool. I knew my best policy was to say as little as possible and was rewarded with a smile from his fair colleague who had come with him in the boat, apparently the stewardess.

A little later the warden contacted me on R/T and promised that an army diver would arrive around lunchtime. Shortly afterwards I was visited by the skipper of "Spirit of Merseyside", the Fairbridge Drake training ship. He was a charming Irishman called Jimmy Dowey with a delightful sense of humour. Hearing of my troubles with the prop he brought his crew in their inflatable to my boat and suggested that they might take me as deck cargo to their next port of call, or perhaps lift my stern with their mainsheet, sufficient for me to get underneath and disentangle the prop. There were other equally Heath Robinson suggestions and he ended by offering me a meal aboard but I had to decline: I knew I would have difficulty in walking.

Sadly it was not to be his year. I heard from him on my return and learnt that he had lost his brother later that summer and also lost a crew member overboard while in dock in Cardiff. On the first occasion he had been off the coast of Spain when he was contacted to be told that his brother's boat which was being sailed single handed from the North Cape had been found without anyone aboard some 80 miles east of the Shetlands. His brother, who sailed single handed for many years with an artificial leg, had been engineless when some calamity befell him. By a strange co-incidence, friends of mine were returning from Norway that same night and the watchkeeper thought he heard a voice crying out at 3am. Despite a search they found nothing but on reporting to the coast guard they were told that they were some 100 miles south of the position of the casualty and that the dinghy was still on board. As if this were not enough our Skipper had earlier lost his bosun, blown off the dock in Cardiff while he had been absent from the boat, taking leave in Ireland. Naturally he had been held responsible and at the end of the season lost his job as Skipper. I was not the only 'unfortunate' on this trip!

The Fairbridge Drake Society, who own Spirit of Merseyside, is an organisation formed in 1929 to rescue, motivate and train young people at risk, aged 14 - 25, to enable them to grow to full maturity and make a constructive contribution to the society in which they live. In addition to the Schooner there with me at St Kilda the society have a barge called Turbot at Liverpool, a garden centre in London and various other centres of operations where they carry on their excellent work. Judging by the faces of the youngsters in the inflatable that hung from my quarter, they were all very happy and enjoying themselves. I was sorry that I couldn't take up their offer of hospitality.

St.Kilda to Loch Claish

Another boat had suggested that I could go aground at low tide on the foreshore and do it myself if I couldn't get a diver, and so I watched the receding tide very carefully and found that there was indeed one spot where I could safely go aground, provided that the army were not awaiting deliveries, as it was where their L.S.T. supply ship came ashore.

By now I was in acute discomfort because my leg had swollen up and was extremely painful. I would have the greatest difficulty in getting the dinghy launched and so decided against going ashore. I suspected that I had cracked a bone in my leg and that if I did go ashore I might have to see the station M.O. and then find I couldn't get back under my own steam to the mainland. I certainly didn't want that! I thought I was going to have no choice, though when the army C/O called me on R/T and asked me to go and pick up the diver. I started to unhitch the dinghy but the skipper of 'Spirit of Merseyside' saw my predicament and brought the diver over in his inflatable.

Not only was this helpful, but proved essential because we were able to use his painter under the boat for the diver to hang onto when he submerged. He was a young man in his early twenties wearing a wet suit and he went under the transom some nine times before he was able to free the prop. He would accept no reward, asking me to put my offer of ten pounds into the collecting box for cancer relief. His main concern was to get back to camp in time to watch the football match on TV.

Later, the skipper of 'Spirit of Merseyside' came alongside with his young charges and asked *'Was I going round Muckle Flugger'*. I confirmed that I was and his face lit up. *'You really are going round Britain, then! Good man, I'll look out for those little tan sails in Lerwick'* and off they went. Looking back, I am only too sorry that I did not get out to the Shetlands....I wish I had and feel I let that delightful man down, a gentle man.

My sailing club, the North West Venturers whose burgee I was flying, have a special plaque on which is inscribed the names of the boats that have got to St. Kilda and the year of the cruise. There were about 5 or 6 names on that plaque and I had hoped to get mine on but now I couldn't get ashore to post the essential card from the army post office and I certainly wasn't going to ask anyone else to do it for me. I think this hurt more than the physical aches of my body. Anyone who has set himself a goal and fails to get there must feel as I did, a deep sense of depression. Later I was to discover that they had accepted my arrival in Village Bay as sufficient to get my name on that coveted plaque. Such little things we value.

What is so special about this little island, or group of islands - there are four of them, Hirta (also called St. Kilda); Soay; Dun and Boreray (4 miles NE) rising hundreds of feet straight out of the sea - that make them a place of pilgrimage? Firstly they are the most westward part of Great Britain, some 40 odd miles from the west coast of the Outer Hebrides and subject to sudden changes of weather making visits by small boats dangerous in unsettled weather. Secondly, they are a nature reserve with a resident warden from the Scottish National Trust living on St.Kilda, the largest island of the group which has been declared a World Heritage Site. The main island is also occupied by the Ministry of Defence who operate an early warning radar lookout post.

There are only two possible anchorages on St. Kilda, in Village Bay on the South East corner and a temporary anchorage in Glen Bay on the North side of St. Kilda. Elsewhere, a cable off shore and the depth drops to 30 metres. This Island is brilliantly portrayed by Hammond Innes in his exciting book 'Atlantic Fury" where he also describes an Easterly storm in Village Bay (which he calls 'Shelter Bay'). Reading it later brought my visit back to me with extreme clarity. Of course he fictionalised his Island but the similarities are clear to see, albeit seen through a looking glass.

I was fortunate to arrive at St. Kilda after a prolonged spell of high pressure so my first night was free of swell despite a North Easterly from which I had a lee in the bay. However, the weather worsened while I was there and a day later there was an extremely unpleasant swell as the wind veered south east. No one stays at St. Kilda in a South Easterly and on the Saturday night all boats departed except for myself and 'Monacho'. I stayed because I could not yet get around the deck and thought I might have trouble getting the anchor up and then getting back to the cockpit again.

The night proved to be all I feared: I rocked and rolled in the considerable swell, twice almost being thrown out of my bunk so that finally I slept on the cabin sole, which was very hard on my shoulder blades. I was delighted when morning came and I could officially wake up.

At around 8 am the skipper of 'Monacho' came over to see if I was alright and if I would be leaving. I confirmed that I would and that 'yes, I would be going through the Sound of Harris again'. This was to be his venue but he said that first he would take his charges round the 'Stacs' (rocky pinnacles) and other Islands. He looked rather careworn, as did his stewardess who was with him. I suspected that they had had a bad night like me.

I raised anchor without too much difficulty and motored out of the Bay before raising sails and heading eastwards. A little later 'Monacho' also left and went off round the Islands. I would like to have seen them but the discomfort was such that I just wanted to get to a safe anchorage and have a quiet night.

Later, I spoke with 'Monacho' who asked me to keep an R/T contact with him on the hour. I was touched by his concern. Another boat had heard his call and called him, so naturally I listened in!

'Hello, Cubby. Where were you last night?
'I was at St. Kilda, laddie'
'Wasn't it uncomfortable?'
'It was dreadful. We all rolled the long night in our bunks and there were few for breakfast this morning'
'Why on earth did you stay, man. You heard the forecast?'
'Well, you see, there was this wee yachtie and I didn't like to leave him'

I turned off at this point, very abashed and yet full of admiration for this man who had stood by a 'white native' while all his charges suffered. God Bless you, Cubby! I suspect he hadn't finished with me because when I reached, in very misty conditions, the entry to the Sound of Harris which he had already transited via the Leverburgh Channel - I was taking the Stanton Passage - the coast guard called me and asked me where I was. At that very moment I had just located my first buoy after taking a slightly wrong direction in the mist so I told them and they asked me to advise them as soon as I was through. Their call was so apposite that I can only assume that 'Monacho', who were watching for me from the other side of the channel about two miles away, had advised the Coast Guard on a private channel that I was possibly in trouble.

Once again I counted those buoys through the channel, the mist just leaving enough visibility, comparing every one with the chart and ticking them off as I passed. The Clyde Guide gives bearings and back bearings to follow, which is fine if there are two of you, but on your own and in a shifting mist the only thing is to remember the major landmarks and watch the buoys. It was nerve racking for about 45 minutes, the time it actually took me to transit though it seemed so much longer, and I was delighted to be able to call the Coast Guard and tell them I was safe and heading for Loch Rodel. I would not recommend the Sound of Harris to a single hander!

Just inside Loch Rodel is a small pool with room for about three boats to anchor in complete security and I had looked forward to going in and losing myself again, but there was a rather large catamaran in the pool and another boat so I went further down and anchored off St. Clements church in thick weed. I motored the anchor in to ensure that it was firm and it held beautifully. I had thought I might have to unearth my fisherman's anchor to cut through the growth but all was well. I was so tired that I slept from nine until six the next day, missing the weather forecast but feeling a lot better. My leg was very very sore and my back was bruised from the fall approaching St. Kilda but most of the other aches and pains were gone.

I had been doing so much motoring that I felt it time to refuel and decided that I should be able to get diesel at East Loch

Tarbert, some ten miles north. This would be the second time in an 'East Loch Tarbert', but this time in the outer Hebrides: truly 'Bare Knees' country! Loch Tarbert can be a confusing name for a harbour. I left Rodel at 7.30 and moored at East Loch Tarbert pier at 10.30, having discovered that there would be no ferry until later in the afternoon. The Ferry office let me use their phone to contact a contractor on the Island who sent three six gallon drums of diesel by lorry to the harbour and then we had the nightmare job of transferring it to my tanks. They had no pumps and I couldn't carry 6 gallon drums (one of which was leaking - 'there's a hole in my bucket, dear Liza') from the pier to the deck. In the end, we transferred first into my two 2 gallon portable tanks that I then emptied into my internal tanks. It took us over an hour to transfer those 18 gallons of diesel and the decks stank of the stuff all that day.

By the time I had paid transport costs and tipped the three men who helped me it was almost as expensive as if I had settled for DERV which was available from the local garage! I paid my mooring dues, having filled the water tanks, and set off again, knowing that I could now reach the mainland and get out to the Orkneys without further trouble as I had also bought bread, butter, and other fresh foods. I had also telephoned the family, the first chance I had had for almost a week and sent off all those post-cards to say that I had made it to St. Kilda! I also arranged a broadcast report.

The town of East Loch Tarbert on Harris comprises a garage, a few houses and half a dozen shops. Oh yes, and a chapel (or was it a church?) There was the inevitable gift shop but this time it was selling genuine Harris Tweed: you could expect no less. I was tempted but the boat was so overloaded that I really didn't have room for anything more

My next port of call would be the west coast of Skye. There are not too many safe harbours on this coast, but at 7 pm I was anchoring in Duntulm Bay behind a small Island which gave perfect protection from the light south west wind. There were two other yachts sharing my haven for the night. Most of the time I was in Scotland I found that other boats were rarely less than 30 ft. and the vast majority were chartered. It was the same at Duntulm, with a large Moody and a Westerly 33 both to the North of me. I was told in St. Kilda that anything less than 30ft was a rare sight there, and certainly it would be a very long run for a boat incapeable of an average speed of 5 knots. I was lucky in that 'JUNKETTE' is a slim greyhound of a boat which, with a waterline length of only 21ft was quite able to sail at around 5 knots (hard work without a bowsprit, though).

    I had managed to buy some fillet steak at Loch Tarbert and had a splendid meal before retiring to listen to some tapes. The loading of diesel had resulted in some escaping into the under berth locker on the port side...where I kept my fresh vegetables. I had to wash the potatoes and onions very thoroughly and repack them before I could eat. The system for storing fuel in 'Junkette' is through side deck filler pipes into the keels. The level of fuel could be judged by dip sticks, but it is impossible to guage exactly how much is needed and if, like me, you fill up when you can rather than adding a little now and then, you often overfill so the excess ends up in the locker beneath the bunk and the result is that the smell of diesel fuel stays with you for a day or two and anything stored there must be protected in plastic bags.

    My leg was now going rather dark and bruised and was very painful so for the next few days I would be going to bed early. I had a few books with me so I refreshed my memory at this stage with what Libby Purves had done on this coast, where she had been, to see if it helped me. Middleton's report was not going to be any help since he had gone through the Bowling canal. Libby had gone up to Kinlochbervie and then straight through to Stromness but it was a bit much for me as a single hander in my state of health. I thought first I might go to Ullapool and then on to Loch Roe and, in easy stages, round Cape Wrath.

    Next day, after leaving Skye I found myself uncertain whether to go to Loch Ewe, the nearer, or Ullapool but eventually decided on Ullapool as I thought I could not really spare the time to see the gardens at Inverewe, which I would certainly have done had I gone there. These gardens are superb. This area of coast is washed by the gulf stream and as a result has a very mild climate. Palm trees have, until very recently, grown at Ullapool on the sea front and still do at Plockton. In the gardens at Inverewe, the Rhododendrons and Azaleas do particularly well and this was the time to see them at their best. The decision to go on and miss them was not an easy one to take but the state of my leg convinced me! As it was, I did not reach Ullapool until after 8 pm and was lucky to find a vacant mooring buoy.

In the morning I went ashore loaded with my washing as I had been told there was a very good laundry at the camp site, and indeed my information proved accurate: it was excellent. While the clothes were whirling round I did my shopping for food and by midday, all was done and back on board.

I had discovered another problem: a little earlier in the cruise I had found a lot of water in the port cockpit locker. I keep my water tanks here and assumed that in filling then I had accidentally spilled some from the hose. When it happened a second time a few days later and I found that a tank I had thought full was empty, the truth dawned: I had one with a leak in it: a five gallon tank. Now, in Ullapool, was my chance to replace it and indeed the local ironmonger not only had one but filled it for me!

I managed to carry it all of 25 yards and from then on I was emptying some out over the sea wall every few yards until I was able to carry it with just short pauses, my leg being very painful indeed. I got back finally with about 3 gallons in and felt exhausted. Ashore once more for a drink in the pub and it was ghastly. There were few people about, a few early visitors and no one wanted to talk which was sad because I had had many happy memories of this town. The Yacht club was deserted so I returned to the boat. I had thought of trying to find a Doctor to look at my leg but worry about the mooring (the owner might return while I was missing) and my general depression made me give that idea up. I very nearly decided to call the whole idea off there and then, and I guess that if just one person had commiserated with me, I would have, so it is as well that I met no friendly soul.

The next day I moved out and headed for the Summer Isles where I thought of spending a night. However, when I got there and saw the extensive fish farming set up I decided to go on, especially as at last I had a favourable wind. But it was not to last and soon it backed from North East to North West and once again headed me in a rising sea. North Westerly winds in the North Minch can soon produce some violent and unpleasant seas and for the next few days I was to have pleasant morning sailing and dire afternoons in short sharp seas due to the Northerly winds bucking the North going tides, now the stronger spring tides. Since leaving Skye, the wind had turned to the North and it was much colder. I felt great sympathy with the winchmen on the 'Search and Rescue' helicopter which was practising in the area, landing crew men on the stern of accommodating steamers and a bulk carrier travelling up and down the Minch.

These northerly winds meant that a passage of 24 miles in 8 hours was a major achievement. It was now more than ever that I valued my spray hood. Sailing into a wind is never pleasant but with the effect of a favourable tide making the apparent wind move ever forward and faster, and being from a cold northerly direction anyway, sailing became even more unpleasant. Not only did I have wind against tide but I got this effect that all sailors are aware of: the apparent wind moving ever forward as your speed increases. I had decided to go for Loch Roe but had some difficulty in recognising it from the pilot and relied on my DR position being correct when I turned towards the cliffs. There it was, just as the sun came from behind a cloud and I motored into a lovely little anchorage, completely calm and unruffled called 'Bo Pool'.

I launched the 'Sweat' and rowed ashore at low tide, having some difficulty in getting the dinghy through the thick kelp. There was a small landing cove very weed infested but eventually I got ashore to find a horrid litter of plastic bottles and discarded rubbish from picnic parties. I must have spent well over an hour on my hands and knees gathering up the debris and trying to bury it under some bushes and stones.

The view was incredibly beautiful: I thought of 'Brigadoon' and imagined an American cast gambolling in the heather and ferns. The nearest house was about a mile away on the far side of the pool and the only sounds were of birds and sheep.

BO POOL
Note the 'Sweat' in the little bay.

Back on the boat I had a good meal and considered my position. My leg was very painful but I couldn't really spare the time to try and find a Doctor and I kept hoping it would get better after a good nights sleep. Unfortunately it was at its worst when I first got up but after some excersize it seemed to get a little less painful. Those first few minutes were excruciating.
Next morning, 18th May, I had a gentle North Easterly - and I was heading North North East! At least it wasn't westerly and I shouldn't have such very unpleasant seas. Once again I was tacking up the North Minch, against the tide but in sunshine and smooth water. Aware now of the unpleasant nature of sailing into

a headwind with the tide after midday when the wind tended to veer west due to the heating of the land, I decided to motor sail and reached Loch Claish by early afternoon, a trip of 34 miles. On the way I had time to observe the antics of the seabirds: Gannets swooping down like World War 2 Stuka dive bombers (perhaps the designer had studied the Z shaped wing formation of the birds!) and the small Guillemots. This coast is very rich in bird life, I suppose because of the close proximity of the Gulf Stream current which must bring much small marine life and which certainly helps when travelling north.

    I had passed Loch Laxford, where John Ridgeway operates his adventure school and was full of admiration for John and his students, ready to brave the elements this far north, often with the most primitive of shelters. I would liked to have stopped and talked to them but I knew my leg would protest at too much walking. Even so, had there been a free mooring I might well have been tempted but all were occupied and I pressed on to Loch Claish. After my cruise was all over I heard from Anthony Cook who had been gale bound in Loch Laxford for a week. I would guess he got there about three weeks after me, at the time I was getting gales at Peterhead on the other side of Scotland, so I was very fortunate in my timing.

    I turned in towards Kin Loch Bervie and headed for Loch Claish, the small harbour which backs onto the much larger, and busy fishing harbour and found space to anchor close to the jetty so that I could quickly row ashore (as quickly as getting 'The Sweat' off allows!)

    Libby Purves gives an excellent description of this place in her book and of the Deep Sea Mission which, like her, I found very welcoming so that I was glad to buy a meal ashore for a change. What Libby did not mention was the sad display of plaques on the wall, commemorating the loss of fisherfolk at sea: usually very young men who had presumably not had time to find their sea legs. There were four young men finishing a gargantuan meal and it was as though I could see a dark cloud over their heads as I read the notices. All, though, was not 'doom and gloom': the car park was full of new cars, the property of the fishermen in this booming port and a tangible sign of the results of their efforts. There is little else other than a mini supermarket, a single hotel and the inevitable Ice plant.

In the morning when I was having breakfast I heard a horn close by sounding 'J U' and, on looking out of the hatch I saw a man on the jetty who called me. *"JUNKETTE, where are you going next?"* It turned out that he was a coast guard from Scrabster (over a hundred miles away?) who was looking to see where I had got to. I had been unable to raise the Coast Guard once I had left Skye as I was out of reach of Stornoway C.G. and also of Pentland. I could hear Aberdeen, surprisingly, but they could not hear me. Much later I was to find that other sailors in the North Minch suffered the same loss of contact though I believe that in some of the summer months a temporary Coast Guard look out is manned at Handa.

I explained that I was heading for Loch Eriboll but needed the services of a Doctor. He suggested that the nearest was at Scourie but that meant reversing my steps and I'd no intention of doing that. He then said that there was either a Doctor or nurse at Durness. I said that I'd try and hang on until I got to Scrabster: I realised that I would not be able to sail across to the Orkneys until I had some treatment. By now my leg had gone almost black and was very swollen and painful.

The coast guard wished me well and asked me to report in when I reached Eriboll. I quickly cleared the decks, raised anchor and motored out towards the Minch. The wind was very light indeed so I motored into a virtual flat calm and headed North. The coast line here is remarkable with such outstanding headlands as Stoer Head and 'The Shepherd': tall granite 'stacs' or pinnacles of rock rising shear out of the sea. Beyond these rocks and cliffs the landscape is very barren and unfriendly with vast stretches of bracken and scree. I imagined what it would be like in winter when the seaman's mission in Kinlochbervie would be a very welcome place to come to from these barren wastes. It was in these areas that Ridgeway's adventure school worked!

STOER HEAD AND STACKS

Loch Claish to Wick: Round the Top!

The sun was shining, the sea calm and the engine running well so I was able to sit back and consider the sea surface gleaming in the low rays of the sun, quite brilliant. Once again I marvelled at the Guillemots and their diving feats. Sometimes they would submerge just ahead of the boat and then reappear well to the stern of me, often in groups of seven or eight so I supposed there must be schools of fry shoaling around me.

I reached Cape Wrath without trouble, keeping well clear of Duslic rock which was only half covered. The name 'Wrath' means turning point, and looking at the headland I had just rounded, with its pronounced peaks, I could imagine the pleasure that the raiding Vikings must have felt in knowing that they were moving into richer climes, rich in plunder with softer bedding further south, and all the connotations that could mean to those hungry men of war. Thinking of wars, I looked to see if there was a range flag flying as the north coast here is a major gunnery range, but could see nothing on the cliffs as I turned East, no flag.

At last I had cleared the West side of mainland Britain and I was wondering if I would be able to go further North to the Orkneys and Shetland. At least with the firing range quiet I would not need to sail four miles further out. I was worried about fog, but so far the weather was beautiful and clear. It was the fear of fog that decided the skipper of Grace O'Malley to go straight out to Stromness.

By five o'clock I had reached Loch Eriboll. There is an anchorage on the west side of the entrance called 'Rispond Bay' which would have been handy for a quick exit but I had seen a curious orange contraption in the far distance down the loch and went right in to investigate. I anchored in North Bay of Ard Neakie, alongside a small lighter with the name 'Kellman Marine' stencilled on the side. The orange object turned out to be a giant crane and Jim Kellman was building up a Mussel farm, using the crane to level the road, raise rocks, tow heavy loads ashore from his boat and do the thousand and one things needed on such a heavy manual job. For instance, he had a mile and a half of nylon rope too thick for me to encompass with one hand (twelve inch circumference). This was the ground rope for the nets and buoys round his patch. He had begun his enterprise, with a little help from the Highlands development board, some two years ago and was hoping to collect his very first harvest of mussels later in the season as they have a three year growth period. Later, when I was sailing down the east coast I heard that Mussels there were not being harvested because of a disease they had succumbed to and I wondered if it would reach the west. It has been suggested that the disease might be due to intensive salmon farming!

Jim Kellman lived in Inverness and used to travel the 90 odd miles at weekends to tend his farm, mostly alone. Apparently he had been told to move his rubbish and hide his crane as there had been objections that he was spoiling the view (and how!). I asked how he could hide a crane and he said he wasn't sure. There was a gleam in his eye and later I saw him dismantling the crane into small pieces and loading them onto a flat bed truck. I think he was hoping to hire it out to the fishermen in Kin Loch Bervie.

He told me there was a stand pipe for water in the adjacent field so I set off with a two gallon can, but my leg was so sore that I came back on my hands and knees while he had his back to me. I sat on his new roadway and chatted until I felt fit enough to get up and walk down the beach to the dinghy. Jim Kellman offered to let me tie up behind his boat as his mooring was very strong, but the thought of raising the anchor and moving over to him was more than I could face. Physically I had nearly reached the end of my tether.

The next morning I set off bright and early, and once clear of the cliffs, picked up a good south westerly which sped me along, past the Kyle of Tounge and islets at nearly six knots for six hours. I would have liked to have stopped at the Kyle of Tounge and go ashore on some of the Islands. The weather was perfect for such a venture and good weather on the North coast is at a bit of a premium. If I hadn't been sailing so well I would have called on 'Rabbit Island'. As it was, I soldiered on, my arms soon aching from the strain of holding the tiller against the excess weather helm - oh when would I be able to get that bowsprit replaced? - trying various ways to use tiller lines to control the boat. None worked for very long in that stiff breeze and I was reluctant to reef down while the sea was creaming along so happily under the forefoot, so I had to give up the idea of lunch and enjoy the ride.

Then the wind suddenly died completely and the fog descended. Visibility was down to about 30 meters so, on engine, I foolishly headed inshore, looking for the headland I would round to enter Thurso Bay. I should have relied on my DR as I had another four miles to go on the clock. Instead I nearly went aground on the reef off Ushat Head and I turned just in time to avoid it. I was later told that this is a favourite area for surfing as the waves are really quite spectacular: I can personally vouch for that as the white water swirled in the fog but a few feet off my keels.

Of course I had Decca which would give my position more or less exactly, but I got out of the habit of using it since, while sailing, I couldn't leave the helm. As soon as I saw the broken water and turned out to sea, now on engine, I did check and discovered that my DR was correct and I had just been very silly. When the rig is working properly, ie the sails balanced with the bowsprit in place, I can easily leave the helm and go into the cabin to read the chart and Decca, but since leaving Port Patrick I was denied this luxury except when motoring and used to have the chart up in the cockpit with me together with binoculars and a handbearing compass for what George Taylor, the editor of Practical Boat Owner magazine called 'eyeball navigation'.

Finally I came to Scrabster harbour and called the H.M. but could get no reply. I had hoped he would be able to tell me where to moor but as I came into the inner harbour I saw a yacht with two men aboard and headed for it, asking them to take my ropes. There was a little hesitation and they didn't seem keen to have me alongside, but at that moment the engine decided to 'take off' in a cloud of white smoke. Luckily I was out of gear so I shouted to the men to hang onto my ropes while I tried to stop the engine, which only proved possible by putting my hat over the air intake.

Eventually, I tied up and tried to find the harbour master, without luck, so instead went to the harbour hotel and had a hot meal. I met a charming American flyer who was working at the American base a short distance away. He hadn't been in Britain very long and was enjoying the hospitality but missed the warmth of his native Florida. He was amused when I told him about the taxidermist in Crinan and he thought he might try to get down to see his work. I then asked the landlady about Doctors and she suggested I go to Thurso Health Center the following morning, Thurso being just two miles away. There is little at Scrabster besides the harbour, a gift shop and the Hotel although it is quite a busy little port, handling the ferries to and from the Faeroes as well as a small fishing fleet and the yearly pilgrimage of the Royal Yacht to visit the Queen Mother at the Castle of Mey just a little east of Scrabster. The Faeroes inhabitants come over for their 'duty frees': drink on the island is fearfully expensive, as are clothes so the inhabitants come over for a trip to Thurso or Wick to replenish their supplies just as we 'pop over' to France with the same purpose!

Scrabster does, though, have a small but adventurous Yacht Club whose members regularly sail to the Orkneys, Shetlands and to Norway. For people who regularly sail across the channel from South coast ports that may not sound much but in these Northern waters, clear of all obstacles from the American coast to Norway, you can have some big seas and suddenly changing conditions to face. Also, the gulf stream crosses over the top of Scotland and through the Pentland Firth, helping produce the fiery effect of 'the merry men of Mey' on an ebb tide, so the sight of a diminutive Caprice yacht in the harbour came as something of a surprise.!

The Pentland Firth had been my 'bete noir', my fear ever since I had set off, so much so that I had decided to avoid it by going right outside everything and up to the Orkneys, even perhaps the Faeroes and then round to the Shetlands to miss it, yet here I was, wondering if I had time to go due North to Stromness or whether I would have to go due East and 'into the mouth of Hell'. The Clyde Cruising Club guide says 'The rate of tidal streams in various parts of the Firth is higher than that experienced in almost any other part of the sea round our coast'.

While in Scrabster I was told an apocryphal story of this tide race: about how a Battle Cruiser the story teller was serving on went east across the race against the ebb tide in a force seven. The boat 'fell' into one of the huge 'holes' that suddenly appear in the sea, and the jolt was so great that the main bearing studs broke and the rear gun turret shifted. Another heave and it shifted again, this time to slide overboard, taking everything in its path. Imagine me in a 26 footer, even if I only had a flare gun to go overboard!

The next morning I awoke to a grey day, and going ashore met the Harbour Master and explained my strange arrival. Apparently he had been calling me, but in the hiatus of the engine blowing up I had turned the R/T off and not heard him. I made my peace, explained that I was going into Thurso to find a Doctor and asked him to recommend an engineer who might be able to look at the engine and determine what was wrong. I said I hoped to be back by lunch time and went out to phone a taxi.

With my usual luck, just after the taxi arrived and picked me up, a bus appeared, one of the two a day that went to Thurso! Thurso proved to be a delightful town with a good selection of shops and a thriving, and very busy, health centre. I had to wait over two hours to see a Doctor: apparently there was one Doctor who looked after visiting seamen and went out on the Life Boats when required. Imagine my surprise when I met 'her', a delightful young lady who, after a careful examination of my leg, thought I had in some way got an infection and gave me an antibiotic with orders to return two days later, on Wednesday.

This delay was going to put all my plans in jeopardy if I was to reach Suffolk by June 29th (my sister's birthday) and I nearly decided to press on 'and take the tablets'. If the engine hadn't failed I would have done, but as it was I was stranded. On return to the boat I found an engineer had already been and in his haste to examine the engine, had broken part of the casing, being unable to find the appropriate retaining screws, and bits of cover were spread all over the cockpit. It did not auger well for our relations on his return, but eventually sanity returned and I greeted him civilly (just) and suggested that the fuel pump governor might be faulty.

He turned out to be one of those profits of doom. 'You wont get it repaired for a week at least....I don't think they'll have a replacement 'cept from Glasgow' etc. I suggested that he might get a part by return post from the manufacturers in Devon and he went away to phone while I repaired the casing damage. On his return he asked how much oil I had in the sump and was it overful? We checked and it was. 'Ah, they told me that if you have too much oil the engine breaths in the fumes and begins to fire on them'. We drained off a gill of oil, and tried the starter. Hey Presto! Success! All was well. Later I got a bill for £50 for that advice and 'help'! That was one of only two bad moments in Scrabster: for the rest I count the town as one of the most helpful and friendly that I have ever visited.

When the engineer had left (his dirty finger marks and foot prints on the deck removed), I prepared myself a meal and retired early to bed, feeling very unwell. At about eight o'clock I woke to a hammering on the hull: the skipper of the boat I was tied up to was livid because the engineer had put his dirty, greasy hands over the man's lovely new pram hood. He demanded I moved my boat so I had to dress again and see the harbour master who found me another berth further in the harbour. When I had stopped the previous night I had forgotten to bring in my log line, a cord that hangs from the back of the boat with an impellor on it to record the distance travelled. Now, feeling very depressed, I did not notice it so when I motored the boat round to the new berth the log line wound itself round the prop. It was not strong enough to stop the engine and I did not notice it until the following morning when I found it tight round the prop.

Fortunately my new berth was in a very shallow part of the harbour and at low tide I was able to stand in a couple of feet of water and cut the offending cord away. I thought of Cubby on Monacho and wondered what he would think of an idiot Skipper who twice got rope round his prop! The water was very cold but a relief to my leg which did not seem to be getting any better.

As I had to hang about for a couple of days I began to talk to local people and became friendly with the lady, Irene Jones, who operated an RNLI caravan selling trinkets to visitors. When she heard I was going round Britain for Cancer Relief she said that she thought a friend of hers was on the local committee. Irene was as good as her word and that evening I met the Bews, a lovely couple, he a butcher in Thurso, who invited me to their home for a meal. I had a wonderful dinner preceded by a bath in a most elegant suite where a Russell Flint print of two maidens in a roman bath, which I much loved, looked down benignly at me. Looking at it from the scented water I remembered how, in 1948 I had gone to a Bond Street gallery with a friend to see an exhibition of Russell Flint paintings. At that time they (originals) had cost about £40 each. Now, the print looking down at me would have cost at least £50

Being a butcher, Denis had provided a piece of succulent Aberdeen Angus beef that was almost too good to be true and showed once again that meat in Scotland was generally excellent. May, his wife, could also cook a Yorkshire pudding, and having been brought up on these delicacies I could enjoy it the more. At sea, your diet is strictly limited so one of the greatest joys ashore was that of eating, which is why Yachtsmen, almost without exception, remember their favourite ports as those where a good meal is available. Eating well and bathing are the twin dreams of those on small boats!

On Wednesday I returned to the clinic, no better for the antibiotic and the Doctor decided that an X ray was called for in case I had a cracked bone. An ambulance took me to Wick, to the Caithness General Hospital via a couple of outports where we picked up other patients. The sun was brilliant and it was warm even this early in the year so far North.

When we arrived in late morning I discovered a large granite building only recently opened by the Queen Mother. Who else but this great lady who spent her summers at the Castle of Mey which she saved from certain ruin by first re roofing and then overhauling inside and tastefully decorating for her own use - she was dearly loved by all Caithness. The hospital is very well appointed inside and it seemed to me to be just about the right size for the area it served, light and airy, clean and functional without appearing soulless. Outside, it dominated the town, standing on a hill above the town centre. At the moment it looks preposterous and heavy, but it will mellow with time, I suppose.

An X Ray showed no fracture but the Doctor diagnosed excess bruising of the bone and much congealed blood. I was admitted for treatment! I had no hospital gear with me, no pyjamas, soap or towel etc. Instead I had a bag of groceries for the boat, but I need not have worried: within 24 hours I had all I needed, thanks to the kindness of the people of Wick and area. Although the boat was 22 miles away and I was a total stranger I had at least one and often two or more visitors at every visiting time. Folk drove the 20 miles from Thurso every day and I saw members of the Yacht Club, the Supervisor of the Deep Sea Mission to Seamen, a school teacher, and oh so many others. One of the first people to visit was the skipper of the boat who had asked me to move. He was very embarrassed and apologised for his ill behaviour and gave me some cakes cooked by his wife. I was utterly charmed because it could not have been an easy thing for him to do.

The hospital physiotherapist had the task of easing my leg and at first nothing seemed to help. Then he tried ultra sound and the effect was almost instantaneous. After the first treatment I could walk, slowly, without a stick and that lasted for about an hour. From then on each application gave greater relief and I was released from care by the following Monday.

Although an ambulance had taken me to hospital I had to make my own arrangements for getting back to Scrabster and here one of my new friends, Ron Jones, the husband of the RNLI lady turned up trumps by offering to come and collect me. He drove me around some of the villages in brilliant sunshine - I had been lucky in that my visit to the far North had coincided with a period of exceptionally fine weather - and I was able to share his enthusiasm for the area. I learnt that there were a lot of English people as well as Americans living in, or near Wick because of the work at Dounreay power station and a couple of service establishments. Most had come to love the county and their Scottish friends, but a small minority regretted moving, comparing the area with their beloved southern shires and complaining too frequently. My own experience was of extreme hospitality and outstanding friendliness. I knew I would return.

After a long talk with the H.M. who disabused me of my ideas of the Pentland Firth - 'get there at the right time, right conditions and you'll have nothing at all to fear, especially going East on the flood' - I decided to leave on the next morning, Tuesday 29th May. I now had no time to go out to either the Orkneys or Shetland, and Wick was to be my next port of call as I turned south at last. I knew that I had to be off Dunnet head by around 9am to catch the tide right for the Firth so I was up early and off at low water, having moved the boat into deeper water the night before.

At Dunnet head the wind dropped to a whisper and I had to motor east until off John 'O Groats when the wind piped up and the sails began to draw in a southeasterly breeze. With the tide helping I could sail close hauled in a calm sea and the fabled 'Merry Men of Mey' race was almost without movement. I sailed inside Stroma Island where there is now a harbour, although I felt no wish to stop as the weather could change dramatically the next day, feeling the tide pulling the boat through at great speed. Passing John O Groats from seaward gave me a strange feeling: from the sea it looks so welcoming but from the jetty, looking out into the greyness of the distant Orkneys you have a very different sensation.

With little wind it took me just under one and a half hours to reach Dunscanby Head from Dunnet Head, a distance of around 12 miles: ie the tide had been running at around 4 knots the whole way, and this at 'neaps' (small tides). In spring tides it would have been a real helter skelter. I met Dunscanby Race as I approached the head and this was my first turbulent water, which fortunately lasted for no more than half a mile. This race is caused when the East going Pentland stream meets the North going tide from the North Sea, best sailed through at neaps! With the tide still under me I was soon through it and in another half mile definitely turned south, admiring the strong lines of the headland and the further Stacs, more needle like pinnacles of rock.

DUNSCANBY HEAD

When I reached Wick harbour that idiotic thing happened which every skipper fears a novice will do: throw a rope without the end being tied on board. Yes, the helpful Harbour Master stood to take my lines and there I was, watching the neat coil fall irretrievably into the water. 'You will be able to see it at low water and get it back' he announced, but at the neap tides now running there was no way I could reach it. A good coil of 15 meters of mooring warp lost! I realised that I was still very tired... at least, that's my excuse.

Being in Wick again seemed strange and I was struck with the lack of amenities: water was the other side of the harbour, a good quarter mile to hump a jerry can. No letter boxes: I had to find the main post office to post a letter, and few telephone facilities, certainly none in the harbour. On the plus side was the fact that the charge of £4.60 would have allowed me to stay in the port for up to seven days: very different to the idiotic charges on the south coast. I was very aware of harbour charges, mainly because so far I had paid very few, my charitable status giving me an advantage. At Scrabster, for instance, my boat had been looked after for over a week yet there was no charge at all.

While in Wick I was struck again by the heavy appearance of the hospital, brooding over the town. It certainly makes it's mark. In the harbour my heart was in my mouth as I saw two young lads standing fishing off the wall, with the sea just covering the rocks about 30 ft below. They were like mountain goats, but I couldn't bear to look for more than a moment. I turned away to find a sign writer putting a name on a boat in 'Ye Olde English' script: GECKO OF WICK. He was so sure of his strokes of the brush that in no time at all he had completed the first colour of deep blue and began the highlighting in cerulean blue. I wished I had had the time for him to treat my boat in similar fashion but I gathered that he was fully booked for the week. I was once responsible for employing graphics artists and their abilities and artistic professionalism, like good illustrators have always impressed me. I wonder sometimes why fine artists tend to 'look down their nose' at the work of illustrators! It was a little time before Andrew Wyeth was accepted because his work was too detailed: too much like that of his father, who was an illustrator. But who, having seen Wyeth's 'CHRISTINA'S WORLD' can doubt either his ability or poetic vision. Incidentally, it was another artist who explained the meaning behind that painting: Rolf Harris who tells us that Christina suffered from Polio and that we were indeed looking at her total horizons.

I had brought painting materials with me at June's suggestion (she is a professional artist) but in fact made very little use of them until it was all over and I could work from the stability of my own home. The moving platform of a boat is not ideal for sketching, even with pastels, my favourite medium, and when in harbour I was always too busy looking around and talking to anyone with the time to spare who could tell me any local history.

Ahead of me lay the Moray Firth and stations south. My post of the last six weeks waited for me at Inchyra village, near Perth and it was time I was on my way. I had wanted to be clear of Scotland before the end of May but that was now impossible so I was going to have to move on quickly. I had been invited to visit Inverness (Radio Highlands were carrying reports of my voyage), and friends had a cottage some few miles inland but I wouldn't have time and instead, would have to cross the Moray Firth diagonally. The voyage so far had not been without its traumas and I knew that the worst sea conditions were likely to lay close ahead. The North Sea is known to be unpredictable and prone to Easterly winds, putting sailors against an often inhospitable lee shore. It was time to move on.

Wick to Edinburgh

I left Wick at 8am., and finding a pleasant North Westerly behind me, switched off the engine and handed over to 'George', with a little assistance from a shock cord to help the inherent weather helm. All was well for about 30 minutes when the autohelm failed again and 'George' went sick! I attempted a repair on the move and an hour later had it going. It worked until I got to Stonehaven, three days later!

I was now crossing the Moray Firth diagonally, well inside the oil platform position but in a 'submarine excersize area'. Having met the Skipper of Dalriada I was very nervous of Subs: without an engine to hear, they could easily hit me with their periscope. A yacht is very small and often lost below waves or swell when the Commander is conning the horizon. When attending an Open University summer school, one of my fellow students turned out to be the second in command of a nuclear submarine and we talked about the problem of yachts. He agreed that we made problems for sub-mariners because we were not easy to detect. Imagine, then, my fear when scanning the horizon at mid day I spotted a brilliant flashing on the water to the North of me. It was too small to make out other than a point of light but I guessed it was the glass of a periscope flashing in the sun. I thought of signalling back with a mirror, perhaps the letter 'D', but the sun was behind me. From then on I kept scanning the horizon and wondering whether to use the engine, but I hated the noise of the thing and liked the quietness all around me.

That quiet seemed to have changed in quality as I looked round, and I realised that although there was nothing but sea in sight all round me - no land whatsoever - I could hear an engine. There were no aircraft in sight and I realised that I could hear the engine noise of the submarine. It is a strange effect at sea, a soft humming noise like a power station and it seems to be everywhere, all invading. Then I saw the flashes for an instant, closer now behind me. I switched on the radio, on radio 2 as loud as I could and put the portable face down on the cabin sole. I just hoped 'they' would hear it. It was nearly mid afternoon before I could relax.

As I approached the coast east of Frazerborough I was within range of the coastal radio station and was able to call the BBC and make arrangements for a broadcast the following day. Shortly afterwards, the wind died on me and as I slowly coasted South I was delighted to find a school of Dolphins around me. I went below to find a camera, but when I returned they had all gone! I was just cursing my luck when they returned and gave a great display of flashing Dorsal and Tail fins, white bottoms shown like Folies Bergere dancers. I noted that whenever I went below they would vanish, but as soon as I could be seen on deck they would return. Great exhibitionists! They stayed with me for almost an hour and greatly enlivened the end of a long sail.

I arrived at Frazerborough at 9pm: a long time at the tiller, waiting for 'George' to take another 'sicky'. (Oh, those Australian soaps, how they affect the language; I once found myself saying 'this arbo'!) I was not to have a quiet night, though. I was tucked away into a small corner where I thought I would be out of trouble in a busy fishing harbour but ... just behind my mooring was the 'Ice' plant and fishing boats kept pulling up and loading ice throughout the night and it was all very noisy. Do you ever have the feeling that you are not wanted?

The cost was not exhorbitant for harbour dues and the harbour master very friendly but I was pleased to leave and head for Peterhead. The wind had now gone southeast and was heading me, what there was of it. Also, I had an adverse tide, stronger inshore but I was unable to sail far out because of cable layers working a mile off shore, and had to put up with a long, slow motor sail into Peterhead. After all the glorious weather I had had on the west and north coasts of Scotland I now got into a cold, dark and dank atmosphere which was to last, on and off, for the next three days. It is evidence of the superb weather that I had had in the past that I should count three days of inclement weather as a long time!

Peterhead is very busy indeed, but much better for yachtsmen than Frazerborough because you can anchor in the southern harbour where there is a quiet pool in the south east of the bay, and you can row ashore to shop in the excellent town. I had intended just an overnight and left the next morning at 6.30 am, but outside the harbour I met head winds of almost gale force with rain and mist so after a half hour I decided I was better off waiting for better weather and returned to re-anchor and have breakfast. There was another small (27ft) boat not far from mine and the Skipper rowed across, offering to take me ashore and show me the shops.

Peter Russell, sailing his boat ELIZA all on his own, was on his way to the Baltic. Apparently he sailed about 3000 miles every summer, all on his own, He made me feel most inadequate, especially when I discovered that he had a Steel Knee Cap and could not straighten one leg. His base was the Forth but he was rarely there. He intended to sail to Russia round the North Cape next year and return by the canals and the Black Sea. He had asked the Royal Yachting Association for advice, and they said, 'Tell us about it when you've done it: you will be the first'.

After shopping, Peter came aboard and we compared notes. He had had similar trouble to me with his autohelm and now had two, one providing a spare while he repaired the other. The problem is the ingress of water and he had improved the reliability by covering his with a plastic bag. He told me to strip mine down when it failed again and, after drying it, spray it with WD40 before re-assembling it. Later I did just that in Stonehaven and it worked, and was still working when I finished the trip some three months later. However, I did buy a spare in Edinburgh (a different make) just to be sure, but after fitting it up I only used it once, just to be certain that it would operate properly.

The trouble is, as I've mentioned, the ingress of water, and this comes about because of the neoprene gasket which is extremely difficult to fit properly, especially on a moving boat. Once I had mastered it I had no more trouble although I did have to take care of 'George' in heavy rain with a cover over as I had had to butcher the bottom of the case to refit the socket pin and it was no longer watertight. Poor George. He never came to terms with the excess weather helm after I lost the bow sprit and was to fight back until I got to Portsmouth and had the 'beak' replaced: the only Kingfisher with a bowsprit.

Because of a rough sea and high winds I stayed a full day in Peterhead and was able to enjoy the facilities of the town to the full. Peter introduced me to a dodge that I had not thought of: every time he enters a new port he heads for the information bureau and picks up any relevant leaflets about the geography, history or entertainment of the area, all at no cost and often very useful. The young lady in the office was extremely helpful and we left with an armful of leaflets. The next day, though, saw me leave at 6am with a fair wind from the North East and I sailed on Jib alone at around 5 knots. I enjoyed being at the tiller, and not raising the mainsail meant that the helm was more manageable. It had been misty for the first couple of hours but when I sailed past Aberdeen the sun came out and the dark clouds all went away inland: the easterly component was bringing drier air from the continent. The run was so good that I was able to moor in Stonehaven harbour while there was just enough water at 1pm.

The autohelm was now defunct so I stripped it in the hot sun, dried it out and put in WD40. It took me till 4pm to manage to get it all together and working but from then on I had no further trouble. I then had a chance to walk around the town and I admit to liking it very much indeed. It is a lovely harbour full of friendly people and quite a big town in the background. Rather like Wick, I could not find any letter boxes and had to walk into the main drag of the town to find the main post office to dispense my cards.

I had a chat with the Harbour Master who had very great sympathy with my cause: his daughter had had cancer diagnosed and he did not yet know whether her treatment had been fully successful. He operated a fishing boat mainly used for chartering fishing parties, so he gave me a supply of diesel at a ludicrously low price. Since I had only been able to buy 4 gallons of DERV in Scrabster I was delighted to have red diesel again ready for my journey South. The weather stayed kind after the last three days and I was able to enjoy my break in Stonehaven. I learnt that Dunlop of tyre fame was born here and the town are proud to own him.

Another skipper owned a boat at the next bay down the coast which, although exposed to the east, he believed was a good anchorage because he had had a very heavy concrete casting put down. I saw his boat the next day and I must say that I wouldn't have slept at night with the thought of what an Easterly gale could do. I do hope he never came to grief, but I cannot help feeling that some people ask for trouble. I was told that in gale conditions the sea had been known to come right over the harbour wall at Stonehaven, and that is a goodly height!

I left the next morning at 7.30 am (Oh these lovely misty mornings!) headed for the River Tay and Tayport. The weather forecast suggested northwesterly 5 rising 7, but I found a slight south westerly and motored south. It was an uneventful sail except for being intercepted by the RNLI who used my boat for a simulation excersize. I think they had heard me on RT and wanted to see who it was who was fool enough to sail round Britain alone. For a moment I thought they were going to overrun my log line and only by dint of some rude gestures did I manage to get them to change direction and approach on my starboard quarter. It was pleasant to have company, even for so short a time, but soon I was buoy spotting as I entered the Tay, aware of the sand banks south of me awaiting the unwary.

I arrived at 3pm on Sunday, June 3rd and found a free buoy in the river at Tayport, which saved me having to go into harbour with all the stress of tying up single handed. A colleague from Inchyra up river near Perth was expecting me and I said I would be anchoring near the Bridges. As it was, I was a mile east of them. Unknown to me my friend sailed his 22ft boat the 15 miles from Inchyra as far as the road bridge, dropped anchor and began to call me every hour. I was only a mile away but never heard him because I had switched off and flaked out on my bunk. Tony called me until midnight and then took the flood tide back to Inchyra! We had missed each other by mere minutes and I proved yet again the foolishness of switching off my R/T set.

Some years ago an elderly dinghy sailing friend asked to join me on a cruise and together we sailed down to St. Ives. I can still remember his complaining about the radiotelephone. There are always a few fools who misuse the medium, particularly at weekends, and not always amateurs: many is the time I have heard fishermen using coarse language in an attempt to embarrass women sailors. Anyway, Harold hated the disembodied voices and he became almost paranoid about them and insisted that I turned the R/T off whenever we were in port. I suppose his influence lingered so that when I reached Tayport and picked up a buoy, it was not too unnatural to switch off. I still have not forgiven myself for Tony's wasted journey.

With respect to radiotelephones, I actually believe that they are among the best friends a sailor can have. Used properly they let interested parties know where you are, allow you to help others in trouble and, in the unfortunate event that you need help yourself they are a godsend. Unfortunately there are idiots who abuse them or allow young children to make use of them, bad enough on an intership channel but downright criminal on the distress frequency.

The following morning I took the flood tide up river and arrived at the little pier at Inchyra village at 1.30 pm. I tried to tie up but the tide was under me and I was swept up the side stream to ground just in front of my friend's house. What a way to arrive, so undignified, broadside across the stream: again a problem of being single handed and unable to grab the jetty and tie up as I came alongside. My friend had seen me and together we warped JUNKETTE back to the jetty and tied her up. Tony Train, a member of my Association, had all my mail for the past 2 months and I had a glorious afternoon opening letters and parcels from home.

That evening we went to Perth where golf first was banned because it prevented archery practise, but with the advent of gunpowder and decline of 'bow' making, the 'bowyers' turned their hands to making golf clubs. In days of yore Perth rivalled St Andrews as a centre of golfing. King James 1st and his Queen are buried under the flagstones near King Street on the site of a Carthusian monastery: where else do you walk over royalty?

After a meal we had wonderful drive through the banks and braes of Tayside, past stately homes almost hidden by rafts of trees and up onto a ridge to see the rich rolling farmlands, a magic landscape. We returned to Inchyra, which is a tiny village of maybe a dozen houses between the adjacent railway line to Perth and the River, close to the village of Glencarse. It is a lovely area and I spent the next three days resting and exploring the neighbouring countryside. Walking was a very great pleasure after being cooped up so long on a 26ft boat. Having for so long had such pains in my leg I took the opportunity to indulge myself, with short breaks in local hostelries where I could talk to the locals over a pie and a pint.

It was very lush farmland and I took a walk one morning past the Glencarse home farm where even that early in the year the 'corn was as high as an elephant's eye' - it was truly a well kept farm but sadly no one about to talk to. A little further and I saw a weasel running along the side of a brook: the first I had ever seen in the wild. I mentioned this later in a local pub and found there was no shortage of apocryphal stories: about the man who, bending over a stream, was attacked by a wild mink which jumped on his neck and sank its teeth into him. Unable to get it off, the man strangled it and then went home to have its jaws opened by his wife with a pair of pliers. Yet another story of a man attacked by four weasels: could that be a 'wad of weasels'? The story I liked best was an imported one from Kenya where, in describing the origin of a run of small hills, the local tribe talked of being terrorised by a giant. They sought help from the Lion "too big"! They asked the elephant, "too tall", and from the Giraffe, "Too strong for me"! But the tiny termites said "leave it to us". As the giant slept they covered him with their small clay balls, working non-stop through the night. When he woke and tried to get up he was smothered and all that could be seen were his knuckles.

    I was also to see another creature I had earlier missed: a linnet, but this time it was a corpse in the grass and golden buttercups: 'and no bird sings'!

    The next day I had a call from a new member of our Association asking if he could come and see JUNKETTE as he lived not far away. I was delighted when he arrived and took him for a sail up to Perth. He had just bought a Junk rigged boat and was eager to see how they handled, and leaving the jib furled, we sailed JUNKETTE. (Note the 'god like' upper case treatment!) We sailed up against the tide so that he could see how easy it was to tack in the limited space of upstream Tay. Later, after helping me obtain some red diesel from a farm factor, he offered to take me home for a meal. He stopped at a phone to speak to his wife and then set off. *"Have you come far?"* I asked.

    "No, it's not far: about 60 miles." He had driven 60 miles from Linlithgo to see me and by the time he returned me to the boat and got home again he would have driven 240 miles for an afternoon's sail. Now that is what I call hospitality: that generous freedom of spirit, which I found stronger in Scotland than almost

anywhere else. Those who say the Scots are tight fisted could not be more wrong.

I mentioned that there is a rail line at Inchyra. It has an automatic crossing controlled by lights and bells. The service is quite frequent so I had a chance to time the interval between the onset of the light and bell warning, and the arrival of the train. Just 28 seconds so the large notice that read SLOW VEHICLES TO PHONE BEFORE CROSSING was very relevant. I only hope that the inhabitants were reasonably fleet of foot!

I was able to watch the salmon fishers at work on the Tay. They operate as a team of about three. One takes a small boat out loaded with nets, which he slowly discharges over the side as he rows up river. When the net runs out he heads for shore with the bolt rope and while one man holds the inward end of the net, the other two walk the net back downstream until the three of them slowly draw the net in over the mud. It is a slow operation, each cast taking about an hour, and while watching two casts retrieved I saw them catch only one Salmon of about 3 lb. Hard work and only occasionally well rewarded. But then, fishing was ever thus.

The day following the 'fishing' excersize we heard gale warnings. I was concerned at the position of JUNKETTE against a somewhat insubstantial jetty but a member of the local yacht club offered me his newly laid mooring in the river and I went out on the tide and picked it up. Later, when the tide had dropped and the boat aground I got down to inspect the mooring and found a concrete drum just showing above the sand. I decided that perhaps it might move with the weight of JUNKETTE and could leave me high and dry on the bank. With Tony's help, I ran out my new anchor to the water's edge some 12 meters further from the bank but we were unable to get more than the bare tip of the anchor into the hard stone and sand of the river bed. We left it there as being better than nothing and I went to sit out the storm. In fact, after finding the boat riding happily in the rising wind I went to bed. In the morning, at low tide we found the anchor well and truly buried in the river bed. The mooring block had moved slightly towards the bank until the anchor took hold and held the boat and block steady. If ever I had wanted an illustration of the effectiveness of Simpson Lawrence's new Delta anchor it could not have been better presented!

It was now Thursday and I decided to move on as I wanted to be in Edinburgh for the weekend. I took my leave from my host and sailed down the river on the ebb to pick up a mooring at Tayport again, to wait a favourable tide the next day. The eastern sailors have a philosophy called TAOISM which is the art of using the elements to your advantage, especially when sailing, the art of willing compliance, of going with wind and tide and I have always been happy to follow that dictum, both in sailing and in life. The Tibetans, so close geographically to the eastern mystics, spend much time teaching their young priests the art of dialectics, of argument. Like Cicero they develop the ability to sway by reasoned argument rather than by force of arms, by compliance with logic.

From Tayport I did consider taking a short cut across the shoals toward the River Forth since I have a shoal draft boat which draws only three and a half feet. But discretion came to the fore and I took the long way round, enjoying views of St. Andrews until I cleared Fife Ness and headed down the northern side of the great river. It was a fresh but warm, sunny day and I enjoyed the sailing, heading for the small town of Elie where a local pointed out a visitors buoy I could use. I could have gone into the harbour but the hassle of tying up when single-handed meant that, as ever, I tended to stay at sea, afloat and alone. On this occasion I was quite happy as I had just had four days ashore with plenty of people to chat to, and I would be going ashore for a couple of days in Edinburgh. Now I could digest all I had seen, all the 'richness' of the green valleys of the Tay, a truly beautiful river. If you try and take in too much at once, like a Japanese tourist flashing his camera at everything, you end up with a meaningless kaleidoscope of memories. Unfortunately I never had the chance to visit a distillery: that was one memory I would have liked to return with, perhaps with a bottle of Macallan Anniversary malt but I never went up the river with similar name on the east coast, the Tey!

    It was Saturday morning, June 9th when I dropped my mooring and sailed out into the Forth at 10 am. There was little or no wind and I coasted down with the tide to the Fairway buoy. After calling the coast guard I heard a friend call me and later I saw his Junk rigged boat SHIMONI tacking in the light breeze off Inchkieth (Inch Island - 'kieth' means Island in Scotland). This was just after lunch and for the next two hours we seemed becalmed and for some reason Godfrey seemed reluctant to start his engine and head for the harbour, saying he had some problems with his power unit. Eventually, two more boats joined us and then all became clear. They were members (flag officers) of the Forth Corinthian Yacht Club (Godfrey's club) who had come out to escort me into Granton. It must have been a wonderful sight as we sailed, Godfrey's Junk in the lead and we three following in arrowhead formation into the harbour of Granton. I was very moved by the kindness and thought that had gone into my welcome.

    The Royal Forth yacht Club had made a visitors berth available to me, so I was able to tie up safely. I put up sail covers and generally tidied the boat before the club launch came to take me ashore to the welcoming arms of two yacht clubs and to Godfrey Hick who took me by car to his home in the Moorfoot Hills, south of Edinburgh.

    The Hicks live on a fine estate of about 800 acres in Heriot where they farm sheep and trees. It is a family co-operative with chalets around the grounds in which members of the family come for weekends and holidays and share in the tasks of tree clearing, brashing and weeding: all those things to do with forestry, the sheep farming being in the hands of a professional farmer. The main house, a nineteenth century building, houses two families, one of them in a converted (beautifully) hayloft while I stayed in the main house with Godfrey and his wife Ailie. On a tour round the house I came across something totally unexpected: a Bechstein grand piano in the drawing room. Neither of the Hicks played and I did not dare try to play it as Godfrey confessed it was in need of tuning. It would be very difficult to get a tuner to call so far from the city. The 'Tree' specialist of the family (Ailie's brother, Charlie) came over on Sunday and explained their forestry plans. They were putting up plantations of hard woods after experimenting to find which trees withstood the rigours of the Scottish climate best. Lyme trees and Sycamore seemed best but they were putting in a very catholic selection including Cherries, Mountain Ash, Maples (including a sugar maple) and Beeches. There were one or two big Ash trees but it was the Lyme trees that were spectacular. I always think of cold climates as being the habitat of the Birch and Larch so it was a delight to see large leafed deciduous trees being cultivated. Of course, the main stands of trees were conifers, of which there must have been many thousands, but the hardwoods were being planted on the lower slopes by the burn that ran through the grounds.

    The burn was interesting in that at some time it had been dammed to provide a pool above the house in which the family could swim, a pool complete with sluice gates and bypass culvert. A lot of thought had gone into that operation and I had a lesson in 'Burn' management. If you play around with a stream by removing bends, deepening or cleaning, you could well be in trouble when the winter rains come and produce some unexpected results. In general, leave well alone, the burn will look after itself! The bridges over the burn were real 'boy scout' affairs and indeed one that had decayed was replaced by the local scout group who had made the sort of bridge that Prince Charles would have been proud of. It could well have graced 'Loch 'Na Gar'. It was here that I learned that a Scottish blue bell would be a harebell in England and an English bluebell would be called a Wild Hyacynth in Scotland. A 'brook' would be a 'burn', a stream called a 'water'.

Godfrey took me back to Edinburgh and we toured the local chandlers, looking for a possible inflateable to replace 'the sweat'. We didn't find one at a price I liked but I did buy another self steering gear, a Navico this time, to hold as a spare.

While staying with Godfrey I was told the story of Inchkieth, the Island in the Firth of Forth where we first met. Apparently it is owned by Tom Farmer and he has offered it for the use of 'Allandale Animal Sanctuary', run by Miss Allan who lives on the island together with 'endangered hens, geese, ponies, 10 dogs and some goats....oh yes, and a pig'. Miss Allan is a relative of mine host's wife, and her plight in looking after these animals on an island without a boat was featured in a Noel Edmunds TV show one Christmas. Miss Allan was then shown a motor launch named "Pride of Inchkieth". She was at first furious to think someone should use the name of 'her' island, until Noel explained that it was being donated to her sanctuary by P & O Ferries as a surprise gift. It is now to be seen regularly in Edinburgh, stocking up with supplies for the animals.

Edinburgh used to be called "Auld Reekie": indeed a few older inhabitants still call it so, but, thanks to the clean air act it no longer earns that name. H.V.Morton explains the origins:

"There was a man of Fife yonder - a Laird called Durham of Largo, who regulated evening prayers by the smoke of Edinburgh, which he could see from his door. When the reek grew heavy as Edinburgh cooked its supper he used to call his family to the house with 'Its time, noo, bairns, to tak' the buiks and gang to our beds, for yonder's Auld Reekie, I see, putting on her nightcap'! (A propro of nothing at all, H.V.Morton was the brother of my old headmaster, G.F.Morton!)

The history of Edinburgh, the Capital of Scotland, so rich in story and in mystery - was James VI Queen Mary's son? - is available in so many guide books and travelogues that I have no need to subscribe further except, perhaps, to remind readers of the enormous literary output from the city with people like R.L.S.

(his father a builder of lighthouses), Scott; Burns, and original thinkers like Hulme and Adam Smith. Edinburgh did as much for the 'Period of Enlightenment' as any city in England: it is a fitting place to stage the annual arts festival.

I was now ready to restart my journeys and although it was suggested that I meet the members of the Royal Forth after their afternoon's racing, I decided to use the favourable evening tide and start back south. I did not want to arrive near the Farne Islands (Grace Darling country) in the dark and preferred an overnight sail now that I was refreshed. It was with very great sadness that I left the Scottish scene and my heart was full as I sailed through the fleet of racing dinghies.

Edinburgh to Amble: and Freddie!

From Edinburgh, sailing through the fleet of the Royal Forth's sailing dinghies in their evening race, aided by a favourable wind I was soon to be faced with another calamity. As darkness fell some 8 miles from Edingburgh I discovered that I had no navigation lights apart from a stern light. I had lost my bicolour at St Kilda and had omitted to replace it since I thought I had a perfectly satisfactory masthead tricolour, but this failed, as did the anchor light and when a fishing boat flashed his lights at me all I could do was shine a torch on my sails. From then on, whenever I saw lights on the water I steered well clear of them.

The result of all this was that I steered a somewhat strange course and was unable to take my usual catnaps in the cockpit. It was a very long night and by 8am I began to hallucinate. This was about the time I was passing Berwick on Tweed and I thought how strange that a town, the first northern fortress of England, which had had a castle built in the reign of Elizabeth 1st should have that fortress pulled down in the late nineteenth century, to make way for ... a railway! All that was now left was the lovely old bridge at Tees Mouth. The town had boasted a cousin of

Elizabeth, Warden Hunsdon who was the protector of the Emilia of Shakespear's sonnets. I found myself trying to remember those sonnets I had learned as a schoolboy:

*Tired with all these, for restful death I cry.......*or better recalled

Shall I compare thee to a summer's day?
Thou art more lovely and more temperate:
Rough winds do shake the darling buds of may

My thoughts were then diverted to H.E.Bates... my mind was wandering, and you might think this is a short period to take to reach this state but I had been awake and working for 24 hours, and concentrating steadily over the last twelve. With a following wind I kept jibing through falling asleep and I had to force myself to sail a mile or so out to the east so as to take the wind on the quarter, but then I'd doze off, to wake when the sails again jibed. By 10am the wind began to get up and here off the coast of Northumberland I ran into some short seas.

Perhaps I should say that I ran 'from' some short seas as suddenly, because for the first time in JUNKETTE I was pooped by a wave coming over the port quarter which filled the cockpit. I was only wearing lightweight trousers and pumps, and of course I was drenched. It wasn't cold but I could not make out why the cockpit was taking so long to drain when I saw that the round plastic knob from the gear lever had come off and was sitting over one of the cockpit drains, making a perfect plug. How it got there I had no idea but when removed and replaced in its rightful position the cockpit quickly became dry. Fortunately, the boat had rounded up and was in no danger. Bless the old girl, she looks after herself better than I do.

By now I was thoroughly wakened and rather outraged that the sea had got the better of me. I hauled in the sheets, backed the jib and lashed the tiller so that I was hove to and then went below, stripped off and dried myself. I put the kettle on and had a cup of tea. The boat was riding quite happily and making only little leeway so I decided 'to hell with it' and fried some bacon while I found some dry clothes. The wave had come into the open hatch, drenched the chart table and there was a hell of a mess in the cabin but I quickly dried the chart and desk before sitting down to eat. I forced myself to take my time: I suffer from high blood pressure and reckoned that my system needed a pause, so I left the boat to her own devices for the next thirty minutes. Then, with the boat still jumping a little, I started to clear up the mess of food on the cabin sole, books all over the place and pencils, pens and rubbers hiding everywhere. There was stewed rhubarb to be scooped up from the engine casing, mixed with tea bags and sugar. After a short while I'd had enough and went out to the cockpit again to renew the fight.

  The pooping came about because I was travelling too fast, despite a triple reefed main. I see from my log that I was touching seven knots and occasionally surfing down wave crests at 9 knots, but instead of feeling invigorated or excited by the speed I'm afraid I was slumped down on the cockpit seat and not looking at the sea very much, struggling to stay awake so I did not know how confused it was. It seems foolish looking back that I had let the worsening weather creep up on me without attempting to do anything about it. With such winds I would have been better running with a small jib alone as I had done on the run to Peterhead, but tiredness plays some silly tricks.

  When I came on deck the wind had risen to about a seven and the sea was quite nasty so my first job was to lower the main. I found I had just the same problem that had hit me at St Kilda. The gaff got the wrong side of the lazy jacks! Damn silly to do the same daft thing twice and I had to fight with the sail for many minutes before I could douse it. I decided then that soon I would have to redesign the angle of those lazy jacks to avoid this problem. On jib alone I set out to try for Holy Island rather than head for Amble, my original intention. The pilot said it was a very good foul weather harbour but I had no large scale chart and I was worried about the many reefs in the area. Grace Darling had won her spurs in these seas and I had no wish to become another entry into an RNLI log. The pilot I was using was the C.A. Handbook which had a chartlet of the entrance so that when I got closer to the 'island' (not an island at low water) I began to refer to it closely as the entry channel is a 'dogs leg' round shoals. Coming from the north there is a reef called the Plough Seat with a buoy to mark it. In my tired state, I found myself using the CA chartlet turned through 90 degs. but assuming North was still 'up'. When I found I could not line up the two leading beacons I realised my mistake: just in time to avoid hitting the reef. It was time I got my head down. I had now been on the tiller for seventeen hours and it was quite enough: the perils of single-handing! I started the engine and dropped the jib, taking the easy way out rather shamefacedly.

I finally got into Holy Island harbour and the relief from the wind was immediately apparent. I tried three times to pick up a buoy but even there the wind was sufficient to throw me off the buoy before I could go forward with a boat hook. In the end I dropped my anchor, but was still too close to another boat and had to raise it again and try once more. Because I was so tired I got it wrong yet again and only on my third attempt was I satisfied that it was holding and that I would not drag down on anyone. The effect of being seriously overtired has to be experienced to understand how dangerous it can be.

To me it is rather like the effect of an excess of drink when my reactions are slowed up. I remember once in London just before going to my rifle club a friend asked me to join him for a drink. I had one small glass of beer and then rushed off to the range under Victoria station. I used to fire a pistol and my scores were typically around 85 but this time I shot a 42! Just one glass of beer had affected my reactions so that I was firing too late. Is it any wonder that so many car accidents are caused by alcohol. You just have no idea how much a few drinks slow you up. Being overtired has an identical effect as far as I am concerned. Incidentally, an 85 may sound low to a rifleman but the 99.9 possible on a rifle range becomes about 86 with a pistol at 25 yards! This would mean that you could hit a 10p coin at that distance every time! I know I couldn't do it now....I cannot always see a buoy at 300 yards, but thirty years ago I came second in my group of the Surrey open competition.

After anchoring I looked at my watch: half past twelve! I didn't attempt to make lunch or even a cup of tea: just dropped on my bunk like a dead man and slept until the next morning. After breakfast and a proper clear up of the mess I made my fortnightly broadcast to Radio Manchester, on the 'Susie Mathis' show before slipping off the lashings of 'the sweat' and then rowing ashore (to a rocky foreshore where I had to drag the dinghy quite a way up towards the steps) and had a look around the island. What impressed me most was the way the locals had turned old fishing boats into bothies by slicing them in half, upturning them and fitting doors to the open end. They made perfect huts on the beach for all their boating tackle, the planks covered with tin, corrugated iron or tarred tarpaulin or old sail-cloth. Beside each little hut was a frame for drying nets.

BOTHIE: HOLY ISLAND

The 'Island' is an Historic relic (St. Aidan had spread the Gospel to the Kings of Northumbria after his crossing from Iona). There are records (Bede) of a visit by the Abbot of Iona, Adamnan who gave King Aldfrid the journal of Arculf, the very first of the religious pilgrimages to the East. The village has now had to come to terms with the tourists who drive their cars over at low water: there are at least three cafes, and an ice-cream van plus a mobile fish and chips van which sit out on the car park: vanguard to the daily influx of visitors. Over coffee I met another cruising family who had watched me arrive and anchor just astern of them. They were Tynesiders and had built their own 36ft steel boat, a gaff rigged ketch called 'Min Eskede'. They were going on to Amble and told me to look out for 'Freddie' who would come out to meet me. They were not about to tell me who this Freddie was, just 'you'll see when you arrive'. I enjoyed my short stay in Holy Island, a good, safe and roomy harbour in a gale with most of the things the visiting sailor needs. The approach needs careful conning as there are numerous reefs, but the pilot makes entry much easier with clearly marked beacons (though I found it difficult to identify St. Mary's Church belfrey). There is between 3 and 7 metres of water in the harbour and several visitors' buoys   After lunch I raised anchor and left just after the steel ketch, and since he knew the waters and I had no large scale chart I followed him through the Farne Islands, sailing west of Farne sound and seeing the Longstone light in the distance. The weather had moderated and we motor sailed in a very light breeze until Coquet Island came in sight.

    I had memories of Coquet Island where, many years ago in the boat of a friend we had tacked to and fro in front of the island, waiting for the tide to rise sufficiently to get into our moorings in the River Coquet. In those days it had all looked run down and very sad in the river, with dilapidated buildings and mud berths. I was due for a shock!

    The entrance to Amble, (or rather 'Warkworth Harbour' where the fishing fleet berth: the Marina at Amble is another quarter mile up river) is vividly portrayed in Libby Purves' book

'One Summers Grace' where she shows a photograph of the broken down pier head at the entry, a solemn reminder of the power of the sea as the broken end hangs drunkenly seawards.

    The tide runs very fast across the entrance and, with the threatening pier end balefully staring as the tide pushes you towards it, you have to concentrate on your helm, at least if you are making your first visit. Imagine, then, one's reaction when you suddenly see a large fish swim up at the side of the boat and then lazily swim under the hull to reappear the other side, its dorsal fin 'nicked' by too close an approach to some propeller or other. This is Freddie, the dolphin, who welcomes every boat to enter the river. 'Freddie' is now an institution much loved by the town folk. He has been at Amble for the last seven years, all on his own, at least no Ms. Freddie has been seen and he comes out to every boat that enters or leaves the river. In 1988, early in the year, the fishermen once returned to harbour with a mine in their nets. The navy were called in to detonate it but the locals were worried that the explosion might hurt 'Freddie'. The navy responded by sending two divers down to play with the dolphin and get him to move into the river and over the sill of the Marina. Once safely out of the way the mine was exploded and Freddie was then allowed to return to the sea. Apparently he gave every indication of enjoying his contact with the navy. Perhaps we are all wrong: perhaps it should be 'Felicity'. What lady could resist a sailor?

    The Marina is a superb place to moor your boat on the East coast. It is well equipped and in pleasant surroundings, quite unlike what I had remembered from the days before it was built. I was made very welcome and given free berthing and a list of all the Camper & Nicholson yards where I would be allowed free accomodation for the remainder of my voyage. Some months later I was to meet again the young lady from the chandlery and her husband when they visited Padstow on holiday in August.

    Colin and Margaret Power, owners of 'Min Eskede', the steel ketch I had met up with in Holy Island invited me aboard to see their boat and to have an evening meal of fish and chips with them. They had spent ten years in building the boat and it was a tribute to their fortitude over so long a period and to Colin's workmanship and astute buying policy, that they now had a truly beautiful floating home. Colin, a policeman in Newcastle *('I'm no longer on the beat, a desk job now.' 'Oh, a Sergeant?' 'Well no, Chief Inspector actually!')* had attended ship breaker's yards all over the north east to buy bits and pieces from many famous boats. I admired some slatted doors. 'Oh, they are jalousies, the slats keep the birds out and the netting keeps the insects out.' At last I knew what a 'Jalousie' was, having seen the word many times in Graham Green's and Hemingway's novels but never knowing what it meant. Altogether, Colin and his friend bought three tons of teak, and a goodly quantity of the finest quality was now aboard 'Min Eskede'. Someone had told him that if he bought his deck fittings in Turkey he would pay a quarter of the price wanted in Britain so he brought back through a bemused customs over £200 of blocks, tackle etc. Colin obviously deserves to be where he is: a very big man, in more ways than one! His wife, Margaret, and I had one thing more in common: we were both Yorkshire born and bred and I delighted in hearing my own dialect again after so long away from home.

I had loaned my 'bosuns chair' to a couple on another boat and was amused to find the lady up the mast at the cross trees, offering up a radar reflector while her husband stayed on deck directing operations. Leaving her hanging like a fly in the rigging, (I noted the biological difference in that she kept her knees tightly together with her ankles well apart for stability whereas a man would have been sitting with his knees well apart and ankles together) he calmly and slowly took his time in straightening things on deck, doing a general tidy up before he consented to lower her down. I was in Andy Cap country, for sure.

The following morning, June 15th, I filled up with water and set off for Hartlepool. As I left the Marina, Freddie showed his/her broad back and scarred dorsal fin in a grand farewell gesture. Min Eskede were also coming down to Hartlepool but in the very light winds I motor sailed and, to get the best of the tide, headed about 2 miles off the coast and soon lost sight of them in the misty conditions. I never saw Sunderland but did spot Seaham at 5pm. Somehow I had got well ahead of Min Eskede, probably because they would have had to face the adverse tide closer to the shore, and I heard them say they were going to stop at Sunderland for the night. I would liked to have stayed with them and learnt more about Northumberland, county of the small pipes and a holiday home to the master art critic Ruskin. My knowledge of the area was limited to Newcastle and its environs. Here I had been introduced to Newcastle Brown Ale, called 'Journey into Space' by the city's taximen - with some justification: they like strong beer when they leave the pits, many now sadly closed. Sad, that is, to the life of the area since, with shipbuilding, mining made up the major industry so that now there is very great unemployment. That Tynesiders are adaptable is borne out by the success of the new car plant but they need much more than that to take up their energies.

My particular memory of Newcastle was the cleanlines of the workers. I spent a little time in the city in the 50's and travelled by bus from my digs on the west side of the town. After work, instead of dirty, odourous workers on the buses, you were faced with well washed, shiny cheeked chattering and happy people. They speak a special Geordie dialect - a hand down from the invading Danes -making much of what they said undecipherable to a foreigner like me, but the lilt of the pipes was in their voices and their friendliness undoubted. They had the prettiest women and they had also, in common with the other North Eastern counties, voracious appetites. A meal was often served on an oval meat plate so that there would be enough room for it all. For breakfast in Corbridge I well recall sitting down to such a plate filled with bacon, sausages, two eggs, fried bread, potato cakes plus two fish cakes, tomatoes and mushrooms. You could demolish a house single handed on that lot... or raise 'seventeen tons of number nine coal'.

Sunderland I knew hardly at all: a place one drove through on the A1 on route to Newcastle, but I did spend time at the

Sunderland Empire with Barney Colehan (another great name from the past, now passed on) as we were considering venues for a television programme. Unfortunately, the stage ramp sloped so much that it would have been impossible to handle television cameras on it: they would all have been sliding down into the audience. A pity because it was a magnificent building, typical of Edwardian music hall and would have provided a 'perfick" backdrop for a variety entertainment. (Sorry, I don't expect that H.E.Bates spent much time in Sunderland, even though he had been on my mind a morning or two ago). But it is a tough audience in Sunderland and Newcastle, especially on a Monday night: many are the acts that got 'the bird' and the slow hand clap off stage. I think it was at Sunderland that you had to exit through the front of house, through that hostile audience if you were a flop!

But now I was moving on, towards my home county of Yorkshire where, whenever I visit, no matter what part of the county, I feel at home. First, having sailed past Seaham I was now approaching the colliery country of Easington and Black Hall,, moving ever closer towards Hartlepool and the Tees, the last bastions of the county of Durham.

Hartlepool to Wells next the Sea

At 5.30 in the afternoon the tide turned my way again and I was soon approaching Hartlepool. I considered going into the Victoria Dock and finding Kafiga landings, used by yachts, but rather than have the fag of trying to moor single-handed when all I needed was an overnight resting place, I called the H.M. and asked permission to pick up a mooring buoy in West harbour. I found a buoy just inside the harbour that was only on rope, intended for the lightest of craft, but as the wind was non existant and the barometer high I reckoned I would be O.K. for the night.

Later I was to discover that I had been lucky in not taking a mooring at Kafiga! I could have locked in to the main harbour as friends of mine did a year later. I understand that these are extensive and give easy access to the town but are very busy, carrying car exports to the continent among other things.

The next morning at 6.30 am. I dropped my mooring and motored out in a dead calm, to be greeted by thick fog some half-hour later. Had I chosen to go up the Tees I would have come to Middlesborough, but I pressed on South. I was tempted because I had fond memories of nearby Billingham, the home of ICI's biggest industrial complex in Britain and also the centre of the International Folk Festival, held in a few weeks time. The shopping centre of Billingham is fitted with a large stage in the square for the festival and here visiting folk dancers from all over Europe come to perform during the summer vacation. It was here that I first saw a display of Cossack dancing and wonderful, fiery Flamenco dancing. It is a wondrous time and events go on late into the evening, shared with the adjacent theatre. The square buzzes with many languages and happy laughter with brightly dressed children everywhere. I vaguely remembered Hilaire Belloc's poem about a Flamenco dancer: it went

"Do you remember an Inn, Miranda? Do you remember an Inn?"

Had the month been August I think nothing would have held me back. As it was I sailed on into the morning mist.

At 7.15 two yachts flying spinnakers and drifting up the coast came out of the fog, taking advantage of the very light southerly wind. The fog stayed until nearly 9 am. but then lifted and I could again see the coast.

The mist kept playing games with me so that although I passed an invisible Whitby, where the differences between the English and Roman churches were resolved at a Synod of 663 AD. - a resolution as invisible today as was the town - I could clearly see Robin Hoods Bay. How did it get its name? It has been suggested that it was built on the site where Robin Hood's arrow fell after a very long flight from Stoupe brow nearly a mile away, but what was the Sherwood Forester doing so far from home? The bay I knew well as a child but this was the first time I had seen it from the sea. Once again that curious transformation of emotions took place. I had always looked out (in memory at least) from golden sands into a bright, if chilly sea. Now, looking the other way, the cliffs looked dark, foreboding and cold, and only the sea seemed light and warm. Robin Hoods Bay is also the finish of the Lyke Wake Walk, that marathon of long distance walks, some 40 miles, starting at Osmotherly on the North Yorkshire moors. David Bean joined the walk and reported for television back in the late 60's and his report left you in no doubt of the desperate tiredness that the walkers felt at the end. The coast line forms much of the Cleveland Way, a 150 mile stretch from Helmsley to Filey, and of course the infamous 'Trans Pennine Walk" ends on this coast. For my part I was glad to see Scarborough Castle appear ahead of me. There used to be a rail line linking the seaside resorts but I think it was one of those axed by Beeching in 1965. Now, in these days of the health fanatics it is again the walkers who transit those cliffs, people like Wainwright - alas, no more - and Bean.

Approaching Scarborough from the sea makes you wonder what to make of it. The harbour for the fishing fleet can be clearly seen as you enter the bay, but the yacht and small boat harbour has an entrance only about twenty foot wide. This is a very small aperture when seen from the sea but the only way to provide a safe refuge from the storms of winter: the East coast can be a very bitter foe for sailors! It was Saturday and I had been in a hurry to try and dock before the Post Office closed in order to pick up my mail, but the lack of wind had made me nearly three hours behind schedule and I would now have to wait until Monday. The same thing had happened in Oban a few weeks before.

I tied up just behind another cruising boat who asked if I was the one sailing round England. "The Harbour Master is looking for you: he's been asking every boat if they are the one".

I thanked him and went ashore to find the H.M. whose base is on the end of the pier where he performs the harbour master tasks together with those of car park attendant. He greeted me warmly and explained that although he had been expecting me he had not known the name of my boat. Apparently his wife was the chairman of the local Cancer Relief committee who had been told to expect me. Soon she arrived, together with a Yorkshire Post representative to take photos, and welcomed me to Yorkshire, asking if there was anything I needed. I would have liked to have asked for a bath, but the moment didn't seem appropriate and I let it go.

Later I asked the H.M. if he knew where Alan Ayckbourne lived. He pointed to the town, to the roofs rising in serried ranks. "You see that cream wall, well move right, see, there is a dark red roof and two grey ones. It's the red roof". I studied the situation and tried to plot a couple of land marks that might help me as I climbed up the town (Scarborough is extremely hilly). Amazingly I found the house almost the first time. I had only to ask one lady who pointed to a house three doors away, 'they live there'! I knocked and the door opened on a face I knew but could not put a name to. 'I'm sure I know you' I started.

"I'm Heather Stoney"

"Of course, I've seen you in the radio studios. Hello, I'm Ralph Hill"

"Come in, we were expecting you"

Heather is Alan's wife and Alan and I had known each other in Leeds when Alan was a radio drama producer. They had just got back from opening some fete and were surrounded by their booty. "'I'm sure that people save this stuff for Tombolas and hike it all over the country, giving it away and then winning something else" said Alan with a grin, holding out a particularly repugnant bottle of bath salts.

We hadn't seen each other for many years: I had known Alan when he had just got his first play into the west end. In those days he was a radio drama producer and lived in Leeds. I still remember the row there was when it was revealed that he was living in a Leeds council house while having two, or was it three, west end plays running at once. A year or two later Jimmy Saville was to go through the same hurdles in Salford! It must have been strange on Saville's estate to see a white Rolls Royce outside the door. I don't expect the absurdity of it occurred to either of them at the time: they only suffered when the press made an issue of it. Jimmy, by the way, did a great amount of good work in Leeds as an unpaid hospital porter, a job he still carries out at the hospital where my mother worked as an auxiliary nurse during the war. He certainly deserves all the honours given to him: what other single individual has raised over a million pounds for charity by his own efforts?

I stayed for tea in Alan's large and friendly kitchen (yes, rooms do have a personality): this was the one where obviously Heather and Alan came together when he was not working, rather like the farm kitchen which is the centre of rural family life. Perhaps that is why so many of Alan's plays have a kitchen scene and here we had a yarn about the old days. Heather is now his business manager and has given up her acting career, looking after Alan's affairs being a full time job. Listening to them, I realised that a lot of water had passed under a lot of bridges and you cannot put the clock back. They offered to get me tickets for the show on at Alan's Theatre in Scarborough but it wasn't one of Alan's plays so I said thanks, but no thanks. I was glad to have made the contact after so long but did not want to stretch rather thin ties. I like Alan: I found myself comparing him with Havel of Czechoslovakia, the former writing gentle domestic comedy satires with a class battle, the latter gentle political comedy satires with a personal integrity battle. Alan has apparently progressed to black comedy but the comedy has become real for Havel who is now State President. All we need now is for Arthur Miller to become president of the USA.

Scarborough is a very pleasant town, clean and fresh with plenty of entertainment, excellent theatres and first class accommodation. There is a well-endowed park (Peashome) which has a lake where, very many years ago, I used to watch mock battles between model battleships, cruisers and submarines. There was also a bandstand and a wonderful Yorkshire brass band. Those bands were famous throughout the North and there was much rivalry between the east and west of the Pennines: the war of the roses has never ended. Not far from the park was an area we knew as Scalby Mills where we could go swimming in the river - there was a rock ledge that made a perfect diving board - and a walk through wild woodland deep in fern and huge leafed plants ideal for hide and seek. There were also the 'Funiculars' - trams that ran up and down the steep foreshore cliffs, but we rarely used them because of the cost.

Scarborough was where we spent most of our family holidays before the war and I remember playing in the sloping sand. My elder brother was sliding down the sand hill like a slalom racer when he got caught up with a piece of glass that badly cut his leg. There was a mad dash to a local doctor to fix him up. Peter was always the adventurous one and the family had a habit of losing him when he went off on his own, once in Epping Forest until a passing motorist brought him to us.

I had called at the yacht club in Scarborough but there had been no one around on the Saturday. On Sunday I went for a walk in the town and from the high vantage point I saw the yachts racing in the bay. When I returned, as the tide was falling, imagine my surprise to find the club house deserted: they had all gone home to dinner (in Yorkshire it is eaten at midday) and no one was seen again that day! I never did meet any member of the Scarborough yachting fraternity. I did talk to fellow cruising skippers tied alongside and one, who had his hand in plaster told me how the previous week he had tied up in the dark at Kafiga landings in Hartlepool and on walking down the jetty, had fallen through a hole and broken his finger. Another skipper was having trouble with his main halyard and had got his wife to go up the mast and replace it, using the jib halyard to hoist her up. Once again a lady doing the climbing. Of course the man is stronger at the winch, and the woman generally being lighter, it makes sense she should go aloft, but it does illustrate that women are equal at sea.

On Monday morning I went into the town and collected a two-week backlog of mail from the post office. The GPO is in the middle of the town and what struck me most were the number of cafes, diners and chippies that I passed: far more than you would expect, even in a seaside resort, especially a rather up market resort like Scarborough. No wonder that the folk in the streets all looked very well fed if not to say 'plump'! The 'over fifties', almost without exception, waddled rather than walked and all looked very pleased with life. I thought how it compared with the sights and sounds of Whitehaven in Cumberland,. There was a town severed from most of its former employment and bereft of tourists: a town that made me think of Steinbecks 'Cannery Row' with weedy, wind swept back lots, 'For Sale' signs, paper packets blowing in the wind. But like Steinbeck's folk, Whitehaven had some of the kindest people in the world. Scarborough, by comparison was positively pompous in its self sufficiency.

At 11.15 I dropped my mooring and motored out of the harbour, heading south. Once clear of the bay I was able to stop the engine and with a couple of reefs in I sailed close hauled past Filey Brig, where, as a youngster, I used to fish for Mackerel and where I took my first Scout group as a very young troop leader, our scoutmaster having been called up to serve in the navy. My memory of that particular time is cooking rice, and misjudging the quantity so that we had enough for the whole week cooked in one go! We had rice as a pudding, with fish, with eggs...you name it and we ate it. It was early in the war so we had little wish to throw anything away. The eggs, though, did not have shells on them. They came in packets, dried! The 'Brig' at Filey is a finger of rocks that juts out into the sea, to be covered at high tide, but a superb fishing spot when the tide is turning at low water, especially when the Mackerell are running

As I approached Flamborough Head the tall ship 'Scott Bader Foundation' passed me with a fine show of canvas and the bone fairly in her teeth. These fine training ships are a joy to see as you sail round the coast, giving a chance to youngsters to enjoy the sea in a way which, only a few years ago would have been impossible to any but those who made it their livelihood. I sailed first past Flamborough Head and Bridlington (where I once saw a huge Tunny fish hauled up the beach from a Yorkshire fishing cobble: bigger than the boat that caught it), and I left the heavy cliffs to come past the softer and gentler shores of Humberside, past Hornsea and Withernsea in a quiet, sleepy sea.

As the wind was still southerly and unlikely to change directon I decided to anchor off Spurn head on the South side and dropped under Beacon Hill at about 7.30pm. The water here was quite still as I was in the lee of the land, land being eaten away by the sea at a fast rate. Spurn Head has the only full time RNLI crew in the country but it looks as though their station may become an island in the very near future. The cost of sea defences to stop the erosion would be enormous and no one has the funds. With global warming and the anticipated rise of the sea level, the days of Spurn Head are strictly numbered. But then this has always been the case: the place where Bolinbroke landed at the end of the fourteenth century to depose Richard II vanished long ago, and even then Shakespeare called it 'The naked shore of Ravenspurg' in Henry IV since that town had vanished before Bolingbroke got there!

The next morning I had a very long sail ahead of me, over 60 miles, so I set off at 6.45 and motor sailed whenever the speed dropped below 5 knots. If I did not get to Wells in time to enter the river I would be in real trouble as there is really no place to go along the coast of Norfolk and Suffolk except for Yarmouth and that would add another twenty miles or so. In fact, deep fin keelers leaving Scarborough and going south have no where but Yarmouth, some 110 miles away, to find refuge.

Crossing the Wash was uneventful though I did see a magnificent Dutch schooner, too far off to read her name but she did look beautiful in the afternoon light, running with foresails goosewinged. However, as the afternoon slipped by the skies darkened and just as I was approaching where I thought the Wells fairway buoy ought to be, a rain squall hit me and I could not see a thing. A full half hour passed before the rain dropped and then I saw the buoy - fortunately my direct reckoning was spot on as my Decca set had finally packed up - but it was now half tide and I did not know whether I would be able to enter. Talking with other yachtsmen I gather that the fairway buoy is often very hard to find, possibly because of the tides which run fairly fast down the coast, but also because the coast is so featureless at this point.

I called the harbourmaster who came down to the entry to guide me in by RadioTelephone. It is a very tortuous entry, a real snake of a route, well marked - once you have spotted the fairway buoy - but at half tide there is little room for error. Fortunately I could see the shoal water pretty well for myself and was able to steer clear of the shallows until I was well into the river. Then, with about a quarter mile to go I went aground, just the correct side of a port hand buoy which seemed to have moved, or the bed of the river had shifted. I dropped anchor... there was nothing else I could do, and set about making myself a meal as it was now 7pm.. The H.M. reckoned I would come off in the early hours so I thought I'd get some sleep, setting the alarm for 2am.

Shortly after the alarm sounded I came off the sand and hung to my anchor. At 4am the pilot boat came up and suggested I go up stream and moor at the town quay. In the early morning light I raised the anchor with still about an hour of tide to run and motored up to the quay. Now I had a problem: what could I moor to? The top of the quay was about two foot above the gunwales and there were no ladders, no chains, no rings. By standing on the cabin roof I could make out some rings on the top of the quay, about a foot in from the edge. There was no one about to take my lines and I kept circling, wondering what to do. In the end, I took my courage in both hands, motored up to the wall and jumped from the cabin onto the quay holding both head and stern warps and hoping that the boat wouldn't pull me back into the water. I discovered that the rings were set into the surface of the quay which is used as a car park and I had to lift them to get a rope through. It was a nerve racking five minutes until I had made the boat fast. I just hoped that I had not taken someone else's place. Incidentally, I discovered later that it is not unusual to have a car park over your mooring warps and when the time comes to leave you find you are a prisoner!

Fifty minutes later I watched the pilot boat return with a heavily loaded motor barge, water lapping the gunwales, helping pull it round the tighter curves of the river until it reached the far end of the quay and tied up. The Pilot boat skipper came to me after he had moored up and explained that the river had a large rise and fall and that I would need a ladder to get off at low water. He returned with one off the barge and invited me to join them both for a cup of tea later in the morning: 'come about eight, we'll have eaten by then' he said.

I met 'Eric', the Skipper of the pilot boat, and 'Nigel' the Skipper of the barge, over a cup of tea in the small and cosy cabin of the barge. Nigel, a friendly and talkative Yorkshireman, had built the Pilot boat himself in his garden in Sheffield. He had been a miner, but reading the signs of recession in the industry, had learnt to weld and proceeded to make him self a 38ft. steel boat. He decided that Wells would be a good place to launch and began fishing trips. One day he heard of a barge being for sale, a steel barge, so he bought her, replated her bottom where thinnest, fitted a crane and grab bucket and began to use her as a dredger, lifting sand and shale from out in the estuary and selling it ungraded, loaded straight from the boat into lorries. He could sell as much as he could lift and was filling 3 or 4 lorries a day. The barge drew 9ft when fully loaded so could not be used at neap tides when he would use it instead to keep open the main navigation channels.

The Pilot boat, Nigel's Sheffield creation, now no longer used for fishing and skippered by a retired 'Coastal Master' - Eric - was used as a pilot for the very occasional visiting coaster and as a tug for the loaded barge. These two men were delightful company and full of amusing stories. All the 'furniture' in the barge was steel, the chairs, the table, the shelves. 'I can't work in wood' says Nigel, "Steels' my material. You can do anything with steel. When we wear a hole in't bottom, I just weld a patch on. Why, this old girl is just like a pair of old trousers, more patch than trouser". They had now developed a huge trench where they had been dredging up sand and it left Nigel sometimes worried. *"At first, we'd dredge until we were bumping the bottom. Then, if she leaked we didn't have far to drop. Now, if she leaks, standing on the deckhouse ain't going to save us. We fills her until the water, on a calm day, is just running over the gun'les. O' course, if it's a bit rough then we takes a bit less. Wi' that weight o' sand in her your welds 'd better be good"* he finished, philosophically.

The pilot boat was being used intermittently for a P.D.James thriller that was being televised by Anglia TV and I met the producer/ director later in the day. Nigel, with his pilot boat was making good use of his 'investments' and helping the town in more ways than one. It was a town that I soon came to like very much indeed, where the saleslady of the antique shop spent much time trying to sell me a fascinating plate which I could never have afforded but which gave us both much pleasure in discussing. A place where the shore side pub had a steady clientele from 1030 of TV staff, fishermen, shopkeepers etc and who were very willing to serve coffee in place of beer. (My liver won't accept alcohol much before midday). Coffee in the friendly atmosphere of a pub is very warming.

I was introduced to this pub by a character I met who was living aboard a tiny Hurley 22ft yacht as he sailed round the south coast looking for somewhere to over winter. Living in a small boat is an art in itself, especially if you are over 5ft as there is never sufficient headroom. This young man complained of back-ache and spent most of his time off the boat, either in the pub or walking over the attractive sand dunes. He told me he had bought the boat in Hull and was looking for a cheap place to lay up. For the life of me I could not make out what calamity should so affect him that he would see satisfaction in living in, and sailing such a small boat. Perhaps his marriage was rocky or he had been made redundant but whatever it was, his present mode of life could not have been very pleasurable. It was not as if he was using it like

Charles Stock in 'Shoal Waters', a diminutive 16ft boat Charles used to explore the byways of the Suffolk and Essex shoals: instead he spent most of his time in the pub. On the day I left he thought he would come with me but providentially for him, he could get neither his ancient inboard or his vintage outboard engines to fire and stayed at his anchorage. I wonder if he is there still!

LOW TIDE: WELLS

On my second morning at about 11am., just when I was considering my next move after hearing of gale warnings, a voice called me from the quay, and there stood an old friend, inviting me to his home for a night's rest, a bath and a meal. At first I could not make out who it was because the tide had dropped me about 12 ft, but climbing the ladder I found myself face to face with one of my sailing companions from the 1960's, Bob Gell. Peter Williams (who had died earlier in the year and the cause of this voyage), Bob and I had sailed on the Norfolk Broads on two occasions for a week's holiday. We did just about everything that is so graphically recorded in 'Three Men in a Boat', and a few more. In those days I used to wear a monocle and a bobble hat, and one evening, after having consumed rather a lot of alcohol, we attempted to board a boat full of luscious girls. Their 'Knights in Shining Armour' came to their rescue and in the rush to leave, I was last and found myself stretched between dinghy and boat. My weight pushed the dinghy out and I went into the murky water. Apparently I rose out of the depths, still wearing the absurd bobble cap and monocle, laughing like a drain. From then on, wherever we were seen on the broads we would get waves and laughter: instant fame!

On another occasion on the southern broads, dear Peter, then in his thirties, who had a fatal attraction to women, had a young lady of seventeen ditch her fiancée and hang around him. The three of us decided to go to the pub and she joined us, together with boyfriend. In the pub, while Bob Gell played darts with the boy friend and Peter sat with the girl, I spent the evening with the pub's oldest inhabitant, hearing tales about the old days of Wherries carrying sugar beet to London, their huge sprit sails allowing them to capture the slight breeze above the reeds while other river borne traffic was being towed or poled (quanted) along. These wherries, generally owned by the Bargee who sailed with his wife, had very little draft, relying on their great beam and load for stability. The spritsail could easily be dropped in the event of a squall with the minimum of effort. He told me of the effect of the 'New Cut' on some of the journeys etc, all this while buying him a constant stream of ale. Looking back, I think I had the best of it.

Bob took me back to his home at Stalham after I arranged for the harbour master to keep an eye on my boat, and took me to see the broads again but I was heartbroken to see so few sailing boats: just hundreds of power boats, bigger and flashier than any I had remembered. He sensed my disappointment and finally took me to a 'secret' broad (memories of 'Secret Water' by Aurthur Ransome, the man whose books had introduced me to sailing) where a solitary dinghy was tied to a short jetty, where moorhens and coots crept quietly across the still waters. I recalled waking at Ranworth Broad early one morning many years earlier to find our hire boat shrouded by mists and a short way away, a Heron standing on a tree stump while below him a crocodile oozed slowly through the water. I had pointed this out to Bob who had joined me, it all looked so real, but the 'wake' of the crocodile was the eddy of the tide pushing past a half sunken log.

My first visit to the Broads for sailing had been in the war when buzz bombs could be seen passing over on their way to London. We would watch the fighter pilots try to fly up in advance of them in their Mosquito aircraft and then try and get alongside in order to tilt the wings of the rockets and force them out to sea. It was a dangerous occupation (those Mosquitos were made of plywood) and we did not mind too much when the pilots would sometimes swoop low over us, their slipstream causing our boat to sway madly. They deserved their moment of play. Ransome, although later a war correspondent, had no thoughts of conflict when he wrote 'Coot Club' and 'Swallows and Amazons'. I wonder what he would have thought of these harsher days. His books brought the Broads to life for me, as did Alain Gerbault's book 'Fight of the Firecrest' bring to life a cruise at sea and fill me with a desire to sail myself.

After a very pleasant stay in Stalham I was returned to my boat, refreshed and ready to move on. I had been spoiled and the boat looked very small again (and a long way down as the tide was out). I now had no Decca: it had been reporting 'antenna failure' as I had crossed the Wash and had been no help in finding Wells. I suspected that the aerial was waterloged, but there was little I could do about that. Before leaving I asked Eric if there was somewhere I could buy some diesel. Apparently he had a tank and supplied the fishing fleet so I filled my two portable tanks, intending to transfer them to my main tanks and come back for two more, but when I asked how much he refused to accept a penny so I just held on to what he had given me, abashed by his kindness.

I left Wells with great reluctance on Saturday, 23rd June and headed down the coast for Southwold, another long trip of around 60 miles. There was little wind after the previous days' gale and I had to motor sail for quite a lot of the way. Off Lowestoft, the tide across the shoals turns the sea into a brown whirlpool so that it looks just like brown windsor soup. What wind there was headed me so I motored on until I noticed the temperature gauge was very high indeed. I raised the engine cover to stop the engine and just as it stopped, the header tank cap blew off, forcing steam and rusty water everywhere. Luckily my face was turned away when it blew so I was not hurt other than a small scold on one hand, but the chart table was a mess and the inside of the spray hood was coated with a fine brown spray of droplets.

I realised that the sand had blocked the water strainer, so let the engine cool as, close hauled, I crept onwards towards Southwold. Later, putting the autohelm into operation, I went to check on the engine. In no way could I turn the top of the water inlet seacock to get at the strainer. I had no spanner big enough and the unit, which had only been fitted the previous spring to avoid the very thing that now troubled me, had been fitted without a key to operate it. I refilled the tank and ran the engine again, but after ten minutes it again began to overheat. I switched off and called the harbour master at Southwold, who was expecting me, and explained my predicament. There was still time for me to get to the harbour while there was enough water, but it was getting very late and I would have difficulty finding my way in.

The harbour master said that there was a barbecue on the beach which he was attending but that he would come out to me in his launch and tow me in. He had some difficulty in locating me but finally we made contact and he towed me about three miles up to the entrance to the harbour. He asked if I had any engine power at all and I said it would run for about ten or fifteen minutes.

"I'll drop you inside the harbour if you get your engine started, then motor up the stream till you come to the pub on your starboard hand and you can moor at the jetty there" He said on R/T.

He dropped the tow and I motored in to where the public moorings began and then turned to stem the tide and headed for the jetty. There was no one to take my lines and each time I came out of gear the tide took me back down to the boats behind me. I had three attempts but had to give up as the engine was dangerously hot, and I did the only thing possible which was to anchor in mid stream. Luckily another boat owner saw my predicament, crossed the river and approaching me, came aboard a moored yacht and caught my line that I threw to him. Once secure I was able to pull myself forward and raise the anchor before falling back and mooring alongside the other boat. The tide in Southwold runs at up to four knots and except at slack water it is impossible for one man to moor up without help. I was now alright for the night but would have to move the next day.

The following morning my sister arrived from Saffron Walden and together we moved the boat across to the public moorings. I explained to the harbour master that I would be away for four days and I asked the boatyard to have a look at my weed filter and free it for me. I also asked them if they would be able to make me a replacement bowsprit but although they promised to see what they could do, in the event they had no time and only freed the filter, at no small cost.

Meanwhile I went with my sister to her home, ready to celebrate her birthday, now five days away. I was very proud of the fact that I had travelled almost half the way round Britain and still managed to meet my first definite deadline: to be in Suffolk in time for Paula's birthday on June 29th. June had sent all my post on so I had a chance to catch up on many things I had almost forgotten about.

In Saffron I made a Broadcast so that folk would know where I was and then began to try and get hold of a replacement antenna for the Decca set. This proved to be impossible so in desperation I bought a cheap Dinghy Decca set which would suffice for what I wanted until I could get my aerial down and repaired. I only use Decca when it is foggy (when it is, in my opinion, an essential piece of equipment) as otherwise I rely on dead reckoning. This is fine for long distance sailing but you need much more true readings when coasting, especially in fog. I am always amazed at the speed with which chandlers look after yachtsmen's orders. The unit arrived on the Wednesday following my telephone call on Monday afternoon. I have been involved with many discussions about the relative merits of Decca and Radar on small boats, but there has never been any doubt in my mind that if you do not have room for both then Decca or an equivalent navigation system is more important. To know exactly where you are is far more important than being able to see a ship or rock in fog: if you know where you are then you should not be in a dangerous position anyway. If you have to cross busy shipping lanes in fog then a radar detector is useful: at least you can tell what direction a large ship is travelling in and take avoiding action if necessary. Anyway, Radar takes a lot more power than a small boat can afford and is difficult to 'read' and make sense of in a small navigatorium.

Saffron Walden is a lovely market town some 13 miles from Cambridge. It is a place I have long been fond of, a place where the town planners have been able to retain the original style in all the new buildings, and where a supermarket has been built with matching bricks to maintain the Georgian feel of the street. A warm town which might have delighted the heart of G.K.Chesterton, where the church is but a stones throw from the 'Eight Bells', a place redolent of the late eighteenth and nineteenth century: Father Brown might reappear round the next corner and Quoodle's nose investigates the lamp post. This refers to G.K. Chesterton who had visited this town and, it would seem, loved the coast viz: (from 'The Rolling English Road')

'The night we went to Birmingham by way of Beachy Head......'

'The night we went to Glastonbury by way of Goodwin Sands....'

'The night we went to Bannockburn by way of Brighton Pier....'

A week later I was back on board at Southwold, preparing to depart for the River Deben and Ramsholt. I fitted the little Decca set, checked the engine and at midday on Saturday 30th June I left the Suffolk harbour. In the eighteenth century it had provided so many ships, but which now is noted for the fact that the lighthouse is in the northern part of the town, nearly three miles from the harbour itself. Southwold is noted for its strong tides. These are up to 5/6 knots on the ebb, an event that takes place ever since an abnormally high tide in 1953 that caused the retaining banks safeguarding the fields to break down with subsequent flooding of thousands of acres that can now only release their tidal water through the narrow confines of the harbour entrance. The sea is encroaching so fast on this shore line that at Waberswick, just across the harbour from Southwold, the remains of the town football pitch can be seen at low water where a goal post still stands in the sands, and that in around seventy years!

I left despite a gale warning, being aware of time slipping by and when I had cleared the harbour entrance I met a Southerly Force six strong breeze right on the nose. I had left four hours before high water and had plenty of time to sail the twenty odd miles to the Deben, so I took in three reefs and began broad tacks into an uncomfortable sea full of large 'holes' which kept shaking me up and causing the boat to take a sort of corkscrew action. I recalled that back in the days of William the Conqueror the ground I was now sailing over had been forest and King William used to issue passes to his more able lieutenants to hunt here. I had the fanciful notion that I was being carried over the tree tops and that the wind was stirring them up into wild motion, throwing me from tree top to tree top! In these shoal waters I was reluctant to motor and in any case, even tacking in these short seas I was making 4 knots, mostly in the right direction. At one stage the anchor broke loose and I had the unpleasant task of going forward, life line firmly attached, to restow it and lash it down.

Once I had passed Sizewell Power Station, Aldeburgh and rounded Orfordness (and become embroiled in the overfalls by being too close to the coast) I had a splendid sail with the wind more free and made good time to the Deben. I had been given some notes to help find the Deben channel, but since these involved a greenkeepers hut and some flags on a golf course, I found them impossible to place. I had bought new charts at the January boat show and since I spotted the entry buoy I decided to follow the chart. It was an hour after high water at this time and I had no difficulty, but when I came to leave at low water a few days later I had a chance to see that I had sailed straight over a large sand bar. Apparently the channel had moved following the January gales and the chart was no longer relevant!

In Ramsholt I found a vacant mooring and after a short while I heard a hail and friends arrived to take me ashore. I had decided that to cross the Thames estuary single handed would be courting disaster in view of the heavy commercial traffic I expected to meet so I had decided to pick up crew for the trip across to either Ramsgate or Dover. This crew man would come to Woodbridge and join me in a couple of days. Meanwhile mine host, a prison chaplain called Edward Giles, took me to his home in the country near Woodbridge where his wife Meg made me very welcome.

The following day being Sunday, he asked if I would be prepared to talk to some of his charges about my trip, so I soon found myself in one of H.M. prisons, addressing about thirty young men. I was very nervous about whether I could possibly keep them interested but they seemed to like what I had to say and one or two came and shook my hand after the end of the service. They were all young offenders, and knowing the background that some of them had come from, I felt really sorry for them and only hoped that they would have a better chance when they got out, but without a lot of luck or self motivation I guess the lucky ones would be very few.

On the Monday morning, since both Edward and Meg were working I decided to walk to Woodbridge (about three miles, said Edward). It was the longest three miles I have ever walked, partly because there was no footpath on the busy main road for well over a mile. There was a bus service, but I had no idea when it ran and certainly no bus passed me during the one and a half-hours of my walk. I took a taxi back and discovered it was nearer five miles than three!

At Woodbridge I stared at boats, at Whistocks yard where much building work was going on and at the quiet Essex country town. Somewhere among all those boats was 'Grace O'Malley', which had done a circumnavigation two years earlier. They too were members of one of the world's oldest cruising clubs, the Cruising Association. I had hoped to meet one of the officers of that club while in Woodbridge but as chance would have it they left the day I arrived to start their summer cruise.

Woodbridge is the centre of a lot of pleasure boating and I was reminded that this part of the East Coast, particularly Suffolk and Essex had provided thousands of ships in the past. In the seventeenth century there was an Icelandic fleet of almost 150 ships and a smaller number operating the Faeroes run, all from the south East coast ports. Losses were high and in 1852 the annual losses were around 1600 ships around the coast. That many of these were lost off the Suffolk and Essex coasts is not surprising in view of the shoal waters that predominate here, shoals that closed such thriving ports as Blythborough in the eighteenth century and changed the character of another, South-wold, completely in the twentieth century.

Woodbridge to the Solent

On Tuesday my crew, David Frank, the son of a friend arrived and Edward Giles took us both back to JUNKETTE so that at midday we could leave at low water to set off for the Kent coast, knowing that we would have the tide with us from three o'clock. The weather was fine for the crossing, the wind westerly so we were on a close reach, sailing at 5 knots. I saw the sand bar I had sailed over when I had arrived at the Deben: it was frightening to think that I could have had little more than 2 feet under my keels.

We headed due south, past Harwich, a vague mass of derricks in the distance and I thought of the many years ago when I had regularly visited this area, Chelmsford in particular as an engineer for the BBC. Working in Television, two of the largest companies in Chelmsford, Marconi and English Electric Valve Co. were the Mecca of television engineers. Marconi built the first of the new range of television cameras after the war, using a new design of image tube called the 'Image Orthicon' that was made by EEV. I recall how we used to check the larger (4½ inch) camera tubes for microphony (a shivering of the picture accompanying any loud noise) by the 'Dust Bin Lid' test.. to drop a dust bin lid some 5 yards from the camera and measure the ripple. The early days of television were exciting and quite Heath Robinson. It was about that time that Transistors were being developed but were only available to bona fide researchers. I desperately wanted to get hold of some to experiment with so I did a deal with the sales manager of EEV: he loved cheese and I had a friend who was a cheese factor. In exchange for a Cheshire cheese I got six transistors. One of these was used to make an amplifier to fit inside one of the very early cameras imported from America where the sound for cameraman guidance (production talk back) was woefully inadequate. There was very little room inside the camera case which was why I wanted a small transitor for the job and this was the very first use of transistors in the television chain. I believe that the old Mk.I camera so modified is still in the BBC Training School at Woodnorton Hall in Evesham. Others provided the very first studio radio talkback. Good value for a Cheshire Cheese!

These images flashed through my mind as we sailed through the quiet afternoon and may seem to have no place here but it isn't often that I get this far east and I could not hold the memories back. By 6pm the wind had changed direction and was now southerly, dead ahead as we passed Trinity buoy and it took until 8 to reach South Knock buoy. We had sailed outside all the sand banks of the estuary and found there was far less traffic than I had expected, less than I had met in the Clyde and I think I counted a total of nine ships that day, excluding three trawlers. There was much R/T traffic with the French almost constantly on channel 16 asking ships to speak to them on 14: they were monitoring the traffic lanes further south and were constantly giving speeds and bearings back to ships.

On this trip, there being two of us, I was able to check the performance of the 'Dinghy Decca' navigation system. Once one came to terms with its one key cyclic operation I found it quite effective, the waypoint being a useful feature as you could set up your next buoy and then read off range and bearing which gave us a chance to correct for the tide. On the debit side was the fact that it was working on only two chains: the results were rather slow in updating and somewhat 'hit and miss', two steps forward and one step back, but for a cheap instrument it was adequate.

Decca (or Sat.Nav or any other navigator) is fine if there are two of you, but while single-handing I found I never had time to go and read the thing and then translate the figures to the chart, at least in coastal waters. This had been proved very true at St. Kilda where I tried to use it for giving an exact position and got badly knocked about for my troubles. It was generally easier to read the log, the compass and draw tidal offsets with the chart on my knee. Decca, or any other position indicator is a fine thing to have on board, especially in fog and I would strongly advise any offshore or coastal sailor to invest in one, but the old fashioned D.R. should be kept up in case of equipment failure, yours or the distant transmitter.

We were now in an area which, although I had not sailed in before, I was quite familiar with: this patch of sea was used for all my RYA navigational excersizes in class and I could remember working out the tide, leeway and sailing speed in hourly segments so as to be able to say where I would be in, say, four hours and twenty minutes. In practice one never needs the degree of accuracy that the tests set you but they are a good discipline.

As we approached Ramsgate the sky darkened and all we could see were the very many shore lights, which were most confusing. Now I was very glad to have a pair of young and sharp eyes on the lookout for me. Eventually we found the fairway buoys but were put off when suddenly, from out of a pitch black background we saw a white light flash twice from a stone beacon in the water ahead. We had to wait a full minute for another warning flash. It was all very nerve racking and we were very thankful indeed to finally make out the pier head lights and enter the outer harbour. We didn't realise it then, but we could have gone straight through the lock to the inner harbour, but in the dark at nearly midnight we were thankful to find a pontoon to moor to.

The next morning, when the lock opened we moved into the inner harbour and tied up in the quiet and peace of many moored boats. Although there were some hundred boats they were mostly deserted and the pontoons empty of people. David returned to his family, promising to phone his father who would join me for the trip from here to Lyme Regis. I had decided that because of the crowded nature of the south coast it would again be sensible to have company, and this time I was proved right because I was to discover that the Solent was like Piccadilly Circus! Only I was not really travelling all round Britain single handed, first the Crinan, then the Thames Estuary and now more than half the South Coast!

June was staying with relatives at nearby Dover so I phoned her and she came and collected me for us to spend two days together in that famous town and I had a chance to see the great activity in the harbour with ferries leaving or arriving every few minutes. I had decided not to visit Dover by boat because of all this activity and it looked as though I had been right.

I took the chance to find a tool shop where I could buy a spanner with jaws wide enough to allow me to unfasten the weed trap on the engine water seacock. I had no wish to be caught out again! We did locate one but it was away at the back of the town, about a mile from the front where we were staying. I asked the shopkeeper if there was a simpler way to get back and he gave directions to a little back passageway that would lead directly to the shopping center. There, just behind the main drag of shops we found this stream surrounded by trees on the one side and high wooden fencing on the other and all the noise of traffic somehow magically disappeared. There were ducks swimming in the stream and I was amused to see one which was sitting on a black plastic rubbish sack floating in the middle of the water: the decomposing rubbish must have been warming the bag up nicely! You would have had no idea that you were so close to the center of a busy town. I had just bought another camera, my third, so made use of it to record the scene. Unfortunately the heat and moisture of the fo'csle was not good for the negatives and when I got home most of my photographs were very poor.

Too soon I returned to Ramsgate, to find my crewman, Steve Frank waiting for me. Steve, now retired, is a Brazilian who has lived in Britain for many years. He had owned a small sailing boat in Cornwall but found it too far to be worth the trip from his home in Dorset. He was delighted to have the chance to take to the water again aboard JUNKETTE and I was to be glad of his company and permanent good humour. He had many interesting tales about his homeland and about the 'Jangadas': light balsa wood boats used by native fishermen. They weren't so much boats as rafts and the men would often fish up to 20 miles offshore, aided by the constant wind pattern, light morning zephyrs which strengthened throughout the day to give a brisk on shore breeze in the evening.

The facilities for the visiting yachtsman in Ramsgate are excellent, with one odd foible. After 6.30 pm the Gents washroom and toilets are closed and the 'Ladies' facilities become unisex. It is all right once you have become used to it but the first time can be daunting. Presumably the difficulty is the Yobos who roam the dock area after night fall. Just beside the Harbour offices is a quaint Victorian building with the words 'Ramsgate Home for Smack Boys', a reminder of the sea fishing days when Ramsgate was a very busy port fielding dozens of 'Fishing Smacks' to comb the thriving channel waters and shoals.

With Steve for company we left Ramsgate harbour and headed west in a freshening breeze. The weather forecast gave a force 5 from the southwest, but was soon updating this to a strong wind warning. We were making little progress, tacking against rising seas. In an hour we had only made some 2.5 miles over the ground and our plan to anchor at Folkstone was rapidly going out of the window. As we approached Dover the wind rose to half-gale force and we heard the harbour master quoting wind speeds at the eastern pier head of 35+ mph. I decided to try and go into Dover and wait for things to cool off so I called the harbour and was asked to wait for the arrival of the harbour launch. By this time we were only a quarter of a mile from the pier head and were getting the back scend from the cliffs: waves were hitting us from all directions and we were very relieved when the launch finally appeared and shepherded us into the outer harbour.

APPROACHING DOVER IN A GALE

The crew of the launch asked if anyone had contacted me in Ramsgate as apparently they had asked for me in Dover and were told I was in Ramsgate. For the first time on this trip I had failed to let anyone know of our plans, primarily because we were uncertain about the weather. I never did discover who was looking for me.

We anchored in the outer harbour where I had been warned that the holding was poor, but in our case we had to 'motor' the anchor out when the launch came to take us all to the inner dock. I was greatly impressed with the way the Harbour master controlled the heavy traffic. He was polite, precise and clear in his directions and at no time did I feel I was being a nuisance in going into the harbour. I was treated to just as much courtesy as the master of the largest ferry. The method of dealing with visiting yachts was interesting. They could either remain at anchor in the outer harbour in an area reserved clear of the ferry routes or be corralled by the patrolling harbour launch who would then herd a bevy of boats to the waiting pontoon just in front of the lock gates at the inner end of the inner harbour. Here, all the boats would tie up and their dues would be collected. Then the bridge would rise, cutting off all ground traffic to the ferries, the lock gates would open and all the yachts smartly cast loose to find their way into Wellington dock. The lock and gates would be quickly shut behind them to allow the busy traffic to and from the ferries to resume. The lock gates open for a short time about an hour either side of high water.

June had spotted us in the harbour and came down next day to whisk us off for a meal. When we had arrived they had been 'blessing the port' with the RNLI in full dress parade on the lifeboat. The wind had been so great that the service was nearly abandoned so June and her family were not too surprised to see us arrive. The following day was beautiful with blue skies, the typical clearing after a warm front passes through, and we had a pleasant, if unplanned, day in the port. I had the feeling that pleasure boats were being welcomed, preparatory to the expected loss of Ferry traffic when the Channel Tunnel opened, or was I being cynical?.

Those ferries are quite a sight to see as they raise their skirts in a shower of spray and daintily 'float' up the beach (in fact, on long concrete ramps in Dover) ready for their next load. I believe that when crossing the channel the passengers see very little of the scenery because of the curtain of spray that surrounds them, but they are a very fast form of cross channel transport and would ever, for me, be preferable to an underground train journey. The river Conway in North Wales has now been tunneled for road traffic and I find myself worrying whether the sea is going to break through: I can't get through quickly enough, but the channel tunnel....! Oddly, though, I don't worry about the Blackwall Tunnel in London, or the Mersey Tunnel in Liverpool, perhaps because they've been there long enough to prove safe.

The next morning saw us leaving Dover at midday, sailing close hauled into a steady west north west breeze, heading for Folkstone which we reached by 2pm. As we approached Rye we heard the Coast Guard warning of a wreck in the approach channel to Rye harbour and I was reminded of an episode very many years ago when I had worked in London. I had an Uncle who had two daughters but no sons and he befriended me and took me on long walks. He was a senior manager with one of the leading insurance houses and very knowledgeable: I think he used me as a sounding board for some of his ideas... .should he fall in with Lord Pakenham and insure the Indian Railways, for instance! I was happy to be a listener and only made the occasional grunt. Uncle never drove so we went by bus, rail or hire car. In Rye we had boarded a bus to take us along the coast to Hastings. Uncle was describing the typical features associated with the Kentish man and to illustrate his ideas, asked me to note a girl at the front of the bus, to note her high cheek bones and deep forehead, her ruddy complexion. This girl and her companion shortly got up and left the bus, jabbering away in Dutch. I pretended not to notice and was quietly amused but much later, while studying history I became aware that Kent had been invaded by the Jutes after the Romans left in the 5th century, and no one is sure where the Jutes came from. It could have been Jutland (though the similarity of sound is too apposite and the Angles were thought to originate there or from the eastern banks of the Rhine or...they could have come from Holland!

Travelling west from Dover is hard work because of the tidal pattern. Passing Dungeness and going west you have only two hours of fair tide whereas when you are sailing eastwards you have 10 hours of a fair tide right up the Kent coast.

At five oclock we were off Dungness and by 11pm were anchoring off Eastbourne to await a favourable tide along the coast. Eastbourne is said to have the highest sunshine rate in Britain: well this year there was so much sunshine everywhere that they were going to be hard put to keep their record. The stay there was short and at 3am we were again on the move towards Bognor Regis where we intended to wait a fair tide round Selsey Bill. We reached Bognor with an adverse tide, literally fighting every mile at the end until we anchored off the town, the tide sluicing past us at around three knots. An hour later the pressure dropped and we raised anchor to get to the Bill at slack water. The wind was freshening and as we approached the Solent we had a fine sail in about 20 knots of wind from the South West. We headed for Gosport and the Camper & Nicholson Marina in Portsmouth where we had been promised free berthing. The tide out of Portsmouth runs very fast and we were glad to have a good engine pushing us through. It was very many years since I had been in these waters which were far more familiar to Steve who acted as navigator, much to my relief as there were a lot of boats about, not to mention a plethora of ancient forts, sunken walls and submarine barriers.

The history of this area is fascinating. The whole of this part of the south coast still bares the names of Roman forts and towns and now, with the raising of the 'Mary Rose', more recent history from the 16th century, perfectly preserved in the mud of the Solent and available for student and holidaymaker alike to enjoy. As an Island nation since the passing of the ice ages, our maritime history has been of interest to almost every schoolboy and continues to be made today where landing slips built in the Forties for war purposes can be found all around the coast. There are gun emplacements in Dover, old mine fields near Lyme Regis, Battle of Britain airdromes in places like Goodwood and Fordingbridge and so many more. It is now interesting to see how we are reverting to one of the old Roman cultures, that of Wine production in Sussex, but using the grapes of the Vandals, of Germania: the Muller Thergau grape, better suited to our Northern climes.

Camper & Nicholson made us very welcome and I put out a few calls to contact friends and family. The non stop run from Dover, despite adverse tides,had not been in the least tiring with two of us to share the helming so I was all ready to go visiting. Shopping in Gosport was strange: we could not find a general grocery! We could buy shoes from several shops, TV's and Radios, books and chemists, but no Grocer unless we walked the considerable distance to a supermarket. The advent of shopping centers and supermarkets has been the death knell to the small grocer, and quite often the centers themselves are a fair distance from the harbour so that visiting yachties have quite a trek.

I met with my first stone wall with the Cancer Relief organisation. I rang head office in London to tell them where I was and all they could offer were some telephone numbers. They seemed unwilling to make any contacts on my behalf or to speak to the press. They assumed I could do it all, without any contacts, from a pay phone! I suspect I must have got the 'office temp' when I rang, but it was to happen again on the south coast, I'm afraid.

Some friends who came to visit me heard the story of my broken bowsprit and suggested that I try Camper & Nicholson's workshop while I was there and gave me the name of the foreman. I had tried twice to get repairs done without success in Scotland and Suffolk so did not expect much help as it was the height of the season, but I hadn't counted on the goodwill that attended me.

C & N said that if I left the broken piece as a pattern they would have one ready in four days. I did not dare ask a price, but thanked them most heartily and used the time to investigate the Solent.

First we went out to the Beaulieu River where I met up with another friend sailing a Kingfisher 30. We agreed to meet up in a couple of days in Poole. I went on up the river, past Buckler's Hard - where in Drake's day, the great warships had been built of good English oak - to join an aged friend who let me tie up alongside his boat not far from Beaulieu itself. He is an eighty year old sailor who was on the verge of deciding to give up his hobby at last because his legs were beginning to fail him. He sailed a 22ft boat and had been with her all on his own to the French canals where he had unfortunately suffered an explosion in the engine well. Donald Booth was a much travelled man and it was a delight to moor up alongside and have a chat with him. Even at his advanced age he was experimenting with his rig and had fitted a wishbone arrangement that I didn't much like the look of, I'm afraid. However, his boat was still giving him a lot of pleasure though I suspect his wife would be pleased when he did give up as she often walked down to the river bank to see that he got home safely.

The next morning we left the Beaulieu river which is very shallow, we had gone aground three times on our way up but were more fortunate on the return, touching the bottom only once. This river must be a gold mine for the Montague estate as they have all the mooring rights and it isn't cheap, especially considering the lack of facilities!. We headed across the Solent for the Isle of Wight and Newtown River. This little Creek is quite lovely but in mid July was absolutely packed with boats, as was the whole of the Solent area. I saw one of our association boats and rowed across to have a cup of coffee with them.

The boat, LIZA, was spotless and I discovered that they kept her in Gosport, in the C & N Marina. As they had to travel from Croydon for a sail it was much easier with two children to be able to board from the comfort of a pontoon rather than getting out a dinghy and rowing out to a tidal mooring. There is much talk about the rising cost of moorings on the South Coast and there is no doubt that it is high compared with most of the rest of the country, but if you compare the facilities you have at a Marina with those of the average country club or golf club then you are no worse off and probably pay a little less unless you have a very large boat.

When I left the Young's boat I had only a short row back, but the tide was flooding and it took me a very hard fifteen minutes rowing to reach my boat. For some of the time, to the amusement of the children, I was almost going backward. Later in the day we put the outboard on the dinghy and went up the Shallfleet creek to the boatyard and walked up the stream to a charming country pub for refreshment. The whole area of Newtown River is saltings and the many birds in the reeds and shallows are fascinating. A nature photographer could spend a week here and not be bored. The area seems also to be a haunt for Scout and Guide camps which is hardly surprising as there is so much for the kids to do. The smell of woodsmoke from the campfires in the evening is in my memory still.

From Newtown Creek we sailed out of the Solent, past Bournemouth (full of memories for me as I had spent much of my RAF service in the area) on to more shoal waters, this time Poole bay. I cannot remember ever seeing so many boats moored up as I did off the channel up to the town. Coming from the Northwest where a dozen boats makes a crowd, it was always a surprise, and not always welcome, to see so many boats. In Scotland I had sailed for a day without seeing a single boat on more than one occasion, but down here I was seeing hundreds every day.

We tied up at the town quay and now began a delightful visit. We were well and truly in the center of things and there was always something to watch, people of all types to study and an amazing diversity of shops. I fell in love with Poole, with the bustle and happy laughter, with the true holiday atmosphere. But a short walk from the quay is 'The Dolphin Centre', a huge complex of shops of all kinds, big enough to serve a city the size of Liverpool or Southampton. It is strange how some places affect you more than others, often for a reason you find it hard to state, but Poole remains a very happy memory for me. Let me mention just one of the attractions that held me spellbound: a picture gallery right on the town quay with a huge selection of paintings and sculpts. I must have spent over two hours in there, for once thrilled at the quality of paintings on display. Too often picture galleries in resorts show the sort of chocolate box landscapes that sell so well, almost as though the Pre-Raphaelite Brotherhood was reborn, but without their grand illusions. The one in Poole, though, showed Flints, Impressionist prints and some lovely soft watercolours by modern artists that could have been seen happily beside Copelands and Turners. I was very tempted to buy but knew I couldn't carry paintings safely on the boat.

I was visited by the South West Organiser for Cancer Relief, my first contact with them since Scarborough so I was glad to be able to hand over the contents of my collecting boxes which had been getting rather heavy. I wore a Cancer Relief banner along the side of the boat and would hang a collecting box from the nearest pole or post. People were very generous and I rarely left a town without a sizable collection. I found that most people confused what I was doing with Cancer Research. Their work is to look into the root causes of Cancer whereas Cancer Relief is to bring succour to the sufferers in the form of Macmillan Cancer Nurses or to their families with financial help if the breadwinner is stricken. I liked to think that I was doing something for the here and now.

I feel great sympathy and support for the work being done in Bristol to help Cancer sufferers by counseling and diet. I'm not sure about diet but I do believe that reduction of stress is one of the best cures. I also believe that faith healing works, not only for cancer, of course, but my own experience has been one of relief following someone else's 'prayers' on my behalf. I'm not sure what I mean by 'prayers', certainly not a call to a deity, but direct helping as though by thought transference. On two separate occasions when things were getting out of hand with my own symptoms, friends who have been aware have sat down and willed me well, unknown to me till later, but in each case I was much improved. I know, it could have happened anyway, but the co-incidence is too marked to ignore.

We stayed in Poole for two days, hoping to see Peter and Lorna whom we had met at the mouth of the Beaulieu, but no luck so we moved out and began our journey back to Gosport. As we approached the Needles, the wind freshened and we decided to reef. The tides in the Solent are unusual in that there are two high tides in parts of the Solent area since the water enters from each end, and at differing times because the main mass of water in the channel moves slowly east as the tide rises. The result is that there are two periods of high water slack between Cowes and Ryde and we needed to reach the Hurst narrows at low water slack so as to have a good tide to take us to Gosport. We had left Poole on the half ebb and were now having to sail fast. The weather helm was forcing us to reef early so I decided on motor sailing. Would you believe it: we again got a jib sheet round the prop! I just couldn't believe it. I'm afraid that I shouted at my colleague though it was no more his fault than mine. Now there was no way we could get to Gosport that day. Fortunately I did have a day in hand, if I could get the offending rope sorted out.

We sailed through the narrows and I thought of anchoring at Keyhaven and waiting for low water but I was told that it was a muddy bottom so we headed for Cowes. The harbour was very full but the Harbour Master said I could use the scrubbing post for the night, but at extra cost to the normal, expensive, harbour dues. My Yorkshire nature rebelled and we set off again to try and find somewhere to dry out. It seemed that there was mud almost everywhere (I had not then thought of the shingle banks in mid Solent) and we began to consider finding a diver. After anchoring at Hampstead ledge overnight, a local fisherman, asked for advice, confirmed the lack of a firm bottom and offered to take my crewman, Steve to Cowes to find a diver. Two hours later there was a VHF message to say that no diver was available and that Steve would bus back to Shallfleet. I raised anchor and sailed into Newtown Creek.

I anchored where we had been two days earlier and as the day was sunny and warm, decided to have a go at the prop myself. Steve, my crewman, had already tried as he felt responsible for our predicament, but had been unable to hold his breath long enough to achieve anything. Also, he badly cut his arms on the barnacles on the hull of the boat. I first put on a long sleeved shirt to protect my arms and then threw a rope over the stern and pulled it tight up to the rudder so that I would have something to hold on to keep me under water.(I had done this sort of thing before!). Then, to the amusement of other boat owners, I went overboard, armed with a bread knife in my teeth. Because the water was shallow it was warm and quite pleasant, apart from the tide that kept trying to pull me away from the boat. I tied a rope round me and fastened it to the stern ladder and then began to dive under the boat. The water was very cloudy and this made the job harder as I could not really see what I was doing. Bit by bit I got the rope free and was very tired and breathless at the finish as it had taken me about half an hour of continuous labour to free it. I don't know how many times I dived but desperation drove me on - I knew that there would be little possibility of my getting into Gosport Marina without an engine and I had a date there with a new bowsprit the very next day!

Despite the protection of a shirt, my arm was heavily grazed. Obviously the fouling of the bottom was far worse than I had expected but I had to wait until I got to Lyme Regis before I could do a scrub down. I started the engine to try it out and motored further up the creek, to hear a hail and find Steve being dinghied to the boat. He had taken a bus from Cowes to Shallfleet and found a skipper about to leave for his boat in a dinghy and the man had offered to ferry him out. He was delighted to find me so close, even more so when I told him the good news. We immediately raised anchor and set off for Gosport, arriving at 5.30 pm. on 17th July. Life was to be very different from now on.

FROM THE SOLENT TO PLYMOUTH

The next day was spent mainly watching the shipwright fit the new bowsprit and provisioning for our journey west. Camper & Nicholson had beefed up the new spar, which was beautifully made and fitted with apparent ease. I had witnessed the fitting of the prototype and it had taken many visits back to the bench to fair out the bottom section to suit the deck camber and my greatest concern was the state of the roller reefing extrusion which was now showing a crack. The makers were not prepared to come to Gosport to assist and I had no time to go to them so we tried taping and keeping at least two rolls of sail round the spar.

By late afternoon everything was completed and ship-shape so we left on the tide and sailed for Newtown again where we anchored once more off Hampstead Ledge at nine in the evening, a beautiful evening too. The new bowsprit made boat handling a joy again and although the winds had been too light to really test the helm we had found there to be almost perfect balance. It was amazing to think that for over a thousand miles I had put up with such discomfort with the excess weather helm where a second pair of hands would have been so useful, and here I was with a perfectly balanced boat AND a crewman. From now on, sailing was once again a real pleasure and my speeds over the ground greatly improved.

On Thursday, 17th July we left the Solent, sailing past Yarmouth at 3 knots in the lightest of breezes and again admiring the statuesque Needles as we went through the narrows: a most impressive sight, the early morning sun turning them into shining white pillars. Very soon we were sailing past Bournemouth again, full of nostalgic memories for me. When I had been in the RAF at Christchurch, there had been one very hot summer and we had spent some time that year attempting to help put out the forest fires which plagued the area. I hoped they were not having trouble now, some forty odd years later.

I had once returned to my old station, now part of a farm, to find some of the old buildings now hen houses, the airfield at Ibsley overrun and I was very depressed. There had been some enjoyable times in those far off days, fighting off huge moths in the warm summer nights in the nissan huts where we lived, or scrounging wood for the central brazier in the cold winter nights. There were nights of endless card games, days of wine and roses, of first fumbling love, of Saturday meals in the White Heart at Ringwood. Drinking '28 claret at 30 shillings a bottle and listening to the local gentry discussing the way their offspring rode a horse - *'Daphne has a good seat but you should see Elizabeth. My dear she is such a slouch'.* I think I might have liked 'Elizabeth'!

While in the R.A.F. in Ringwood I came to know one of those people with a natural talent for shooting, a chap call Jimmy Gough who once, with a catapult, shot a Pheasant from the back of the truck while on the move. The driver stopped and Jimmy hopped over the gate to retrieve his prize. One day he came to us holding a brown paper parcel which he carefully unwrapped. Inside was a silencer, the first I had ever seen. He had made it himself, a steel tube fitted with 6 thin steel baffle plates. He screwed it on to the end of his .22 rifle, which he used for shooting rabbits (nothing so common as a 12 bore) and raised it to fire. I stopped him and suggested that if any of the plates or the tube were out of line it could blow the breech back into his face. He looked shocked, this hadn't occurred to him, and he then held the piece behind a blast wall before pulling the trigger. There was a slight 'cough' and when he pulled his hand back the gun had just a trace of smoke leaving the barrel. His home made silencer was perfect. By chance I met him some years later in the London Underground. He had a beautiful Cypriot girl on his arm after completing a Mediterranean tour: a real beauty with golden skin. Even his cupid darts were winners.

Now it was all passing my right shoulder, about two miles off as we crossed Poole Bay heading for St. Albans Head in the lightest of Easterly winds. Studland Bay is very impressive: in fact the whole of the Dorset coast line is very beautiful with deeply indented cliffs, sea worn tunnels and caves and magnificent sandy beaches. If it weren't for the overcrowding, keeping a boat at Poole would be pure magic with some of the best cruising grounds in Britain and but a step across to France and Brittany, to all the allure of the Atlantic seaboard. Here, in mid week with the schools just closing and the wild influx of holiday makers only just beginning, it was bearable - just - until you heard the chatter begin on R/T.

Steve was very keen that we should spend a night at Lulworth Cove. Being a Dorset man (at least by adoption) he was very proud of his counties' most noted beauty spot. It was not to be as the range safety officer asked us to sail 4 miles off the coast. I suppose we could have stood on our rights and just carried on, at least two other boats did just that, but I have always been a conformer. Instead we sailed on to Weymouth.

We decided to anchor off the town in the bay rather than go into the harbour, which was very crowded. This turned out to be a true blessing because that night two Mermaids visited us. We had just finished an evening meal in the cabin when we heard laughter close to the boat. We went on deck to investigate and found two young ladies hanging onto the stern ladder. We were about a quarter mile off shore and these young girls, about fifteen, had swum out to investigate. One was from Western Germany (her English was quite good) and the other from Eastern Germany. It must have been very cold in the water at this time so I suggested that they come aboard for a cup of coffee. *'You'll be perfectly safe, we're a couple of sexagenarians'*, I said, but with a burst of giggles they swam off and it was only much later that Steve suggested to me that my words may well have been misunderstood by someone with a limited vocabulary!

The next morning we raised anchor early and in company with four other boats (I did say these were crowded waters) we set off for the 'Bill'. Portland is a Naval base and as we passed the harbour we were treated to the sight of fleet manoeuvres as half a dozen warships came out, only to anchor a mile or so out in the bay. Once past the base we hugged the shore line, about two hundred yards off the cliffs as the best route to avoid the turbulent waters round Portland Bill. As it was, with the weather set fair and wind - now a good breeze - with tide we had a quiet passage and began one of the best sails of the whole cruise, up Chesil Bank - that curious stretch of shingle holding in the waters of East and West Fleet. The wind was still Easterly and we were creaming along at six knots with a perfectly balanced rudder and two reefs in the main while I gave a broadcast via the coastal radio station to the listeners of Radio Manchester. What a difference in our stations: me on a sunlit stretch of glittering water while Susie Mathis was in a dark studio in far off dusty Manchester. Now, despite the earlier traumas round the top of Britain, my 'cup runneth over' and I was having the time of my life.

We sailed across Lyme Bay in warm sunshine, reaching Lyme Regis by three in the afternoon as the wind died away, a day ahead of schedule after some 1500 miles of sailing. I had written to the Harbour master in March saying that I would like to book a mooring from the 21st July, to coincide with their Life Boat week, and here I was on the 20th. I felt very proud of my achievement and myself so far, two of my four deadlines met on time with two still to go, Falmouth by August 11th and Pembroke by Aug. 22nd.

The harbourmaster called me and said that he was coming out to meet me and to stand by for a visitor. A brand new launch came out from the harbour (he had taken command that day) and there was a lady aboard whom he handed over to my deck, a Mrs. Pennington of the Cancer Relief organisation who officially welcomed me, on behalf of the committee, to Lyme Regis. It was a lovely gesture, much appreciated, especially as she was not a sea going person and it had taken a lot of courage for her to come out to me in this way. She and Steve got on like a house on fire as her husband had been out to Brazil hunting up obscure flora: he was a botanist.

Very shortly we moored up in the tiny harbour, called 'The Cobb', just below the maritime museum and then disembarked for a cream tea laid on by Mrs. Pennington. I had been to Lyme Regis twice before, having spent a Christmas here, and was very fond of the place, not least because it housed both a favourite landscape artist - Marie Blake - and John Fowles, the author of 'The French Lieutenant's Woman'. The town, built on a hill side and consequently calling for much excersize in going from place to place, is delightful in itself and blessed with exquisite views both in the harbour and across the Bay both East and West. There are excellent sands in front of the town and in the next bay to the west is the wide sweeping arc of Monmouth Beach, a shingle beach where the Earl of Monmouth had landed in his attempt to topple Cromwell. This is topped by the 'Undercliffe' walk, illustrated so well by Elaine Frank, another Lyme Regis inhabitant. While still young I had undertaken that walk from Seaton to Lyme Regis along the cliff tops, to marvel at the 'Island' of cliff that had separated and hung away over the sea with a gap of some 10 yards between it and the mainland. It is a walk only for the stout hearted: I don't think I could manage it now. (I did, in fact do just this some three years later!) When I had set off in the 40's with a party of about fifteen, we were told not to leave the path as there were many mines laid to seaward!

The Cobb was (and is) a man made harbour, originally constructed of timber to safeguard the small fishing fleet in the sixteenth century but later reinforced, first with rocks and stone and later with concrete so that now there is a perfect haven for small boats. It is a place of endless interest so that when my crew man left me – it was time for him to return to his Dorset home, from now on I would once more be alone but I had plenty to occupy me.

On my second day I refreshed my memories of the town and even practised 'reflex drawing' as propounded by Marie Blake. I visited the museum where I came across a name new to me: Thomas Coram who was one of the very first to introduce a version of 'Children in Need' - in the nineteenth century! Lyme was a place to taste again the delights of the culinary arts and I enjoyed eating ashore. On the Saturday evening I was invited to eat at the Yacht Club as their guest. I was given a cheque for the Cancer Relief fund, and a day later a couple I had not met before, the Mapstone's, invited me to their home in Bridgewater, Somerset, for a bath, a meal and a night's rest.

This was a delightful interlude where I was shown the Quantock Hills and had a chance to see what had once been an opening to the sea in the Bristol Channel from the centre of Bridgewater, now a Marina with no access to the sea at all: to sail you would have to be craned out onto a transporter and carried to the sea! A developer waited to convert the area into waterside housing. As the sea encroached on the East coast it seemed to be receding from the West. Were we being moved away from Europe? Would the channel tunnel have to be lengthened as time went on. Bridgewater is a very vital town and later in the year I was to re-visit and see the Carnival where all the local villages provide floats with the children demonstrating some theme: when I went the following year there were 90 floats and the parade took nearly two and a half hours. It was quite extraordinary and well worth seeing.

On my return to Lyme Regis I was to find an extraordinary scene: there in the harbour was a boat being repainted and it was the identical scene that I had in my house, painted by Marie Blake some three years earlier. It was as though I had found myself in the middle of Constable's 'Hay Wain', so similar was the scene before me to that on the canvas at home. The only difference now was that my own boat JUNKETTE was on the edge of the picture. It was deja vu in reverse: the present moved into the past. I was so intrigued that I invited Marie to join me on the boat to see it for herself and found myself wondering if the French Lieutenant would be walking aboard with her.

Marie is a delightful artist and teacher and, playing truant from her charges, stayed a long lunch hour with me where I plied her with gin and tonics. This was enough to confuse her so that when she invited me to join them for dinner that night she gave me the wrong time and I arrived almost an hour late, to find most of her class departed for the studio. There were sufficient people left for me to have a fun meal and I then joined them for a tutorial on tonal studies, being asked for my comments on some of the student's efforts on display. Marie's formula for painting is to go and sketch the scene from as many angles as possible, preferably by 'reflex drawings', ie. drawings done quickly without looking at the paper so that the 'feeling' of the subject is obtained, unalloyed with objective intrusions, a truly subjective analysis of the scene. These, she contends, should be followed with tonal sketches in either mono or duo colours and the most satisfactory then followed through into a completed painting either in the studio to avoid the problems of changing light values, or by frequent return to the scene. Her students can be seen in the town with their pads in one hand and pencil in the other as they attempt to sketch passers by or the antics of dogs or children on the sands without recourse to looking at the paper. That it leads to a freshness of approach is without doubt, a freedom from the stilted form, from stylised shapes even though the whole process is very structured. I found myself incapable of achieving the tonal studies in any meaningful way: I was what she called an intuitive painter. I painted what I wanted to see! I think she was trying to be kind!

At my friend Peter's funeral in Wales earlier in the year I met his landlady's daughter from Manchester whom I had not seen for very many years. Peter had been very fond of her and was a godfather to one of her sons. He had spoken of me and when they heard that I would be along the south coast they suggested that I phone them in Bristol and they would come over to Lyme Regis for a meal, it being only an hour's drive for them. I did this and then booked a table at a restaurant in the town and, calling at an adjacent florist, ordered a corsage of white flowers to be delivered to the restaurant so that my guests could find them on the table on their arrival. When Eric and Barbara arrived at the boat they told me it was their 25th wedding anniversary that day. I had no idea and was amazed that they should want to come to see me on such a day. On arrival at the restaurant, the flowers made the day for them both: the florist had made a lovely display of small white Lilies with a collar of pearls: it could not have been more appropriate. I was doing it for Peter and I think they both knew why. Peter had adored Barbara, even when she married someone else and he had never seriously looked at another woman, happy to be included in their family as a godfather. You will gather that Peter was a very generous man and a very good friend in whose memory I was making this cruise.

Lyme Regis was very busy at this time, its annual Life Boat week in full swing and the sands swarming with happy families enjoying the wonderful summer. In the harbour 'Sea Seeker' (the subject of my painting) was being scrubbed and painted and Trevor Mapstone and I were busy fitting a wind vane steering gear which he had kindly loaned me as it would give me improved self steering. My next stop was to be Torquay and he decided to join me in his boat for this leg of the journey. His daughter came with him, carrying a young child. Very sadly, some three years later she died from lung cancer. Life just is not fair: can you understand why I am a humanist?

It was once again with a heavy heart that I set sail, only to round up and pick up a buoy off the harbour entrance. The wind vane was far too insecure to leave fixed to the stern and I found myself uncoupling it and putting it back on the deck. We had fitted it in a hurry, without the proper tools and it would have been foolhardy to carry on with it. I then set off for Torquay, closely followed by my friends in their boat.

As I passed Teignmouth on my starboard hand I remembered a time, not long ago when I wrote a poem about loneliness and frustrated ideas. I had been sailing through the night across the Bristol Channel in thick fog and after a long night sail in considerable pain after I had hurt my leg in Ramsey Sound (my legs seems prone to damage!) I wrote the poem in a hospital waiting room in Truro, not too far from Teignmouth where Donald Crowhurst had set out on his fateful proposed circumnavigation in 'TEIGNMOUTH ELECTRON. I suppose I must have subconsciously worked it out while sitting at the tiller in the

Bristol Channel, 'doing nothing much', more or less as I was while sailing this day to Torquay. Sailing alone, no one is going to say to you 'haven't you anything better to do?'

The people in the boat behind, my friends from Lyme Regis, knew the Crowhursts, both husband and wife and they had shared in those awful months of waiting for news. I wondered if they thought of him as we sailed past his home port.

In Torquay we made for the town quay rather than the Marina so that I would be able to 'rattle my collecting box', but the harbour master soon put paid to that and would allow me no more than showing the box on the boat. Since the general public were most unlikely to come down to the jetty it was a waste of time. I was very disappointed with Torquay, primarily because of the extreme rudeness of the yacht racing crowd who seemed to believe that the waterfront of the harbour was their private property. Nowhere else did I meet such outrageous behaviour: an officer of the club, tying alongside my boat without any fenders of his own, suggested that his wife be allowed to cross over my cockpit. I refused and asked if she would take the normal, more private route across my bows. They didn't like this and next day moved their boat alongside my friends who were then subject to similar treatment. A taxi driver was stopped with four letter words and told to wait while a crew carried their Moth dinghy across the approach road. I asked him why he didn't say anything but he was a councillor: 'we have to suffer this, but only for a few weeks' was his reply.

I had a cousin living in Paignton and she came over to visit me and invite me to her home for a night's rest. The stay in Paignton was far more relaxing and it was a chance to catch up on all the family gossip. As children we had lived only three miles from each other in Leeds, but now the family was split up all over England and very rarely did we meet up. I had another cousin down in Devon, but a few miles away and I hoped to see them soon too. In the evening we went to a Bistro, called 'Clodagh's Bar' and run by the one time Song for Europe Pop singer Clodagh Rodgers. I had met her in Manchester but it had been many years before and as she didn't recognise me I made no attempt to speak to her.

From Torquay I split up with the Mapstones who were returning to Lyme Regis and set off for the River Dart at 6 am. I had not gone more than a mile when the boom end again parted. It had worked all the way from Tobermory but the strain had proved finally too great and it broke, at the same point. I turned back into Torquay and carried out hurried repairs which were to last until I reached Milford Haven, but more of that anon. An hour later I was on my way again and entered the River Dart at about 10 am. and headed towards Totnes.

I would have liked to have sailed right up to the town of Totnes, both because I had relatives there and because Totnes was the landing place of Brutus, and later so many mediaeval Kings. However I had no large scale chart for the river and the tides were falling: I had no desire to be neaped, and so I settled for visiting Galmpton Creek where two of our association members kept their boats. I was fortunate to meet one of them, Malcolm Smith with his lovely Kingfisher 20 GEMINI, but after a very few words, finding there was no spare mooring, I set off back again to the main river where I picked up a large mooring buoy. As a result I missed seeing my second cousins who came to Galmpton Creek to find me. I was not enamoured of the Dart, where I was charged a great deal for no facilities, and was glad to leave the next day and head for Salcombe and Kingsbridge. The Dart is very beautiful but very commercialised. There are facilities off the town but higher up the river there is nothing other than unhandy mooring buoys, for which you pay the same as a town side berth. It reminded me of the charges at some National Trust Gardens where you park in a muddy field without footpaths and pay handsomely for the privilege. I have looked at charts of the area and tried to imagine why so many mediaeval Kings and Missionaries should have chosen the Dart and Totnes for their entry to Britain and can only assume that the entrance must, in some way, mimic in smaller scale the entrance to the Mediterranean: in stead of the Pillars of Hercules, the Paps of Perseus, perhaps.

ENTRANCE TO THE RIVER DART

I reached Bolt Head at low water so dropped anchor in Storehole Bay to wait the tide and prepare a meal. At 8 pm. I raised the anchor and sailed into Salcombe, dropping anchor again in Sunny Cove for the night. Later I discovered that the approach to Salcombe had been dredged to a depth of 3 metres right up as far as the town quay and I need not have waited. I was determined to try and reach Kingsbridge the next day, but didn't realise that the quay at Kingsbridge is under the control of Salcombe harbour master. This time I did have a chart for the river and sailed right up to Kingsbridge, going aground only feet from the pontoon in the centre of the town. By dint of powering the engine hard, I slipped over the mud until I could reach the pontoon to pull JUNKETTE in and there I stayed for the next two days. It took a day for the harbour master to catch up with me: not many boats slip through his fingers!

I love Kingsbridge: a really charming town which I had first visited in 1955 when, with a friend, I had gone to find my cousin (the brother of the one in Torquay). All I knew then was that his house looked over the water front. I found it easily because Frank used to play the piano accordion and, in Leeds, led a dance band for local hops. There, in Kingsbridge on a summer evening in 1955 we found a small crowd outside a house on the front from which came the unmistakable sounds of Accordion and Drums. Frank and I were re-united after some 15 years apart.

Like me, he is older and greyer, but lives just outside Kingsbridge now (the house where he lived has become a cafe and gallery) and he still plays the piano accordion for the local folk dance groups. His son and daughter also play instruments and to hear his daughter Debbie with her recorder or a tin whistle is to see someone for whom it is an extension of them. It comes to a life of its own between her lips just as the Clarinet seems an integral part of Emma Johnson when she is performing with an orchestra.

Debbie came down to find me and take me home for a meal and a chat. It was another great day of nostalgia and that evening we all went to Hope Cove for a drink in the water side Inn, a short walk from their home in Galmpton (yes, same name but different place). Later, while her father played his accordion in the garden she did the Broom Dance for me with great zest , dressed in a very short skirt and Tee shirt which did my blood pressure no good at all. D.H. Lawrence, in 'Sons and Lovers' has his hero say that he likes to see his girl 'move under her clothes'. I could see what he meant.

The following day Debbie joined me and a few minutes before high water we cast off and began a slither and slide out of Kingsbridge towards Salcombe. We went aground three times but eventually got into deeper water: even my shoal draft of 3.5 ft. was too much for the estuary this high up. Back in Salcombe arrangements had been made for me to tie up for the whole morning at the town quay (mooring normally limited to one hour) as there was a Macmillan flag day in the town and JUNKETTE was the main attraction. I was visited by the Mayor and the press and spent the morning showing people over the boat.

After midday I took Debbie with me for a short sail out to the channel and saw some sharks not more than a mile from the shore. Later the harbour master said that they had been reported frequently over the past couple of weeks but so far none had come in any closer. It was a hot, sunny day and we were glad of the slight breeze on the water: ashore it had been sweltering. Salcombe is very well equipped for visiting yachtsmen with a fuel barge, rubbish barge and a launch collection service. It is not cheap but at least, unlike some ports on the south coast, the facilities were there. I noted one anomaly: on the town quay the water taps were so low that it was not possible to fill a portable container without a hose, and no hoses were available! There are plenty of moorings for visitors with a pontoon reserved for their use in 'The Bag', about a quarter mile from the town.

While in Salcombe I met an old colleague of Peter's, Stan Taylor, who had retired to the town and had a boat called 'Southern Comfort'. We chatted about times past, in particular about the current changes in the BBC. The old organisation was being slimmed down, not before time, by the rigorous mind of its new (or newer - he had now served some four years) Director General, Michael Checkland whom I had known well in the past and whose signature is in my autograph album, given on retirement. Previous chief executives had been program men but Michael was an accountant and far more business like. He looked for positive returns in staff and facilities and ensured that he got them. For too long we had been carrying passengers: producers who produced no programs, facilities underused because of being badly sited for political reasons, staff inadequately managed and consequently too expensive... and so it went on. Fortunately he knew his limitations and never interfered in the programming decisions of channel editors unless asked to adjudicate: the BBC remains fiercely protective of its programming independence and his appointment of John Birch was to help shed some of the load off his shoulders in this area. Michael was a man I greatly respected over the years though I considered the appointment of Birch a mistake. (The BBC had apparently rejected him many years earlier when he applied to be a P.A.!)

The following morning dawned bright and sunny, but a dead calm prevailed and I set off west again, motoring over a calm sea. I thought of Middleton on KATE who had rowed when there was no wind but there was no way I could have rowed JUNKETTE very far which was after all a bigger boat and a lot heavier. I was surprised to hear a call from the coast guard asking for any boat near Bolt Tail. At this time I was about four miles off and called to offer my help. Apparently some one was in trouble in Hope Cove, where I had been the previous night, a bather, but I was too far away to be of help and my offer was declined.

My next venue was the River Yealm, some fifteen miles west, a most beautiful river, unfortunately brim full of boats. I managed to find a mooring and shortly after I had tied up I was visited by the harbour master bearing a letter. He welcomed me to the river and said I need pay no fees during my stay. There was a regatta and carnival at Newton Ferrers that afternoon and he suggested I might like to see it.

The letter was from a Betty Barlow, the local Cancer Relief organiser who had heard of my visit to Salcombe and had the wit to try and contact me if I came into her area: she lived across the river from Newton Ferrers in the hamlet of Noss Mayo. I had to applaud her ingenuity in reaching me and phoned her, agreeing to go for coffee the following day. She was sorry that she had not known the date of my impending visit as she could have involved me with the carnival and helped make a collection for the charity.

After lunch on board I took the dinghy and motored up to the town through dense moorings of pleasure craft, tying up at the hotel jetty and walking the last mile into the town. It was a marvellous sight with craft of all kinds on the water, races of rowing dinghies of all types - Gig racing is a most popular sport in the far west with teams competing from Plymouth and Padstow to the Scillies. That night there was a firework display and I realised that by chance I had arrived on just the right day for the fun and games.

The following morning I was picked up by Betty and taken to her home for coffee. A delightful lady and I was to find out that she had been secretary for the Royal Western Yacht Club and office manager for Joe Honeywell in Plymouth, Yacht Broker and official measurer for the International races leaving Plymouth, including OSTAR, the single handed transatlantic race. She offered to take me to her old club house in Plymouth and introduce me to some of the celebrities, a chance I jumped at. While I was with her she made contact with the Vice Commodore and the secretary, arranging a visit for me to attend a luncheon party.

Noss Mayo and Newton Ferrers are two villages built on the steep banks of a tributary of the Yealm, facing each other and looking very gothic in their steep terraces: not the fearful gothic but more a fairyland with the cottages painted many differing colours. Noss Mayo is split in two by a stream at high tide, but at low water this almost dries and there is a carriage way joining the two halves of the village. When we had coffee the tide was out and the village re-joined: a picture postcard scene.

Later that morning I raised anchor and sailed out to anchor in Wembury Bay to wait the tide and have lunch. I was listening to the radio and had the good fortune to hear Sir George Porter choose his 'Desert Island Disks'. I had met Sir George when he was teaching in Sheffield and presented an 'Eye on Research' television program from there. The program was about the effect of light on photosynthesis and on colour fastness and I had been called to advise a rather irascible scientist because the cameras in use, Image Orthicons. could not 'see' the flashes of light that he was producing. I had to explain that the charge storage time was too long for the millisecond pulse to produce an image. Fortunately we had just taken on one of the new Vidicon cameras with very small picture tubes which, working on a different principle, were able to portray the light he wanted to exhibit. I think his view of BBC engineering improved considerably during that broadcast. I was also intrigued now to discover that he too was a sailor and had named his boat ANNABEL as a way of saying 'thankyou' for the Nobel prize which he had won: he was generally too modest to explain the derivation...Alfred Noble!

At about the time of meeting Sir George I also met another extraordinary Professor and teacher: Eric Laithwaite. I visited him at his lab in Manchester and he propounded his ideas of linear motion, now in use in Japan for their high speed monorail transport. To illustrate his theme he had rigged up a long solenoid (a steel pipe overwound with copper wire to make a very long electro magnet) connected to a bank of large condensers in which he had built up a large charge. Some fifteen feet from the pipe he had hung a railway sleeper. He placed a thick copper nail into the end of the pipe and then pulled a large breaker switch to complete the circuit. There was a bang and the copper bolt shot out and buried itself into the sleeper with tremendous force. Both men were to give the Royal Society Christmas Lectures to children in later years, both gifted with that wonderful sense of adventure and ability to make others share their enthusiasm.

After lunch I sailed on jib alone towards Plymouth, only a short distance away, passing another pretty Junk going the other way back into the Yealm, a boat called AMICIA. Junk sails do look very attractive at sea: the Chinese believe that man made objects should sleep easily with nature, should comply with natural forces. This is the philosophy of Taoism and the Junk certainly complies.

Entering Plymouth for the first time is very exciting, with the long breakwater in front of you as the first introduction to the harbour. In the winter gales of this year, 1990, the western end was badly damaged, with huge blocks of rock moved like sugar lumps from the bottom of a pile, but the breakwater undoubtedly saved the town from much damage. Past the breakwater and ahead of you lies Drake's Island to the left and Queen Anne's battery to the right. I made for Drake's Island and the Mayflower Marina.

Plymouth to St. Ives

The Mayflower Marina had reserved a space for me and would make no charge for my two nights stay. Camper and Nicholson really went out of their way to help the cause of the Macmillan Fund. This Marina won a number of awards and certainly caters well for its clients. The washing and shower facilities are second to none and there are all the other usual mod cons. one has come to expect as normal for a Marina. The casual first time visitor, though, will not be prepared for the remarkable cuisine of the 'Ocean Bistro' situated in the Marina. On my second day here I took Betty Barlow for a meal and it was truly scrumptious, a gourmet's delight.

There is a snag to the Mayflower: it is a long way to the town centre and if walking, you have to pass through a not very nice neighbourhood. After the Royal Marine barracks you find yourself in what appears to be the red light district of the town: not an area to traverse at night. It would have been more sensible for me to have stayed at the Queen Anne's Battery marina because that was the site of the Royal Western Yacht Club, but not knowing Plymouth I had to choose with a pin! Never mind, I did have superb conditions and I did get to see Joe Blagdon's yard.

Joe's yard is a stones throw from the Marina and well worth a visit, if only to meet Joe, a true sailing man's man. It was not surprising, therefor that when I saw him he had both Michael Ritchie and Geoff Lewis talking to him. But I jump ahead of myself.

The morning after my arrival, I was greeted by a reporter from Radio Devon who recorded a piece for later transmission and then gave me a generous donation. This was most unusual as most reporters are involved in reporting so many charity events that if they were to put a hand in their pocket every time they would soon be very hard up. A little later Betty Barlow arrived as promised and took me to that most prestigious of yacht clubs and the doyen of all racing men: the Royal Western. It was this club that agreed to take on the organisation of the first single handed transatlantic race proposed by Blondie Hasler and, under Jack Odling-Smee and later Lloyd Foster, has continued to do so ever since. It is interesting to note that when Blondie approached the club in 1959, Winston Churchill was the Commodore of the club. Winston would have good reason to remember Blondie of 'Cockleshell Heroes' fame, or 'Operation Frankton' as it was called before the film makers got at it, not to mention Blondie's feats in Norway and Ceylon. Lord Mountbatten had put up his name for a V.C. following the Bordeaux excersize but he was given the D.S.O. to go with the O.B.E. he had won earlier at Narvik.

Blondie Hasler has long been my guru and I was delighted to be in the club which had done so much to further his aims which, before their interest, had looked like foundering in the wayward tides of the Slocum Society. It was Blondie who had designed the original rig on my boat, Blondie who had sailed my prototype with surprised satisfaction and I had the feeling as I rounded Britain that he was watching over me.

Betty introduced me to Commander R.J.Harvey the secretary of the club who showed me around the premises and took me into the holy of holies, the 'Dolphin Room' from which the Ostars and Round Britain races are planned. This is a beautiful book lined room with long, shining refectory table round which I could imagine some of the most illustrious yachtsmen sitting over charts and weather forecasts. We were joined by the Vice Commodore, Donald McDonald and by Mike Ritchie and Joe Honeywell for lunch where, among other things we talked about a possible replacement for JESTER, the boat Blondie had used for the first Ostar and which had been in every succeeding race until lost at sea two years ago. Mike was hoping that a replica could be built to maintain the tradition in future years, a hope all of us round the table shared.

Before I left, the secretary presented me with a most generous cheque for Cancer relief and accepted one of my own club's burgees, hopefully to hang with those of many other clubs gracing their lounge wall. It had been a visit I would long remember and I was very grateful to Betty for organising it at such short notice.

The next morning I left Plymouth and headed for Fowey. The wind was a light southwesterly but I managed to make a course close hauled and reached Fowey by early afternoon. Another beautiful river in the southwest with the towns of Fowey and Polruan facing each other, it was not so crowded as at Salcombe or the Dart and there were plenty of visitors moorings and room to anchor. The harbour master's office operates a water taxi service so there was no need to launch 'the sweat', and since the cost is covered by your harbour dues you feel no resentment for being charged for your mooring.

I tied up alongside another visiting boat, owned by two Portuguese brothers, shipwrights who had bought the boat in Essex and were sailing it to Portugal. The registration papers were slow in being processed and when they got to France they were heavily fined for taking an unregistered boat into French waters. As a result they returned to England and would be seeking work while the slow process of getting the official documents carried on. They had decided to winter in England and I suggested that, since it was so close, they might try Joe Blagdon for some work in exchange for a mooring in Plymouth. They were a delightful couple who gave me hospitality aboard their 32ft. long keeled boat called 'Whiplash' and which was flying, rarely seen in Britain, the Portuguese ensign.

The following morning we all went ashore where the brothers split up, one to return to France to collect his own boat while the other stayed on Whiplash. I had a chance to wander round this lovely town which welcomed yachtsmen with all the facilities you could wish for. The town boasts a church with a tower clock that chimes the quarters as well as the hour. It reminded me of the old Grandmother clock I used to have at home: the chimes were very similar.

On returning to the boat with the older brother, he volunteered to go up my mast to see if he could find out why my navigation lights were still intermittent. I had, by now, replaced my missing by-colour on the pushpit but was still having trouble with my mast head anchor light. After considerable investigations at the top of a swaying mast he found out that the weld had broken inside the lamp housing. He attempted a temporary repair with tape and both the masthead navigation lights and the anchor light then worked. I was delighted, until I came to use them in the dark: he had put the cover on back to front so the only way the mast head nav. lights made sense was if I sailed backwards!

He would accept no reward apart from some whisky in his coffee, despite having very little English money. He was a man of simple dignity and spent some time explaining why he was sorry that Portugal was joining the common market. "They give us money, lots of money. But no one gives money for nothing! They buy our land, the wealthy Germans and French, and we cannot afford to compete!" I thought of the poor labouring man in Wales whose cottages were being priced beyond his means, bought up by wealthy industrialists in Manchester and Birmingham to use as holiday homes. The same was apparently happening in Portugal where the Escudo has so little value that whole farms could be bought for a song in the 'European Free Market'. The rich get rich and the poor get poorer. I passed over a couple of tins of food to them that I would be able to replace: they had been living off rice!

From Fowey I set sail for Mevagissey, entered the small and almost empty harbour and tied up against a vacant yacht. Well I only got as far as tying to their boat when the crew returned and said that they were moving out because the fishing fleet were due to return that night and they would be blocked in over the weekend. I certainly could not afford to lose any time so I cast off and left the lovely little harbour to sailed south- south west as far as Gorran Haven, a pretty 'fine weather' anchorage which I shared with two other boats. I imagine that it would not be so peaceful during the day as I could see several speedboats at anchor, but now, in the soft evening light it was a most desirable resting place.

After breakfast the next day I had a leisurely sail up to Falmouth, a delightful cruising ground with large stretches of well protected waters in the Carrick Roads (apart from Southerly Gales). As I turned into the Penrhyn river the waters were crowded with pleasure boats, assembled for the following day's race for which I had travelled so far, the 'Falmouth Classics', a race ostensibly for classic gaffers but now open to virtually any boat that cares to take part. I had intended to tie up to the jetty of the Green Bank Hotel which fronts the waterside and at which I had booked a room for June and myself, but as I saw it I realised that it might cope with something like the Royal Yacht! In my small boat it was clearly impossible: the walls were some 20ft high without ladders!

I had turned down the offer of free accommodation at the town quay - berths had been reserved for visiting yachts - so had to make my way towards Penrhyn and Falmouth marina which itself was filled to bursting point. They found a niche for me and after berthing I saw June and my crewman and his wife scrambling down the hillside towards the boats. They had seen me arrive from the balcony of the Hotel but, intent on my navigation I had not seen them waving to me.

For my very rare racing events a friend, Andrew Bailey who lives in Shropshire, sometimes joins me. He had traveled with June and his wife all the way from there to join me in the race. It was a very generous gesture and I much appreciated it as without his help it would have been almost impossible to take part in a full bloodied race.

I had been to the Hotel before and we were given a magnificent room overlooking the waterfront so that there was always plenty to see going on. The hotel was also the venue for the control center and reception area for the race so we were ideally placed for the weekend. That evening I met the race organisers in a huge marquee in the hotel grounds that had been erected for the event and was given my race mark, a blue and white strip of cloth with our entry number (which we were asked to show on our port shrouds) together with the following day's racing instructions. I had a short word with Robin Knox Johnson who would be presenting the prizes the following day. It was all very colourful and enjoyable.

On the Saturday morning Andrew and I extricated the boat from the Marina and motored out to join the 190 odd starters for the race. The girls had gone up to the castle in order to be able to see over the whole Carrick Roads and watch our progress. There were so many boats that they were going to have their time cut out to recognise us. We had some difficulty in finding the starting boat and when we did we found that we were in the middle of the first group about to start and had to turn against the stream of boats to get back behind the line. I was amused months later to see a photograph of JUNKETTE in the Practical Boat Owner Magazine trying to force her way through a lot of large Falmouth Quay punts and even larger working boats just about to start racing.

FALMOUTH CLASSICS RACE. 1990

There were so many boats in the race that the organisers had split us into six groups with six different courses to follow. As a result it was very confusing to try and find the course you were supposed to be taking in your group. The boat that thought he had won was informed at the prize giving that although he was first home he was disqualified for sailing the course in the reverse direction. It did not really matter as it was a fun event that was greatly enjoyed by all and the boats had prepared themselves in most curious ways. One boat from Penrhyn had painted his sails in Psychedelic colours that looked quite beautiful in the sun (it was a lovely, sunny day) and another was towing a model of his boat behind him. I'm afraid that like almost everyone else we got confused about the course and I suspect followed three different ones each time round!

Some of the boats had enormous bowsprits that stood out in front of them like huge lances and of course the inevitable happened. One boat 'speared' another, his bowsprit going between the mast and sail of a competitor and the following day we saw the poor victim leaving the harbour under engine, his masts now lowered and on the deck. The purpose of these long spars is an attempt to balance the sails since they carried very large mainsails, used to catch the lightest winds but which meant that without a lot of foresail it was impossible to hold the helm to weather in anything of a blow. The gaffer is a wonderful rig to sail downwind but is not so weatherly as a modern Bermudan rig with its long luff and tall mast. I am a 'gaffer' enthusiast: not only are they superb for cruising but they look so beautiful. However, with the large sail areas and heavy spars, they are a 'man's boat' and take some handling.

In these days of very strong and lightweight alloys developed for airframes it should be possible to develop a gaff rigged boat with all the advantages of the rig yet making them more weatherly. This is what I had attempted to do with JUNKETTE, which has a large Gaff rigged fully battened mainsail and a reefing genoa. Certainly while racing we held our own against much bigger boats: in fact this is why we went wrong, we were so intent on racing the larger work boats that we did not realise until too late that we were on the wrong course!

After the day's racing there was a 'pasty' dance in the marquee and a chance to meet other competitors. First the four of us went into the town for a meal and I watched a very hungry Andrew consume a 'bucket' of mussels, and I do mean a bucket! He must have eaten about 50 of the molluscs: not my favourite food, but they had no ill effect on him and he was as bright as a new pin the next morning. I'm afraid that I was so tired - I had no idea that single handing a boat over a long period could be so debilitating but perhaps it was the fact that having been on my own for so long I could not get used to so much company all at once - that I caved in and had an early night, which was not very friendly but I was incapable of doing anything but sleep. I did, though, attend the prize giving and accepted a cheque from the hands of Rodney Bews of the 'Likely Lads' who was giving the prizes for the Gig racing, of which he is a devotee. The cheque was from the Association of Falmouth Working Boats and from the Famouth 90 race organisers. It was much appreciated.

The next day the girls joined us aboard JUNKETTE and we joined in the 'Parade of Sail' - a wondrous line of boats all sailing towards St Mawes for a picnic on the beach. I regret that I was still 'shot' and stayed aboard while the others went ashore in 'the sweat'. I was not feeling in any way anti-social but I had found that after so long I just could not stand the crowds and was happier watching them have fun at a distance without any feeling of loneliness or irritation. I tried to analyse this at the time but found my mind drifting off to events of the past few weeks: I signally failed to feel responsible for my actions. Fortunately neither June or the others appeared to worry about me, which was fine. It is only now that I feel somewhat shamed by what I had done. I imagine that the people like Terry Waite and Terry Anderson would have similar feelings once they were released from almost solitary confinement.

While sitting on the boat I saw a helicopter come over, clumsy looking things, and it made me think of a story I had told at an Aircraft Factory which I had visited to talk about the work of the BBC. To end on a light note I told the story of the factory that had just unveiled it's latest creation, a fast fighter aircraft. It went through its test flights with flying colours until put into a power dive when the wings came off! There was consternation and much rethinking before a second prototype was built. This too failed in the same way. (In telling this, you drag it out a bit as with all shaggy dog stories). The M.D., after long discussions with design staff called the whole factory together to ask if anyone had any ideas. After several suggestions about metal fatigue and alloy formulations a small voice in the hall said *'Why don't you drill holes along the wing routes?'* There was a lot of laughter but no more ideas.

Back in his office the M.D., being a liberal minded man, decided to go along with the only idea suggested and they built a third plane with a series of holes drilled in the join between the wings and the fuselage. Eventually they did find a pilot willing to take the plane up and of course, you've guessed. It worked perfectly. However, no one would own up to the idea and it was weeks later when the M.D., while in the washroom talking about this to one of the engineers, said *'I wish I knew who thought of it.'*

The attendant turned round and said 'Ah, that was me, sir.'
' *You, what do you know about aircraft design?'* asked the M.D.
' *Well sir, I've worked here man and boy for thirty years and I've never known a piece of paper tear at the perforations.'*

It was dreams like these, thoughts of places I had visited, that went through my mind there in the warm sun off the beach at St. Mawes.

I broadcast a report of the events at Falmouth from my room to Radio Manchester on the Monday and then packed my belongings for a return to the boat. So far I had seen no one from Cancer Relief but after I left the Hotel for the Marina the local Secretary turned up but apparently the Marina, a mile away, was too far for her to come and see me so I saw no one in Cornwall at all. This was a pity as I had hoped to make some sort of arrangements for St. Ives or even Padstow, but it was not to be.

After farewells to June and crew I set off west again, passing the boats now in the second of the week long series of races. What a great event the Falmouth Classic is. The organisers deserve every support and encouragement. From Falmouth I had decided to try and anchor off Penzance, ready for my sail round Lands End. The seas were very lumpy and uncomfortable until I had rounded the Lizard peninsular and I was feeling rather miserable at being on my own again. (Are we not odd! Only the previous day I had wanted to be on my own and now I was missing the company). I looked to see if I could find the aerials at Goonhilly as many years ago I had written up the financial case to provide money for the technical equipment installed for the first ever cross Atlantic television program.

My writing that case had had an odd result,! Some weeks later I had received an invitation to attend the Head of Television Programs' address to senior staff before he left for a tour of Australia. As I was by no means senior staff I could not imagine why I had been invited. Then, during the speech he began to talk about the latest ideas in TV and I heard my words on his lips: he was using the body of the finance case I had written. This, from a past editor of the Times, was greatly appreciated, as was his way of thanking me.

Much later I was asked by the Professional Women's club of West Yorkshire to talk about Satellite communication in a little hall in Otley near Leeds. Behind me were a number of trestle tables all covered with sheets which I, mistakenly, thought to be hiding food! Not so. After my talk about satellite communication and the world service the sheets were removed to reveal hundreds of candles, each with a name flag of some town overseas, eg. Chicago; Perth: Hong Kong etc., all affiliated clubs world wide. Then, as the Chairwoman named each town in this, the 'Festival of Light', the appropriate candle was lit. It was very effective though I did find myself thinking about the fire storm of Cologne and wondering if the central candles would self ignite! But it was a fine display of the ancient form of lighting to follow a talk on the latest advances of TV and Radio. Professor Childs suggests that candles, in the form of moss floating on fat, were used 4000 years before Christ to illumine the caves of the Dordogne where the famous cave paintings can be seen.

There was, I'm afraid, too much mist to see anything on land two miles off and in any case I was concentrating on avoiding the dozens of fishing marker buoys. Both the South and North coasts of Cornwall are covered with lobster and crab lines and it is just too easy to pass too close and get one round the keel. This had happened as I approached Coverack and I had to sail in a complete circle to clear myself of it. I do not like using an engine on this coast for this reason as it is just too easy to get a warp round the prop, and if you tangle while sailing then you can usually sail out of trouble both for yourself and to the fisherman. It is, of course, much worse for the single hander and I used to think that if I got farther off the coasts I would be safe, but not so. In the Bristol Channel, for instance, fishing markers can be seen right up to the 12 mile mark, and beyond!

By early evening I was off St. Michaels mount. The harbour was almost empty and I would have liked to have gone in and wandered over the island as Libby Purves had done, but it was a drying harbour and I wanted to be away at half tide to reach Lands End as the flood began. I knew that I would have head winds until I rounded the Longships light, so instead, I anchored just outside the harbour close to a French boat and settled down for a quiet night and a chance to re-accustom myself to being on my own again.

The following morning, in slight drizzle I raised anchor and, in a very light breeze, sailed slowly towards Lands End. It took me two hours to reach the Runnelstone and a further hour to reach the Longships. The tide had now turned and I had some difficulty in not being swept down onto the Longship rocks in a fitful headwind and growing tide. As I worked my way past, ever tightening the sheets, the wind increased until eventually I was able to turn North East when the helm became more free. I then had a glorious sail, the sun coming out to greet me and the sea smoothed out magically as wind and tide agreed. I put the autohelm on and sat back to write a letter to my daughter back home. It was a lovely sail, but I had left it just a little too late and arrived at St. Ives about two and a half hours' after high water.

I should have anchored in the bay and waited until evening but tried to get in where the channel is deepest alongside the pier and went aground as I tried to turn to port towards the visitors moorings. There is an artificial sand bank across the mouth of the harbour, built to both provide more water for longer for the beaches and small craft and to reduce the pounding that moored craft suffer from the incoming swell as the tide drops. When it was first built about three years ago it was very good but the tide washes it away each year and when I arrived there was not much left. An alternative port of refuge is across the bay at Hayle but you do need guidance to get in and it is only accessible at about an hour either side of high water. I am told that Peter de Savory who intends to improve the facilities both for fishermen and for the pleasure boat industry has now purchased Hayle. There are so few harbours of safe refuge on this coast that he cannot do anything but good. St. Ives is really untenable in a North East gale.

St. Ives is an artists' colony and painters can be seen on every corner. It is a very 'touristy' sort of town with steeply cobbled narrow streets packed with curio shops. Out of season it is very attractive but packed with holiday makers as it was now in mid August, it was not so good. I would like to visit St Ives in May or early June. I did this once on my way to the Scillies many years ago and I found it really beautiful but later in the year, packed with sweating humanity all eating brightly coloured rock, shouting and playing transistor radios at full pitch.. it's not my idea of a great place to be.

After a pleasant day on the sands (I was in no one's way) I floated off at 8 pm. and picked up a mooring. The next day gales were forecast so I stayed put and enjoyed the amenities of St. Ives. On Thursday I motored out of the harbour at midday in gusty conditions and anchored in the bay as I would want to sail East at low tide the following morning. It was very 'rolly' out there and not very comfortable, and the forecasts were not particularly good but I had to be in Pembroke for a reception on August 22nd and that was only five days away. It was time I moved on.

St.Ives to Cardigan

I raised anchor at 8.30 am and set off for Padstow, some 30 miles away in a west southwest brisk breeze and, with three reefs in the main and only half a genoa, was making 5 knots in a very lumpy sea. I hated to think what it would have been like if the tide had not been with me: in that wind and in that sea it would have been horrible!! The glass had been falling slowly for 24 hours and it looked as though we were in for a blow as there was a depression moving in from Southern Ireland, headed for north east England

I could see no other boats as I sailed up the coast until I passed Newquay when I spotted two larger boats inside my line forging up the coast, presumably also headed for Padstow. I later learnt that one was an old friend of mine returning north from the Scillies, a boat from Conway called GALATEA. It was quite cold: a foretaste of autumn despite the sun which kept breaking through the clouds, a big change from that I had had just two days earlier, and I was glad to see Trevose Head a short distance off.

The seas became even more formidable round the head and the wind freshened still further to gale force with rain squalls so that I lowered the mainsail completely and reduced the headsail to a quarter before rounding the head for Padstow Bay. Once rounded there was a lee from the land and everything became a little more calm and I was able to sail briskly but without trouble, past the redoubtable 'doom bar' and into Padstow harbour, still on foresail alone, a great relief from the rain and squalls outside: conditions which did not deter the odd windsurfer in the bay, I had noted.

Padstow had changed since my last visit: it now had a 'locked' inner harbour for the smaller boats, put there last year to protect the harbour and town from storm flooding. It had been completed just in time to save the town from the furious storms that had plagued the whole of the western coasts of Britain in January and February of 1980. I had often travelled by road to South Wales in those months when my friend had been dying in hospital in Cardigan and I had seen the fury of the storms for myself. It was a time when the waters of the river Wye had risen so far that they were but a couple of feet from the main M40 motorway and all the fields to the south of that motorway completely flooded. A time when a small North Wales coastal town, Towyn was flooded to a depth of several feet and hundreds of people forced out of their homes. Without its new defences, Padstow would indeed have been in trouble.

The harbour is accessible for about two and a half hours either side of high water and I had arrived just a little after high water so all was well. Padstow has long been one of my favourite harbours ever since I first visited it with my daughter and a boat called SEA MINT many years ago and I always manage to meet someone I know there. This time it was to be GALATEA, on their way back from the Scillies. I had considered calling at the Scillies but the warning of unsettled weather had put me off and I had been proved right. Then, a little later a couple from Amble Marina in Northumberland came aboard. They were now staying at the caravan site and had seen me arrive at Amble some two months earlier.

The harbour master allowed me to put my collecting box on the harbour railings above the boat and by the Saturday night I had received a very good lot of donations and the box was very heavy. The town was very busy with holiday makers and I had the pleasure of hearing an excellent brass band and watching the antics of the 'raft racers' and 'greasy pole' climbers (where failure meant a fall into the water) and all the other pleasures of a Saturday regatta. I went aboard GALATEA for tea, only to discover that the skipper and I had been to the same school (he

some sixteen years after me) and that he was now head master of a sixth form college. His wife is also a teacher so they are able to have long summer holidays afloat. While aboard, the skipper told me an amusing tale of the sea: while approaching Rostoff for the first time on an unplanned visit, and therefore without detailed charts, he asked his friends to look out for any navigation lights.
"I see one, its green, over there on the port side"
He changed course to bring it to starboard. A few seconds later:
"Its red now"
Again he changed course. Then:
"Its green again".At the third change he had an idea.
"Is there an orange or yellow light?" he asked.
"Oh, yes, it keeps coming on between the reds and greens"!
He had been approaching Rostoff using the overhead street traffic lights as an entry beacon!

My complaint about Padstow in the past had been the state of the water: filthy with dropped paper and 'fish and chip' wrappers, but now all that was gone. Early each morning a man would go round the harbour in a small launch collecting all the debris from the water and leaving the place tidy. When there is no floating trash it seems that people are less likely to throw their dirty paper into the water: they look for a litter bin and there are plenty of those. All Padstow now requires is a police patrol for an hour and a half after closing time: some of the wilder spirits can be a bit of a menace to yachtsmen.

There is a great selection of good restaurants and cafes in the town and a bird and butterfly sanctuary not far away with excellent walks round the headland to see Doom Bar. This is quite a sight in an onshore gale when the spray rises to thirty feet or more, or you can walk across an old railway bridge to follow the disused line to Wadebridge.

In the town there is a large caravan park for visitors, fresh fish tanks and a good chandlery. A trip on the ferry across to Roc brings you to a yacht club very proud of its visitors book signed by Prince Charles, who gave the club the land on condition that they kept it tidy. Padstow is truly worth a visit, especially by boat, and much used by sailors from South Wales and Bristol. Now, with the locking facilities, it is possible to use the harbour as a staging post and to leave your boat at a mooring in the center of the pool, out of harms way, until it is time for you to continue your cruise. This is ideal for crews making to or from Scotland.

Despite adverse weather forecasts I now had only three full days before my reception in Pembroke so I felt that I had to leave, and rather than arrive at Milford Haven in the dark I decided on an overnight passage. The wind was from the North West and about force six when I dropped my moorings at 4.30pm. Out in the bay the only other people on the water were two sailing boards and a dredger. I became so interested in the antics of the board sailors that I did not watch my navigation and was soon in very shallow water off Trebetherwick. I managed to get off the sand by using the engine and was surprised to see that the dredger had begun to move towards me, obviously with the idea of pulling me off if necessary. I stopped the engine and gave an appreciative wave as I passed, steering well clear of the bar before turning more westerly to round the little island of Newland. I did not want to go inside the Island because in the past I had always found it full of pot marker buoys and in this wind there would be no room for mistakes. Because the wind was very fresh from the north west quadrant I had a problem to weather the Island and had reluctantly to use the engine again to get a point closer to the wind. Once again a ship stood by until I was clear, this time a large pleasure boat with a hundred or so people aboard. In the late afternoon it must have given them quite a thrill to see a small boat battling with quite steep seas attempting to sail round the small Island.

Eventually I escaped, stopped the engine and made my way out to sea in gradually worsening conditions as I lost the shelter of the land. I had four reefs in, and close hauled I was only managing three knots. The tide would be east going for another three hours so it was essential that I set as westerly a course as the wind would allow. Since the tides in the Bristol channel run very fast I had set up a way point on the Decca just off Milford Haven so that I could make adjustments for the tide. At night, Decca is not that reliable, but any sudden change, especially at the time of a tide change, would tell me what I needed to know. Needless to say I kept up my DR but that was most unreliable as my speed varied so greatly through the night.

It was a long, long night and with the jumping and jiving of the boat I felt as though I was riding a bucking bronco in some wild west fantasy movie where all the actors are slit eyed and gritty, in speech and appearance. It was how I felt, too! At one point my 'bronco' shied - I felt a change in the feeling of the boat. I could not put my finger on it at the time but I guess it must have been when the inward end of the boom broke. The sail was so deeply reefed that the lacing held the sail to the mast and only in daylight could I see that the shape looked strange. Also, the headsail was fuller than I intended but it was blowing too hard for me to shorten sail further without luffing into the wind and I did not feel like doing anything so unattractive in the dark and wet. The combined effect of both though, was that I could no longer sail as close to the wind as I had wished. Anyway, I was staying in the saddle of this particular 'bronco'.

By 3am. the gale had lessened and gone round a point west, but left behind a thoroughly lumpy and unpleasant sea through which JUNKETTE continued to thrash. I had the spray hood up and this was a real blessing. Without it I would have been thoroughly miserable, but even a small piece of canvas like this can be a blessing when flogging into a gale. For a long time around midnight I had seen a steady white light (steady is a relative term!) where no light should have been. It lasted almost an hour and I am not certain what it could have been though I assume it might have been a fishing boat. But on a night like this, which had been forecast? Obviously I wasn't the only fool.

I did manage to get a couple of cat naps below deck when the wind moderated in the early hours. The Autohelm kept the boat steadily on course despite the heavy seas and I was able to dose on and off for about three hours until the dawn began to show. A check on Decca and I made my final adjustment of easting. I was now 19 nautical miles from my way point bearing 011° and on my present heading and with increased speed through freeing off the sheets, the tide should do the rest. At 8.30am. I could see the chimneys of the oil terminal and knew I was on course.

A previous time I had been in these waters we had got wind against tide in a force seven and conditions had been horrible. I had June with me on her first - and last - cruise (at Neyland she hired a car to take her home) and when we reached Dale Roads, a Nicholson 36 had been knocked down twice and the skipper of a German motor sailer, crossing from Ireland, told me it was the worst sea conditions he had known in his life - and he was a master mariner! I was then sailing a 28ft Atlanta Viking and had found it 'difficult', but as much because of worry about June as anything since the boat, well reefed down, was taking care of herself. It needed a Conrad or Innes - or perhaps Miles Smeaton - to describe that day. Perhaps Homer's presumed blindness was why his storms at sea in the 'Oddysey' were as true to life as a plate of fluffed up mashed potato. His 'wine dark sea' sounds perfect, but for the rest.... The locals in Milford Haven have a much better description: they call it 'the washing machine'.

This time the conditions were good, high water and the last of the east going tide just an hour past - almost slack water - and wind about force five from west north west, perfect sailing weather. The only problem was that I was somewhat out of condition after a heavy night at the helm. Once clear of Dale Roads, I started the engine and headed up river against the tide towards the Marina at Neyland, past all the oil terminals in this huge inland waterway, almost as big as Carrick Roads but not so free to navigation of small boats because of the commercial traffic. At Neyland I moored JUNKETTE, and went ashore for a shower and a coffee before crashing out back in the cabin for a couple of hours after an eighteen hour passage. I didn't even stop to see what had happened to the sail until lunchtime when I discovered that the boom had fractured near the gooseneck and that the genoa roller reefing extrusion had broken about four foot above the deck, the top half being able to turn independant of the bottom. As a result, the reefed sail, under the pressure of wind during the gale had begun to unfurl the top half of the extrusion, tearing the luff of the sail in the process. I now had a foresail with a three foot tear in it and a useless boom. It looked as though my circumnavigation of Britain was to end prematurely!

It was at this time that I met another member of my association, Norman Silk, who kept his boat WOT'S WONG in the Marina. Norman had come to Hesketh to see me off and now here he was, in time to see me probably finish. He had finished his Kingfisher 20+ himself and it must have been one of the best finished boats I had ever seen, certainly the best in the Kingfisher range. He offered to take me the rounds to try and find some wood suitable for making into a new boom but I thought it very unlikely that I would find a seasoned length of Ash or Pitch Pine some 12 ft long. Neyland is another Camper and Nicholson yard and were giving me free berthing, so I decided to try 'Dale Sailing' who are also part of the set up and had their offices adjacent. The M.D. there, while being very helpful, explained that he had no spare labour - it was the middle of the holiday period and he had very full order books - but he did offer me free use of space in his workshops, the loan of tools and trestles, if I could find a suitable piece of material.

In the end, he it was who found me an old dinghy mast which I cut down to length and then adapted by plugging the end with the broken piece off the old boom and making a jury rig for the outer end. In the space of three hours I had a working boom again and was greatly thankful to Dale Sailing for their sensible help. Earlier, before I had met the Dale Sailing people, I had called Radio Manchester and warned them that I might have to call off my attempt and they had asked how much it would cost to put right. I frightened them by suggesting that a new manufactured boom could cost a couple of hundred pounds: I think the Station Manager was wondering if the station could have helped me just to keep the boat on the go and keep the story running:

apparently it was making compulsive listening. As it was, he was saved any embarrassment by my jury arrangements.

The sail loft which lies next to the Marina, COPP SAILS, had made my new sails and before making a new boom I had considered going to them and asking either to borrow a mainsail that I could use loose footed or alternatively have mine modified into a small, loose footed bermudan (triangular) sail. Unfortunately they had just that week gone bankrupt and the offices were all closed up. Under the circumstances, it was just as well as I did not butcher my sail apart from wearing some holes in it! After I got home I was delighted to hear that COPPS had been baled out and were back in business: excellent sail makers they were, too.

The snag with the new boom was that the track which takes the foot of the sail was too narrow to take my bolt rope (the rope sewn into the bottom of the sail which fits in a track like a curtain). As a result, the only way I could anchor the sail to the boom was to tie it in through the drain holes above the second batten. This worked perfectly well, but the sail, in working under wind pressure, rubbed against the ties and by the time I got home I had several small holes in my new mainsail! To overcome the genoa problem I would have to sail with a full genoa whenever possible, or without a foresail if the wind was too great. That would mean all the problems of weather helm again, but at least it would keep me mobile for the last three hundred miles.

I thought about this: it had been my intention to sail across to Ireland and up the coast to Belfast and then across to finish at Ramsey. I would not be able to manage much more than 3 or 4 knots with the jury rig and there were a string of depressions passing over, which meant possible gales. I decided that to go to Ireland would be asking to much of the rig and instead re-planned to sail to Holyhead (if southerly gales, and if North Westerlies then through the Menai Straits) and on to Ramsey, that being quite enough in the conditions. Whatever else, I had to call at Cardigan before I went any further: that was my last essential port of call before the finish on the Isle of Man.

I had called at the Milford Haven Yacht club, expecting someone to tell me about the reception, but the first night of my stay no one said anything. I thought that perhaps they were trying to keep the arrangements secret from me as a surprise but when, on the next night, I had still heard nothing - although I knew that people were coming down from Manchester to meet me - I became worried in case I had the wrong date. I waited until 8pm. and was just about to leave the boat when they called me from the Marina office to say I was being called on R/T. It was the Pembroke Yacht Club from across the water: I had mixed up the two clubs, never having been to the other club in my life.

A car came round to pick me up and on reaching the Pembroke Yacht Club _ found a large crowd of people waiting for me including the area organiser of Cancer Relief from Manchester with his wife. Apparently the local secretary of the Cancer Relief organisation was a member of the Pembroke club and had made the arrangements there for obvious reasons. It was a super evening and I was made very welcome and to feel that I had achieved something worthwhile. I had to admit that I had enjoyed myself enormously during the cruise and that it had never seemed like hard work, much more like an indulgence, which indeed is what I think it has been. The Pembroke club was formed during the second world war when Sea Planes were made and launched from Pembroke. The club ensign (they gave me one of their badges which now resides on the wall of my club) shows a seaplane in flight. The club shares many of its events with its sister club at Milford Haven and has a strong racing section. Like so many Yacht Clubs that I visited on my journeys, they were wonderfully supportive and gave me a slap up meal. All yacht clubs work on the principle of shared facilities: wherever you are, if you belong to a club then any other club affiliated to the RYA will give you free use of their facilities such as showers, bar etc. and it is this aspect of yachting that can be so rewarding.

The next day I dropped my moorings, again with thanks to C. & N. for their hospitality and sailed down river to Dale where

I anchored for the night, ready for a quick getaway to Fishguard. The following morning I had agreed to do a broadcast from the boat as I sailed across St. Brides Bay, but when I woke it was to find a fog so thick that I could not see the next moored boat although it was only yards away. I made my broadcast, but from my mooring and said I hoped to be on my way the following day. I prophesied that I would be finishing in Ramsey around the first weekend in September, a dangerous supposition as it turned out. The rest of the day was spent resting with a quick trip ashore to visit the ever welcoming club in Dale in the evening. ('Why haven't you brought your box?' they asked).

The next morning, while still foggy, was not as bad and seemed to be lifting so I set sail and on a light wind left Dale roads heading for Jack Sound. The winds were so light that I decided to cross St. Brides Bay via Jack Sound rather than go via Broad Sound: it would save time and the tides were right to go through. Jack Sound can be very daunting for the sailor as the tides are very fast indeed and the sound narrow. As it was I had an uneventful passage with the mist just touching the distant hill tops. Once through the sound and headed north west, still in a very light breeze I ghosted along with full genoa and all the main I could manage, quite happy until I suddenly spotted one of the yellow target buoys but yards from the boat. The fog had returned and I had not even noticed. I checked my Decca position and found that I was much closer to Ramsey Island than I had thought: the tide was really under me. I considered turning North for Solva but with that tide and in that fog I knew I would have difficulty in finding it. About this time there was a call from another yacht to any boat in the vicinity of Ramsey asking for conditions. I replied and advised Solva but that I was going to try going south of the Island. I thought that to tackle the sound itself in that fog would be asking for real trouble.

I started the engine and wound in the genoa and sheeted the main in hard: I wanted to have control and the ability to change direction in a hurry. Under minimum revs. I motored forward in thick fog, taking one last check on Decca when I had reckoned I had some three miles to go. According to the Decca co-ordinates I was less than a mile off. The tide was really carrying me. Suddenly, a few yards off the starboard bow I saw a rock and pushed the tiller over hard to swing to port. I held the heading for about a minute before turning west again. It was thick fog and apart from the engine I could hear nothing, no rushing water or breakers. I had a quick glance at the chart. I had come the other way in clear weather and if I was just west of Ramsey, not more than 200 yards from the shore I should be alright for a little. Unfortunately, I couldn't see the shoreline and just had to assume it was there! On the other side, my left hand and further west, were the cluster of rocks and islets known by the collective title of 'The Bishops and Clerks'. I hoped that they remained on my left hand and out of my life, as indeed they had been and now was not the time to change a life long habit!

There was the island on my right and rocks on my left. I inched a little more to Starboard, eyes darting from left to right, my hair turning more grey by the minute. Suddenly I saw broken water ahead of me: right or left, port or starboard? I found I even had a moment to glance at the compass before I decided to turn to Starboard. If I was going to hit a rock I'd rather it was on the island than in the sea. As soon as I could see clear water again I turned north, hoping that I was travelling parallel with the island shore. I still could not see the island and could not, in that tide, go below to read the Decca set. The sea around me was an unbroken grey swell that merged with the fog just yards from the boat. It was eerie rather than frightening but all my senses were on full alert, all leave cancelled.

After about another six minutes and seeing nothing but fog, I came out of gear, put the autohelm on and went below for a Decca readout. According to the co-ordinates I was now just north west of the Island and as if to assure me the sea became more disturbed. Where the tides meet the water is always broken by heavy overfalls and I was pretty certain that this was where I now was. I came into gear, disconnected 'George' and turned to starboard, still in thick fog, and at minimum revs headed to where

I thought the mainland cliffs should be but, not yet trusting the Decca position, looking out for the Island shore line. I also had to look out for an outlier, a small islet off the north coast of the island. Miraculously the cliffs appeared as the fog thinned a little and I was able to see that I was about a quarter mile off and that I had passed one of the most dangerous sea passages in Britain without seeing anything. I reported my safe transit to the coast-guard at Milford Haven and motored on, slowly beginning to realise how lucky I had been.

I have never had a more frightening time than had just happened and I found myself trembling now that it was over. At the time I had been too intent on the helm to react physically but now the reaction set in and I felt weak. I desperately needed a drink but I was too close to the cliffs, still in fog and still in too dangerous water to leave the helm so had to make do with a boiled sweet. I cursed myself for not having made a thermos of coffee: boy, what I would have given for a hot drink. It is at times like this that sailing alone is the most trying. To have had a second pair of eyes watching through the fog would have helped and to have someone now to take over while I made a hot drink would have been wonderful.

It was now 11am and I stopped the engine, loosed the mainsheet and let out the full genoa to run goosewinged in the very light following wind as we crept North. The fog slowly lifted, to be replaced by a thin mist with visibility increased to about a mile. I was able, at midday, to use the autohelm and go below for a well deserved gin and tonic and check my Decca co-ordinates. My DR had gone to pot in the fog with the many course alterations, but using my decca reading as a basis I started again. It was at this time that, checking Decca against my DR I discovered that the simple Decca set I was using which scanned only two channels was giving a strange course like a drunken man: two steps forward and one step back. Over a period of thirty minutes it would agree with my direct reckoning, but if taken in five minute intervals I could have been more than half a mile out. I realised how lucky I had been about getting past Ramsey!

A little later I spotted an inflateable dinghy with about seven people onboard all waving frantically. I sailed over, to discover that their engine had failed and that they were unable to paddle against the tide. In fact they were unable to paddle, period! Not one person on board seemed to know how to use a paddle, so used had they become to having an engine. They were divers, about half being women, but had remained very calm in their emergency. I just wished, for their sake, that they had carried a wing engine and had learnt to use a paddle. It was a big inflateable but later the skipper said there had been no room with all their diving gear for a spare engine. He was wrong and should have made room, those people with him had their lives in his hands.

I took them in tow and at slow speed took them to Abercastle which was their base, about a mile away. It was after I released them, some 100 yards off shore that I realised that they were having difficulty in paddling that short distance to shore: they kept going in circles. I almost returned to tow them right in but instead I turned back on course: now the tide would shortly be against me and as a result I would have a long slow sail against the tide from Strumble Head to Fishguard. Three years earlier I had found myself sailing backwards on that very coast, but then my rig had not been as efficient.

Once in Fishguard I sailed up to the old harbour and anchored in the bay, going ashore for some bread and milk. That evening I called in at the Yacht Club and for the first and only time got the cold shoulder. I asked if I could put my collecting box on the bar but was told that they only allowed collections for the RNLI. No one came to talk to me but as I was about to leave the skipper of the diving party I had towed to Abercastle came into the club and gave me a donation of ten pounds for the trouble I had taken. We had a short chat and a drink together before leaving that inhospitable club. Very much later I received apologies from one of the members who made a personal donation to the cause but it had left a sour taste in my mouth which, I'm afraid, remains.

The following morning I left for Cardigan, much against the advice from a sailor on the shore: "Oh, you don't want to go there! You'll surely be neaped." He was soon to be proved right! I had a fine sail up the coast and at 11 am was off Cameas Head. I called the auxilliary coast guard and was answered by Gareth Williams, Peter's cousin and mooring officer who came out to meet me as I slowly sailed into the bay past Cardigan Island. After pausing for photographs, later to appear in the local paper, Gareth's launch led me into the little bay at Patch, off the Teify Boat Club where a mooring buoy awaited me.

Peter had been very proud of his cousin and had long promised me 'Gareth will find you a mooring when you come to Cardigan, no problem'. The two of them were closer in age than his own brother and Gareth had bought a sailing boat which he had been looking forward to sailing with Peter when Peter retired. I saw it, laid up in the club house yard looking rather woe begone. Gareth had not had the heart to launch it after Peter had died. Gareth Williams had won Peter's respect and love over the years, and was to prove his worth when he went down the cliffs near Cameas Head to save a man's life as the rising tide threatened to cut them both off. For this he was given an award by the RNLI.

Once ashore I was taken to the club house where the commodore, Ron Bell, greeted me and introduced me to the Sunday morning lunch time crowd. There was a whip round with two of my collecting boxes and in a period of only twenty minutes over £85 was collected. These wonderfully warm hearted people, once told of my connection with Peter Williams, had responded magnificently and although I am not a religious person I couldn't help hoping that in some way, if there was a future life, Peter would see their response. This moment made the whole journey more than worthwhile.

Gareth then took me out of Cardigan in his car to his sister's house where I was to stay until Tuesday when I would again be on my way. Dawn and John Steven live a short way outside Cardigan where they had turned their lovely Victorian manse over for Peter's wake. At that time they had promised to put me up if I visited the town by boat and promised me a bath. They live on a hundred acre estate with the fine house some quarter mile up a private road, hidden by trees and pasture. Dawn was Peter's cousin but he had only spoken of her once, when I had met her for the first time at his bedside in hospital. I think he was in awe of her: her life stile was so different from his. They only met once a year, at Christmas time although only living about three miles apart, so unlike my own cousins whom I would see almost weekly and who lived a similar distance from me. But John, Dawn's wife, was wealthy and that can be the biggest barrier of all.

I liked both John and Dawn and felt very much at home with them. The day I arrived they had been invited to a private dinner party by friends a short distance away but assured me I would be welcome, and so I was as I joined about thirty people, sitting round a huge refectory table at a lovely house in the country. I cannot now remember the reason for the party: someone's fortieth or fiftieth birthday (probably the latter), but it was all very relaxed and enjoyable, very like the parties I had had at home before I retired.

John Steven was (and is) a remarkable man. In his younger days he was a keen sportsman, shooting, fishing, squash and badminton etc. He had the funds to indulge himself but worked hard at his given hobbies of farming (he would call it his profession) and cabinet making, his real vocation. He enjoyed things mechanical and would relish the battle between himself and nature in levelling a field with a JCB or ploughing an impossible incline. Driving his 4 wheel buggy up marshy tracks impossible to walk on and cutting up a three hundred year old Ash tree blown down in the gales, armed with a petrol driven chain saw. To finish it off in planks, again with a chain saw using a hurdle to hold the trunk he was sawing, and most of this single handed.

This may sound the energetic work of a typical countryman, but when I tell you he was still doing all this, and building magnificent welsh dressers while suffering from Parkinson's disease you will understand when I say he is a remarkable man. The disease has left him with limited movement of his hands, particularly his left so his handling of tools like chisels and planes is all the more remarkable. There are times when he feels particularly low, and on one of these occasions he asked if I would like to go with him to visit a friend. It turned out that his friend was even worse off than him, a young lady to whom he had taught squash in the past but was now in a wheel chair because, after the birth of her son she had developed M.S. and now, eight years later, could only move the upper part of her body. It was wonderful to watch them together, chaffing each other while she held a tennis ball in her hand and spent the whole time rhythmically squeezing it so that she could try and maintain some movement in her fingers. A visit to Karen was John's therapy: someone worse off than himself.

When I returned to the boat on Tuesday, having made my adieus to the Steven's and been driven down by John I found JUNKETTE high and dry: at high water the keels were not even covered. A quick check of the tide tables showed that I would not be likely to float off until the following Saturday and although I was quite happy to stay aboard, John insisted that I stay with them. While staying with the family I did what I could to earn my keep by doing repairs and helping John in the workshops at the back of the house, where among other things he was making a new face for an old carriage clock. The work was finicky and small and he was having difficulty so I did some of the machining for him on the router.

One day, while chatting about war time days, I mentioned the fact that I liked a glass of wine and had found an Inn in Ringwood where I had been able to buy a bottle of Chateau Latour 1928 for 30/- or £1.50 in decimal coinage. John then took me to see his cellar: a few bottles under a bench in his workshop and there were a couple of bottles of Latour 1955, all that he had left of a case he had put down some thirty odd years ago. Lovingly he took a bottle out into the house and that night we drank to the past in the rich claret. He gave me the cork and the label to keep, a memory of a very happy time. I know one should not count the cost of friendship but I was very touched that he would open a bottle worth at least £100 for me to provide an experience I could never afford.

On another occasion John invited me to go with him on a little fishing expedition. We left after an early dinner and drove about twenty miles to a trout stream, the 'Cothi', where he rented a stretch. We left the car by a church and, carrying a keep net, I joined him to watch him cast for trout for about thirty minutes without success. 'Come on' he says and we re-embarked to drive a little further up the river to try again, but not for long.

"Come on" says John. "The best spot is just a little further up, but we have to take the car".

We drove across a field, through a farm yard where he blew his horn ('let them know I'm here', he said) and up to a hedge. It was now about 9pm and beginning to get dark. He went through the gate and began to dash....I can think of no better word for it: like a thirsty dog scenting water. He ambled across that field like an ungainly bull sighting a cow on heat, making for a low hedge on the far side. I hurried to join him, only to find a fifteen foot bank down to the stream the other side of the hedge.

Nothing daunted, John started down, the fingers of his left hand curled into a fist and used as a walking aid as he clambered down through thickets of brushwood and thorn. I followed cautiously, expecting at any moment to have to dash down to rescue him, but he made it to the bottom, almost trembling with delight at the thought of the fishing to come. I have seen a friends' dog look like this when she said 'Walkies'! Issac Walton would have felt at home with John Steven.

We had reached a pool overhung with trees and a slight shoal leading into deeper water with a small weir about thirty yards away. It was dusk and very quiet: you could almost hear the fishes breath: you could certainly hear them jumping after the late evening flies. John began casting, first one way and then another.

I am not a fisherman but it did seem to me that he was recovering his line very fast.

"*You have to reel in quickly because the water is fast running here*" he said. It was getting very dark and after about twenty minutes he said we had better pack it in. I could hear the fish jumping and pointed this out.

"*Go on, have another go, over there*" I said. "*We might as well make the trip worth while!*" I could'nt bear the thought of his dejection after working so hard to get to the stream, and there were fish there. So we stayed for another hour, but without success. Then began the hard trail back. I had asked John if he had brought a torch but I think he thought it would have scented of poaching: he hadn't. Anyway, a little thought would have made me realise that he could not have managed one, what with everything else he had to carry. It was now 11pm. and every foot or so I had to use my lighter for John to see to disentangle his line from the overhanging branches. I was fearful of his falling in the dark, wondering how on earth I'd get him back because he was no light weight, but his indomitable spirit pushed him on as he went, apelike on clenched hands, shuffling slowly up the bank, his rod held in the crook of his elbow or under his arm.

It took us an hour to climb that fifteen to twenty foot bank and at the top I was exhausted, but back at the car there was a thermos and some sandwiches. We got back home about 1.30 am and I was ready for my bed. Two days later John asked if I wanted to go fishing again.

"*John, I'm going round Britain once and I don't want to do it again. I've been fishing with you once and I certainly don't want to do that again, and certainly not in the dark, thank you*". I said, trying to smile but feeling I was letting him down. I wanted to dissuade him from what had seemed to me a perilous occupation.

He didn't seem offended and instead began to show me part of his stamp collection, but the next morning he was away -'gone fishin'. By 5pm I think both Dawn and I had become a bit worried and Dawn was about to ring the farm when a victorious John appeared, bearing a fish.

"*Not what I wanted really, it's a Pike, but at least the trout will be back again*" and he held up a two pound pike which he reckoned had been keeping the trout and salmon at bay. He gave the fish to a neighbour who was most appreciative: not one of us fancied eating it.

I was curious to know how he had got back up the bank with the fish to carry as well as all his gear but he explained that there were some iron ladders further up the stream and he had waded up to them. The sheer tenacity of the man bewildered me. When his hands shook too much to do any more work on the dresser he was making he would say: *"Come on, lets go see if the bank is holding over the water meadow"* and lead me a half mile walk to the water meadows where he had built a retaining bank to hold up the stream and where there was a quarry, another of his endeavours. Once, when his hands were not good we went to the quarry and hacked at sand stone slabs with chisels and an iron bolster before filling the buggy with several hundredweight of stone which he then drove up to the house before using them to build a dry stone wall to surround a new bed for his winter plants. He just never stopped and Dawn was as bad: she was always dashing about to committee meetings etc. She was well known in the area and had once done me a very good turn.

When I had been visiting Peter at Cardigan during his final illness I was booked for parking on the main road although there were no yellow lines or other indication (the hospital car park being full as the hospital was undergoing alterations). I had appealed but the local Superintendent said that my appeal had been turned down so I paid up, some £25. I mentioned this to Dawn, saying it was a poor thing if, having driven all the way down from Manchester I should face the additional cost of a fine when many other cars had been parked where I was. A short time later I got a letter from Cardigan with a cheque for £25: my case had been reconsidered! Dawn had spoken to the Superintendent, it seemed.

While I was in Cardigan one of my first calls was to the graveside of my friend Peter. As I have said, I was at his funeral service and had seen him interred but when I went to find the grave there was no sign of it. I returned to Dawn, who was waiting in the car and asked for advice. She came back with me and found the grave of Peter's father where, apparently, his remains had been moved as his mother had died shortly after him and the three bodies were placed in the same piece of hallowed ground. Unfortunately, even months later, there was no headstone to record the fact. Dawn left me to pay my last respects and for a few moments I thought of that wonderful man who had made life such a joy for so many people. His spirit was very much abroad at that moment.

Saturday finally came and heavy hearted I said good bye to mine hosts and returned to the boat. Watching John's stumbling walk back to his car brought tears to my eyes: they were wonderful people whom I hoped I would have a chance to meet again. But now I was fully occupied preparing the boat for 'lift off'. Some five minutes before high water at around 6pm I felt the boat shudder and using the engine I forced my way over the sand into the deeper channel and began to thread my way out of Patch, the place where I had got a mooring. Once round the promontory of land where the caravans lay I was not sure of the channel. Gareth had promised to see me out but he was no where in sight and gingerly I cast about for the deep water. I wasn't quite far enough North and grounded but with the engine in reverse and using a long oar I managed to push myself off the sands and found the channel again. At this moment Gareth arrived with Peter's brother Alun and his son and pointed me in the right direction. There are no withies or other navigation marks and so unless you have local knowledge of the channel you are going to be in difficulty.

I waved a goodbye to Gareth, raised the sails and stopped the engine, heading for far off Bardsey. As the evening closed in I watched Cardigan Bay proper drop behind me, ever smaller. When I turned round I saw, for the first time in my life, the famous 'Sun Dogs', a kind of multiple image of the sun in the sky caused by refraction in the moist atmosphere over the water: the conditions similar to those required to produce a rainbow.. This time there were three suns, each throwing a line of light across the water: a larger one in the centre and two smaller, but just as intense, one each side. A few moments later the romance of the scene was further added to when a school of Dolphins played alongside for a short time.

Cardigan to Anglesey: Journey's End

When I went below at about 8pm I had a shock: there was about a foot of water on the cabin sole. I used a bucket and then the bilge pump to clear it and waited anxiously to see if it came again and how quickly. There was no obvious leak that I could detect and for the next few hours I kept collecting a little water, about a half gallon an hour. It wasn't a dangerous amount of water but the big worry was where it was coming from: might it get worse.. .much worse. While worrying about my own condition I heard Milford Haven Coast Guard report a red flare seen at Tenby and a few minutes later Holyhead Coast Guard report a red flare at Rhoscolwyn. It was the season for flares. I just hoped I wouldn't be needing to send one.

Just before midnight I had an exercise in light recognition and believed, from the multiplicity of lights on my Port side that I was passing a large vessel towing something equally large. They were about a mile off and when past I saw the lead ship signalling 'D' by white light, meaning 'keep clear of me'. Shortly afterwards I saw the loom of Bardsey light: I was well on my way towards Porthdinlleyn.

Crossing Cardigan Bay I saw Jock McCleod's boat RON GLAS half a mile off my port beam but I couldn't raise him on R/T: I gather Jock often does not listen on R/T outside the silence periods. Jock has sailed his junk rigged Schooner across the

Atlantic twice single handed and had a very fast sail to Newfoundland from Oban in 1982, returning the same year after a visit to Rhode Island. He designed the rig himself on an Angus Primrose polyester sheathed cold molded hull, some 47ft long with a draft of 6.5ft and a sail area of 810 sq.ft., both sails totally controlled from the central control position. I had been invited aboard when we were both anchored in Plockton one year and it was like boarding a U Boat: you went down vertical steps into the cabin. Inside everything had been arranged so that it was possible to sail the boat from below, safe from wind and weather. Jock has written (with Blondie Hasler) the definitive book on the westernised Junk rig, a book which sadly did not see the booksellers shelves until after Blondie's death.

  Seeing RON GLAS induced a fit of nostalgia which had a very strange outcome. First I tried to remember when I had last seen Jock and then began to work backwards, recalling various cruises. Suddenly I realised that I was remembering vividly a cruise that could never have happened! The places I remembered didn't exist and yet there they were, clear in my mind. Desperately I tried to think of clues. I had been awake all night and I thought I was hallucinating again, but it was all so clear. I remembered being in a more or less disused lock from which, in summer I locked out into a river and a lake with several Islands. The family were with me so it could not have been the Broads. I have never kept a boat at Glasson, so where could it be. I had no answer by the time I reached my next port but several days later I began to realise what it must have been. By dint of isolating certain elements (e.g. the presence of the children), I was able to date this supposed cruise to the late 70's. It was before I had bought JUNKETTE and then I knew. I was recalling dreams that I must have had either under the anaesthetic during surgery or when I was under the influence of Pethidone afterwards (I still remember some highly psychedelic moments of that time) and these dreams had the feeling of reality, even this long time afterwards. It was doubtless this internal mechanism that prompted me to take up sailing seriously when I thought I had not long to live.

The subconscious mind works continuously and comes into its own when left free from conscious prompting. How else can a musician remember a complete concerto without the music, how can an actor remember a long soliloquy? As soon as you begin to say 'what comes next' you are lost. Even as I write these memoirs, partly culled from my daily jotting during the cruise, my memory is being jogged, as it was then, with things I could barely remember in the normal course of events. The most vivid memories came when I was very tired, like recalling the Sonnets off Northumberland, or recalling the history of the Suffolk seaports as I approached Southwold. Sailing gives you the perfect opportunity to commune with the past. I've heard it called 'communing with nature' but the nature is ourselves, the words we've read and thought we'd forgotten, the people we've met long ago, the faces of the sky, the feel of the wind: its all past experience.

At 6am. I passed Bardsey, glad to note that the ingress of water was now very little and slowly sailed up the coast, the tide against me as usual when I sail up from the south until I reached the haven of Porthdinlleyn where I anchored at 9am. not far from another friend of mine in his Moody called HALVIC, doubtless returning from his annual junket to Brittany. Another friend had passed me with his family when I had cleared Ramsey Sound and he too was returning from Brittany. There is quite a traffic of boats to the North French coast every summer from Wales. Porthdinlleyn (known to sailors as PY), a little hamlet below the cliffs a mile south west of Morfa Nefyn and is a perfectly safe harbour in all winds except those from the North through North East, when it is subject to swell and can give a very rolly berth. There is plenty of room for a bilge keeler to take to the beach in front of the single pub, the Ty Coch Inn. There is a life boat station and an auxiliary coast guard station manned in the summer months. It is a very popular anchorage for sailors from Anglesey and Ireland, and is a natural stopping place to await the right conditions for crossing Caernarfon Bar. In the warm evenings you can walk at the foot of the cliffs and find countless golf balls delivered by overzealous golfers from the fairways above. Nine holes on that course have cost me many dozens of golf balls in the past: I always gave up trying the tenth!

After four hours sleep I raised anchor and went with the flooding tide out of the harbour. The midday forecast was a bad one, the wind was rising and the glass falling with westerly gales forecast. Although the wind was South Westerly I knew it would swing to the North as the depression passed over: should I go on to Holyhead as planned? There was unexplained water getting into the boat, a jury boom which would not stand up to a gale and a broken genoa which was useless in anything over force four. I decided to head for the straits and seek an anchorage at Aber Menai while I thought what to do for the best. It was a Sunday but when I had crossed the bar (quite uncomfortable for a short time in the strong onshore winds) I found Aber Menai, the mecca of weekend yachtsmen from the area, completely deserted. In view of the forecast this was not surprising but I reckoned on having 24 hours before the full fury of the depression passed over me and the wind go Northerly. Until then I would be safe.

I anchored in the early evening and after an early meal sat in the cockpit to try and decide what to do. I felt shattered: I had only had three hours sleep in the last 36 hours and was worried sick about the rig. I knew I could reach Ramsey under engine, but what would that prove? I was trying to sail round Britain and had only used the engine when there was no wind. I had not, for instance, bought any diesel since leaving Portsmouth as from then on I had usually had good winds, unlike the excess motoring I had had to do in Scotland during the high pressure period of the glorious summer just past.

I had a gin and tonic but found myself shivering violently and threw it overboard, to be replaced by hot sweet tea. I realised that I was close to a breakdown and as I drank the tea the futility of going on drowned me with self pity and I was soon crying like a baby. How was I going to face anyone if I didn't complete the circle? What was I going to say? I was in the depth of despair. I was in home waters, and looking back now, I realise that this had a lot to do with my decision. If, after having left Bardsey I had made for Holyhead there is little doubt I would have gone on to finish, but the lure of my own mooring, of blessed sleep without further strain was just too much to resist.

When I woke in the morning the glass was still falling, but more slowly: the centre of the depression was close by. I raised anchor, let go the genoa and sailed down past Caernarfon to reach the Swellies at Bangor and shoot the bridges an hour before high water slack: I had the tide with me almost up to Beaumaris. I picked up my mooring in Beaumaris Bay at midday, having completed 2420 miles.

I was about 80 miles short of my goal and the closing of the loop. The distance had virtually been covered by my trip out to Ramsey from Hesketh Bank, some 74 miles, but I realised that I was trying to justify myself for giving up. Despondently I took the dinghy and went to the club house. Imagine my feelings when I saw a large blackboard with the map of the British isles on it and marked with all the places I had visited, with the post cards I had sent pinned all round the outside. Luckily there was no one there because I again broke down and cried. For a moment I considered rowing back to the boat and setting off under engine for Ramsey but then our secretary, who lives in Beaumaris, came into the club house. She had seen JUNKETTE on the mooring in front of her house and had come round to find me.

I told her of my troubles and that I didn't think I could go on. I needed a shoulder to cry on, someone to tell me 'you've done enough'. Brenda did more than that: she actually made me think that I had done rather well and my last thoughts of pegging on somehow died there and then.

I phoned June and asked her to tell everyone, including the commodore of the Yacht Club in Ramsey who was expecting me. I knew I was in no fit state to speak to anyone. I told her I just wanted to wind down quietly and would like to come home but she said she would not be free to collect me until after the week end. "Did I mind?"

I was actually glad to be able to relax and pick up the threads. Brenda asked me if I would be there at the week end. She said that they had tried to find out where I was the previous weekend but that Holyhead coast guard didn't know. Apparently the club had been planning to sail out and meet me on my supposed return from Ramsey. If I had not been neaped in Cardigan that's probably what would have happened: I would have left Wales on the Tuesday, sailed for Ireland and been in Belfast by Thursday, Ramsey on Friday and sailing home on Sunday. But...'the best laid plans of mice and men gang aft a'gley', don't they Mister Burns?

While resting on my mooring I found time to investigate the water leak and found that it had been fresh water. Under the wardrobe locker on JUNKETTE is a covered hatch under which can be found the echo sounder head and, if fitted, a log. This space had filled with rain water while I was in Cardigan when we had one or two heavy downpours, and possibly because of the way the boat lay in a sand trough while neaped, the water had run in through the cabin ventilator. It had then escaped between the deckhead and inner lining to drain down the inside of the hull to this locker. When the boat rolled at sea the water would escape through a small hole in the bulkhead which carried the echo sounder cable to the readout, and the water would then escape into the cabin. My worries about a hull leak had been entirely unfounded and the integrity of that immensely strong hull had been maintained through thick and thin.

On Saturday June arrived with a mass of post and suddenly the clubhouse was full of members. Unknown to me there had been frantic phone calls all over the NorthWest and they all came for an impromptu party which was truly moving. Members had sponsored me for so much a mile, pushed hard by friends like David Swinton and others who had meticulously kept the record of my travels up to date and had caught all sorts of members on their visits to the club house, twisting their arms for support. In the end, members of my club gave more than £800 to Cancer relief and I was told that the final figure for contributions throughout the country amounted to about £5000.

My thoughts about the rig may interest some sailors. It is very efficient and allows me to sail very close winded, but there is a lot of sail to handle, nearly 500 sq.ft., which is a lot for a 26ft boat (actually 30ft. with the new bowsprit). The reefing arrangements require rethinking and ideally slab reefing would be the most sensible arrangement with control lines returned to the cockpit. The angle of the lazy jacks is too great so that it is easy for the gaff to become tangled up with them, and the wooden boom was not man enough for the strain of several tons weight of wind with full sail up.

The sails, made by Copp, were very good indeed and well made: the fact that they were showing signs of wear was solely due to my misuse of them due failure of the spars. The hull had proved wonderfully sound and cut through the water with pleasing efficiency and with very little noise, even in the worst of conditions, probably due to the fact that it is double lined throughout, a factor which adds to the weight but also to the stability. The ancilliary gear had generally proved very good with top marks going to the Simpson Lawrence Delta Anchor and to the Plastimo Olympic compass. Decca had served its turn and earned its place on the boat as had the VHF and my trusty Davis Mk.20 sextant, a gift from my colleagues on retirement. The Autohelm finally proved its worth after initial problems. It had worked non stop all the way round from Stonehaven on the north east coast of Scotland, but the new Stowe log was a failure because of short battery life and poor log readout (now a liquid crystal instead of the former mechanical readout). The little Dingo dinghy was good enough for one man, but seriously overloaded with two, and 'Oh so heavy to lift' on and off the deck. It also suffered from a very weak wooden seat that broke early on in my travels. All in all, the boat and its gear had served me well with the only serious failures being the boom and the lazy jacks, which should have been replaced before I set off: they were as old as the boat! A year later

I re-rigged the boat as a cutter with a taller mast. The result was excellent and I came second that year in the Falmouth Classic race for boats up to 30ft.

After I had laid up the boat I discovered that the rear engine mounting on the starboard side had collapsed and worn the deep sea seal in an extraordinary way. Without the latter to take up the eccentricity I would have ruined a shaft! Fortunately I made very little use of the engine after leaving Portsmouth, but judging by the damage to the seal the mounting must have broken early in the voyage. What did I regret not having? More space for books: so often I wanted to look something up or recall a poem; more tapes, particularly the 'speaking books' - I love to have Martyn Jarvis read to me; and perhaps a Cell Net Telephone as sometimes I could not get hold of the coastal Radio Stations. For a time I was on my own Desert Island: Oh, and I didn't have Shakespears' collected works with me!

Would I do it again, or would I recommend it to other single handers? The answer to both must be 'No', but if you have the time, the right boat and someone to share both the problems and the joys with you, if you have a sense of History, Geography, Oceanography or any other related 'ology' then I can guarantee that you will have a journey to remember all your life and a host of new friends and acquaintances which will greatly increase your Christmas card list. Your photo albums will be filled or, like me, your canvases spilling over into every conceivable corner. You might even write a book about it!

When Brenda, our club secretary, had met me and heard my story she had said *"Well, its nothing. You covered the distance so what does it matter. You nearly made it anyway."* I thought then of something my son had said as a small boy when, at a play park he had tried to cross a rope bridge and fell off right at the last moment, with only a yard or two left to go.

"Well, I nearly made it, didn't I?" He said, proudly!

Lightning Source UK Ltd.
Milton Keynes UK
15 September 2009

143745UK00001B/68/P